D0488754

APOLLO

Bosnian Chronicle | Ivo Andrić

Now In November | Josephine Johnson

The Authentic Death of Hendry Jones | Charles Neider

The Day of Judgment | Salvatore Satta

My Son, My Son | Howard Spring

The Man Who Loved Children | Christina Stead

Delta Wedding | Eudora Welty

The Lost Europeans
Emanuel Litvinoff

⚠

APOLLO

Apollo Librarian | Michael Schmidt || Series Editor | Neil Belton
Text Design | Lindsay Nash || Artwork | Jessie Price

www.apollo-classics.com | www.headofzeus.com

First published in the United States of America in 1958 by
The Vanguard Press, Inc.

This paperback edition published in the United Kingdom in 2016
by Apollo, an imprint of Head of Zeus Ltd.

Copyright © Aaron Litvinoff, 1958
Introduction © Michael Schmidt, 2016

The moral right of Emanuel Litvinoff to be identified as the author
of this work has been asserted in accordance with the Copyright,
Designs and Patents Act of 1988.

All rights reserved. No part of this publication may be reproduced,
stored in a retrieval system, or transmitted in any form or by
any means, electronic, mechanical, photocopying, recording, or
otherwise, without the prior permission of both the copyright
owner and the above publisher of this book.

1 3 5 7 9 10 8 6 4 2

A CIP catalogue record for this book is available
from the British Library.

ISBN (PB) 9781784970819
        (E) 9781784970802

Typeset by Adrian McLaughlin
Printed and bound in Denmark by Nørhaven

Head of Zeus Ltd
Clerkenwell House
45–47 Clerkenwell Green
London EC1R OHT

For Cherry, Vida, Julian and Sarah
who set my tree ablaze with green

Introduction

It's easy enough to imagine Berlin before the Second World War. It was a brilliant, imperial city in which 'everything goes' and from which everything was going, at increasing speed, towards apocalypse. Films, musicals, novels and memoirs make that vanished world palpable. Equally real is the period of the Berlin Wall (1961 to 1989) always in the news, and then its tearing down. Now Berlin has recovered as a centre of power and commerce. It is hard to imagine the Berlin of war's immediate aftermath, in whose corrupt and corrupted ruins past and present vied for meager spoils. *The Lost Europeans* takes us to that forgotten decade and a half. The allies have quartered the Nazi capital between the victorious powers, and the most brutally patrolled fault line in the cold war had not yet been turned into a wall. There is still an awkward flow of people between the sectors; there is still dialogue and the possibility of love.

'One in every five people down there,' says Hugo, glancing from the window of his lavish apartment, 'was a Nazi of some kind. I like the other four. The problem is to be sure that those you like are the right ones.' Christopher Isherwood said *Goodbye to Berlin* in 1939, just as the war was starting. The dark musical *Cabaret* flowed from his book. In *The Lost Europeans*, Emanuel Litvinoff says hello to Berlin. It is two decades, a World War and a Holocaust after the unbuttoned excesses of Sally Bowles's metropolis. In Litvinoff's 1950s, we encounter unapologetic prostitution and the reluctant, guilt-fuelled restitution of the post-war. Isherwood's opportunistic and ambivalent Mr Norris has morphed into Hugo Kranz. Kranz was a performer, his bright early promise betrayed by false love and history. Christopher, Isherwood's first-person narrator, has morphed into third-person Martin Stone, née Silberstein, a Jew young enough to be curious, finding his way and, at last, his heart with a German seamstress from East Berlin working in a West Berlin factory.

When Litvinoff died in 2011 he was ninety-six years old. During his century, Europe suffered a decisive erasure. His Europeans include Jews killed in the Holocaust and those who survived to wander the Europe of the aftermath, unable to come to terms with a culture that dispossessed them. From his luxurious modern apartment Hugo looks on the city 'almost as though it were a solid river flowing with history'.

Litvinoff travelled to Berlin in 1957 to experience the city emerging from calamity and to research his novel. Research for him, as for Isherwood before him, entailed immersion. What was left of the old order fascinated him, but also the division, with the different sectors and their distinct populations and regulations. A sense of the past uneasily coexisted with the complex post-war administrations, a sort of four-way black market in which every vice was catered for and nothing was what it claimed to be. The protagonists set out to repair their broken pasts while many of the Germans they encounter are trying to slough their histories, practicing identity theft of the most urgent kind. The aristocrats quite as much as the punks sport false names, launder their pasts.

The narrator never knows anything for certain. English readers, keen on facts, experience a sinister world of seems, shadows and erasures.

The two Jewish protagonists make different accommodations with history and place. Hugo is a homosexual entertainer of advancing years, betrayed by an aristocratic lover during the Nazi period. He has profited abundantly but bitterly from the post-war German reparations paid to surviving Jews. Martin, born into a Berlin banking family but exiled to England as a boy, belongs to another generation and culture. Hugo is sucked back into the past; Martin, through present love, gains a tentative hold on the future.

Litvinoff, a poet and journalist, turned to fiction in his mid-forties. *The Lost Europeans* is a remarkable first novel, published in 1958 in the United States and two years later in Britain. It has a first novel's faults. It is rigidly plotted, a novel of ideas in which the ideas come first. Characters are sometimes alive, sometimes clauses in an argument. The book does not experiment with the novel form. It shares elements with romance and spy-thriller. It does anatomize the anxieties of a sympathetic liberal imagination in the wake of the war, and of a Jew coming to terms with the Holocaust.

When it was published fifteen years after the end of the war, *The Lost Europeans* had elements familiar from fiction and film. Litvinov borrows his Brownshirts from celluloid, his fades into and out of memory for flashbacks, each scene is visualised from a camera angle. Film rights in the novel were sold almost immediately the book appeared and Litvinoff was able to buy a family home in Hertfordshire on the proceeds. Wolf Mankowitz wanted to write the script and Dirk Bogarde was earmarked for the part of Martin. The film was never made.

There are moments of poetic effect in the book, as when Hugo turns off a light: 'He switched on the darkness and closed the door'. There are moments of miscalculation. At one point, shortly before he returns to London, Martin writes a short passage worthy of the Bad Sex prize, including loins, moist vaginas, impetuous seed and blind womb. Litvinoff's presentation of the homosexual world partakes of the darker prejudices of his period, a decade before homosexuality was decriminalized. Thus the book is singularly of its period: as we see Berlin, we also experience a distinctive British sensibility trammeled in its period.

Litvinoff was born poor, the second of nine children. His father returned to his native Russia before the boy was two, never to be seen again. The family could not afford Emanuel's bar mitzvah. He left school at fourteen, took various jobs and haunted Soho and Depression-time Fitzrovia. Existing on the fringes of the literary world, he wrote nightmare texts, including a vast confessional-apocalyptic novel a la Thomas Wolfe which was lost by his first wife at a railway station. In 1940 he enlisted in the Army and served in Northern Ireland, West Africa and the Middle East. Army and the war provided him with stability: he rose to the rank of Major, contributing poems to anthologies and publishing in 1942 his first collection, *The Untried Soldier*. Poetry continued, and ghost writing, reviews, editorial duties; then fiction and television drama.

His childhood experience of the Jewish communities of Whitechapel was transfigured by the Holocaust. Observing the fate of the Soviet Jews in 1956 (his father's family hailing from Odessa), he dedicated himself to campaigning for the Jews of Europe. It was Litvinoff who, in the poem 'To T.S. Eliot' (1951), first publically upbraided the poet for his anti-Semitism, though he loved Eliot's poems above those of his contemporaries. He edited *The Penguin Book of Jewish Short Stories* in 1979 and published *Falls the Shadow*, his last novel, the title borrowed from Eliot, in 1983. Profoundly troubled by the massacres of Palestinians at Sabra and Shatila in Lebanon and by Israel's Palestine policy, in *Falls the Shadow* he was again in thrall to ideas that stiffened the narrative.

Berlin and Germany itself are now remote from the divided city and the divided post-war nation. The deep scars, even of the Holocaust, come to seem historical. The living tensions of a city still painfully emerging from the sleep of reason and the nightmare of the war, coming to terms with moral and cultural failures, are alive in this novel. Its human drama outweighs its thematic intentions: we are gripped and surprised by what happens, and by the broken geographies that are revealed.

Michael Schmidt, 2016

Part One

1

Coming back was worse, much worse, than Martin Stone had anticipated. When he got into the boat train at Liverpool Street, with English newspapers and periodicals stuffed under his arm, the usual drizzle falling from the grimy London sky, he'd told himself this was just a business trip: he wasn't going to feel anything about it; it would probably bore him. And of course, it did – right down to the coast, across the English Channel to the Hook, and during the long, monotonous journey through the damp, flat countryside of Holland. The border crept up on them so unobtrusively he hadn't noticed it until a German policeman came into the train compartment and asked for passports. Half dozing, he felt in his pocket for his wallet. Then he became aware of the official's hard, grey, searching eyes subjecting him to a professional scrutiny from under the hooded peak of his cap. His carefully sustained indifference crumpled at once. *So they still look at a Jew like that*, he thought with a sudden flood of hatred.

The policeman glanced at the passport photograph and personal details and said: "*Sind sie in Berlin geboren?*' The innuendo seemed obvious to Martin: 'You may carry a British passport, but to us you're just a Jew.' He stared at the German as if he were a lump of filth. 'Yes, I was *born* in Berlin,' he replied in English, deliberately emphasising his cultured accent.

The policeman looked at him again, shrewdly, stamped his passport, and left with a curt, stiff bow. Martin avoided the eyes of his fellow travellers. His heart was beating unevenly. Outside the flat fields spun by identical with those on the other side of the border. But he could no longer look at them with indifference: they were Germany.

The effect of this first encounter with a German official remained with him for hours. During the time he spent in Hamburg waiting for the plane to Berlin he walked around shrinking from the casual contact of passers-by as though they were disease-carriers and searching for signs of abnormality in their faces. People with a history like theirs should be ugly, but they seemed ordinary, as commonplace as any crowd in any city. God had not punished them, Martin reflected resentfully, ignoring the sight of a war-mutilated cripple selling newspapers in case he should feel pity and receive even that dumb reproach. Yet by the time he arrived at Tempelhof Airport and Hugo drove him into the glittering, night-loving city, the feeling already began to pass, leaving him weak and calm, as if a fever had burned out in his blood.

Now he gazed out of the car at the half-familiar streets and crowd of faces swimming by in an electric blue haze with an indifference that could not be explained merely by tiredness. It doesn't matter to me any more, he thought hopefully. It was only the shock of arrival that had affected him, stirring the sediment of his childhood. Even if I was born in Berlin, England made me – the first difficult years at school, the wintry soccer afternoons, evacuation with a hundred other boys in school blazers to the villages of Cheshire; and, gradually, the words coming sweetly off the tongue, not mutilated and foreign any more. After two years in barracks rooms on National Service, he'd felt at least as English as any Welshman.

Hugo drove fast and recklessly, biting hard on a long cigar. He manipulated the steering-wheel with one hand and settled his heavy body more comfortably in the driving seat. 'Does it feel good to come home?' he asked mockingly.

The car swerved to avoid a scurrying pedestrian. 'You bloody Nazi!' Hugo yelled as if it were a great joke. 'Berlin is a form of insanity – and it's contagious. All you need do is change your name back to Silberstein and you can practically take up where you left off.'

'I was nine when I left off.'

'We'll see. It gets you, you know. Look at me, I came in 1952 and I'm still here.'

Martin could have pointed out the obvious differences between them. When Hugo fled from Germany to Vienna in 1934 he'd been almost the same age as Martin was now. According to all accounts he'd been one of the brightest young talents in Berlin. Fifteen years in England hadn't made him less German. Although, God knows, it was impossible to understand how he could bear to come back here to live.

'What would you like to do tonight? Eat, drink, dance, see a play? There are tourist attractions, if you want that sort of thing. Not quite Hamburg Reeperbahn standards, I'm afraid… Or perhaps you'd prefer a peep behind the Curtain?' Hugo sounded like a bored pimp offering a choice of commonplace vices.

'I think I'd prefer some sleep,' Martin said. 'It's been a long journey.'

Hugo stuffed his cigar into the ash-tray peevishly. 'The trouble with you is you've got no curiosity,' he complained. He seemed to interpret the refusal as a personal affront, as if he'd specially arranged the series of entertainments as a private show for his guest. 'Anyway, I hope you've got enough energy to have a drink before you retire.'

Suddenly they turned out of a gloomy side street into an explosion of competing neon lights. Shop fronts glittered like fake diamonds, and a dazzling necklace of bright amber was strung overhead in an apparently endless vista. 'The Kurfürstendamm,' Hugo explained laconically. 'Don't let it fool you. It's practically all front.'

Martin stared sombrely at the parade of well-dressed people walking the pavements and at the steady flow of shiny automobiles. This was a road he remembered well. It had become garish, a vulgar advertisement, but it had not changed that much. 'So this is the Kurfürstendamm,' he said. Hugo's big square hand patted his knee. 'It touches a chord, eh?' he asked, smiling sardonically.

A few hundred yards down the road they stopped. Picked out in glowing emerald-green filament was the name Hugo Krantz. Unlike many of its neighbours, it did not flicker on and off but burned with a challenging steadiness. 'Ici Paris,' Hugo said, waving at the elegant dresses in the windows and the pavement showcase in which crystal bottles of perfume revolved on pads of black velvet. 'I live upstairs.'

Some women stood in front of the shop clutching the arms of reluctant escorts and admiring its wares. 'It makes their tongues hang out,' Hugo whispered gleefully. 'But only a couple of hundred females in Berlin can afford my prices.'

A private lift brought them to a penthouse that appeared to be designed with a reckless disregard for money. Hugo waved Martin to a deep chair by the curved window that formed a glass wall along one side of the room. He turned a switch on the side of his desk and filled the place with soft music, then strolled over to the cocktail bar in the corner. 'Try a German cognac,' he suggested. 'It won't disappoint you.'

The pattern on the carpet was formed of the monogram H.K. On the walls were a Modigliani, a Soutine, a Chagall, some Ben Shahns, and Josef Hermans, and other pictures by lesser known painters, a selection that seemed dictated less by taste than by sentiment, for most of them seemed to be Jews. Over a black terrazzo fireplace was a figurine in the style of Henry Moore, and from it the eye was led through a series of rather feminine perspectives to a slender staircase ascending to the upper apartments.

Hugo brought the drink over and sat down, watching Martin intently for his reactions. 'Well, do you approve?' he asked eagerly, as if seeking reassurance from an expert.

'It seems to have everything one could want – even the view.' Martin nodded down at the Kurfürstendamm. The lights gleamed richly below, mellowed by distance. Little clockwork cars whirred along the highway and tiny marionettes moved predictably along the pavements.

'It's not bad. It amuses one. Looked at in a certain way, you could call it my private flea circus.' Hugo smiled grimly. 'You may not see the joke. On one occasion in the cellars of the Gestapo they sprayed me with vermin killer.'

'You don't seem to love your neighbours.'

'Have a cigar,' Hugo said, pushing over a silver box. He lit one himself and blew the smoke out reflectively. 'One in every five people down there was a Nazi of some kind. I like the other four. The problem is to be sure that those you like are the right ones.'

'And how do you find out?'

'That's the trouble. Sometimes you know, sometimes you don't. One lives on one's nerves. It gives an edge to human relationships.'

The thin, bitter voice did not belong to the moneyed assurance of the apartment, or to Hugo's obese body and the crumpled elegance of his expensive clothes. It turned the sentimental music flowing like warm scented air through the room into a lie. What was true was the pain of the past, the pain of the young man that now spoke through the blurred middle-aged mask of his flesh. Hugo said: 'You're alive here in the way you're alive in an air raid. You live with a mistrust of the existence of tomorrow.' Abruptly, he turned the conversation away from himself.

'Your father was rich. I begged him dozens of times to put in a restitution claim, but all I ever got from him was a hysterical sermon on German blood money. What made him change his mind?'

'He didn't,' said Martin. 'Nothing can change him now. Money doesn't mean anything to him any more. It's a habit he's lost.' He thought of the old sick man alone in their shabby furnished flat in Swiss Cottage, frugally cutting his cigarettes in half to make them last longer and combing through *émigré* news sheets to read the obituaries of his friends.

Only hatred of Germany sustained him, hatred of all he had once loved immoderately. Germany was a passion to which he had been more wedded than to his wealth, his wife, his children.

By hating Germany he committed his own kind of suicide. 'We had what passes with us for a difference of opinion,' Martin went on with a wry smile. 'I didn't see why they should hold on to our property without giving us compensation. I'm prepared to wash the blood off the money before I use it. A percentage for Jewish orphans, or free *Bockwurst* for elderly German refugees.' He omitted to say that his father didn't even know he'd come to Germany; that he had told the old man he was travelling to Switzerland for his firm.

Hugo refilled their glasses from the brandy decanter. 'I like your taste in philanthropy,' he commented dryly. 'Tomorrow I'll have a word with my lawyer. For ten per cent he'll push your claim through in no time. Anyway, here's to all *Bockwurst* philanthropists.' He drained his glass in one swallow and immediately refilled it.

'Cheers,' said Martin, watching his companion closely. Hugo probably drank a good deal. It would account for the reckless driving and that bellowing bravado that obviously concealed a pretty deep insecurity. But what was he trying to do? Drown the memory of the wasted years? To do so he'd have to annihilate his personality with alcohol.

A violin was plaintively playing a coy, sugary melody. Hugo got up abruptly and switched the sound off. But the silence, too, frayed at his nerves. He began talking aimlessly – local gossip about Berlin, political scandal, theatre tittle-tattle – but whatever he said scarcely disturbed the glassy surface of the silence. For a few seconds he paced the floor without speaking, engrossed in an inner dialogue. The ash from his cigar dropped unnoticed on to the front of his silk shirt.

'I suppose your father thinks I'm a rat,' he said at last, 'coming back and settling here?'

Martin felt embarrassed. 'We all thought it was something to do with Marion, particularly after the divorce.'

'Oh, Marion' – Hugo dismissed the suggestion impatiently – 'we never really got on from the beginning. Marion's a first-class bitch. She only stayed married to me for appearance's sake. I suppose it suited us both.' He returned to the window and pulled his chair closer to Martin. Behind the heavy horn-rimmed glasses his grey eyes appeared liquid and dilated. 'Do you know what your father did for me, Martin? I was hardly twenty-two, just a promising juvenile lead. Then I wrote a satirical revue. Not a single management would touch it. Your father read it and signed a blank cheque for the production. Spoliansky did the music, Weber the *décor*, I acted. It gave me the smartest reputation in Berlin overnight. And in those days Berlin wasn't the village it is today. There was more talent to the square mile than in Paris and London combined. I could write my name to any contract. I had a luxury flat overlooking the Tiergarten, an Italian sports car, and an English butler.' And Putzi, he remembered, thinking of the girlish face married to the muscular male, athletic body. The arrogant Portland-blue eyes. The graceful gift of flattery. Putzi von Schlesinger.

He stubbed out his cigar savagely and continued: 'It lasted less than two years, then the dog entered into its inheritance. I went to Vienna and started again. They chased me out. I went to Prague. When Chamberlain came to Munich I knew it was time to move again.'

Martin listened with unwilling fascination. He had no desire for these confidences. The story was, in any case, not unfamiliar.

But perhaps because they were sitting high above Berlin, looking down on the city almost as though it were a solid river flowing with history, he felt unable to break the flow of confessions.

'When I came to London people used to ask me why I didn't go on writing or acting,' Hugo said. 'After all, refugees did make the transition. "Look at Herbert Lom," they used to say. "Look at the Kordas. Look at Koestler." I sat up night after night chain-smoking and writing comedies. In German they were funny enough to give an owl hysterics. English killed them. In the end I gave up trying. I couldn't afford to smoke so much.'

Darkness seemed to have invaded the softly lighted room, and the noise of the city below had imperceptibly decreased. Martin's watch showed it was past midnight. His tiredness had settled into a numb discomfort in his brain, a dry distaste for the unreal, interminable evening.

Hugo continued to drink steadily. He spoke now in disconnected sentences, as if forced into an unwilling confession.

'When I married Marion everybody thought I was damn lucky. A penniless refugee getting the daughter of the biggest button-maker in England. Marriage was, for me, a kind of degrading servitude. I went into business and made money, but Marion got the credit for that. People envied me and despised me. In a sense they were justified. Refugees are a disgusting lot. They can't help it, but neither can lice. Either they apologise for being alive or they parade their sores with the insolence of Oriental beggars.'

The degeneration into self-pity: that was characteristic of refugees, Martin reflected. He remembered Hugo's eighteenth-century cottage in Hampstead, which became something of a left-wing salon. And even if Hugo hadn't succeeded in writing a comedy for the English theatre, he had produced a clever, sardonic book on Central European socialism which got a good deal of attention and gave him the status of an expert. Money, friends, and a reputation for witty scholarship: it didn't sound like the life of a louse.

'Of course, everybody came to my parties,' Hugo went on, as if sensitive to the unspoken scepticism. 'Why not? My income was larger than a Cabinet Minister's, and the hospitality was in keeping. I suppose I was one of the most tolerated refugees in exile, but I'd rather be here.' He nodded towards the street below. 'Even if some of those bastards down there think of me as a *verfluchter Jude*, I belong here.'

'You've convinced me that I don't,' Martin said. He stood up to go. The brandy had filled him with a melancholy muzziness. He went close to the window and glanced towards the macabre ruins of the Kaiser-Wilhelm-Gedächtniskirche. Once in the remote past he had attended a service there with his father. He remembered it then as a huge ugly cathedral smelling of incense and decay, but his father had thought it beautiful. For a moment he tried to imagine what the old man might feel were he standing in this place at this time, but nothing came. Homesick and inexpressibly alienated, he turned back to the room.

'Don't bother to see me to Frau Goetz's,' he said. 'I'll get my bags out of the car and take a taxi.'

'Certainly not. I promised I'd deliver you in person.' Hugo got up reluctantly. I've talked too much, he told himself despondently. I must be lonelier than I think. As they left the apartment he glanced slowly around before turning out the lights. Now it gave him no pleasure. It seemed transitional, a stage setting assembled for a polite social comedy which could be quickly dismantled, leaving the stage empty and bare in readiness for another play. He switched on the darkness and closed the door.

A big, husky young German was just getting out of the lift. About twenty-two, with a pallid, heavy face prematurely shadowed by experience, and close-cropped yellow hair. He was dressed with casual but expensive elegance in the style of an American college boy.

'*Guten Abend*,' he said, startled. His smile came an instant too late, an uneasy afterthought.

Hugo was equally startled 'Hullo! I wasn't expecting you back yet,' he said with strained affability.

'I had a tiff with the girl friend.' The youth veiled his eyes with his thick lashes. There was an awkward silence for a moment. Hugo seemed to be undecided whether or not an introduction was in order, then he drew the newcomer aside and conversed with him in a low voice. Afterwards the young German ostentatiously bade them both good night.

'That's Heinz Dieter Schulz,' Hugo explained as they went down in the lift. 'Secretary, chauffeur, valet.' Somewhat defensively, he added: 'He's a good kid – no father, messed up by the war, a refugee from the East. I treat him more like a nephew than an employee. I bet you never suspected me of being——' there was a pause while he selected a suitable adjective – 'sentimental?'

'It's a German weakness, isn't it? And you insist on being German.' They laughed, aware of the ambiguity of both the question and the reply, but it was a laughter remote from amusement.

Crowds were still parading along the Kurfürstendamm. The pavement cafés were thronged with coffee drinkers. Snatches of music came intermittently from the beckoning doorways of beer bars. Well-nourished men, their faces flushed with food and drink, escorted silken and scented women to shiny cars that waited at the kerb-sides opposite the restaurants. There was a singing of the flesh all down the golden mile of the renovated city, a boisterous brotherhood of good living; and no hint of the pestilential past.

'You have to admit,' Hugo said, breathing the mild air deeply, 'Berlin has a quality no other place in the world has got. Night here is like an injection of benzedrine.' His spirits had suddenly lifted. 'Let's go for a quick run round,' he shouted, slapping Martin exuberantly on the back. 'We'll get a lungful of this marvellous fresh air. The Germans don't deserve to have it all to themselves.'

They headed out swiftly towards the suburbs. Martin lay back on the seat and let the coolness wash over his face like a spring of fresh water. The car sped past big slabs of unlighted buildings and brief oases of brightness until, after about fifteen minutes, the darkness began to intermingle with the branches of trees. For Martin there was a curious familiarity about the district through which they were now passing. The blurred impression suddenly came into focus.

'This is Dahlem, isn't it?' he asked. 'We're near the Botanical Gardens.' It brought an unexpectedly vivid stab of nostalgia. He'd gone to school in this neighbourhood. The sharp fresh smell of the Grunewald nearby evoked the crystal memory of lakes, woods, and country walks, recalling a pleasure he had almost forgotten, the long summer day of a childhood that was abruptly terminated, as if a great black hand had snuffed out the sun.

Hugo slowed the car down and came to a halt alongside a mail-box. 'I think you'll know this street,' he said.

It was a calculated manœuvre. Briefly, Martin struggled with his curiosity, then he got out of the car

'I'd rather you didn't come with me,' he said, and walked rapidly away.

The appearance of the street was curiously changed, like a face which has had its nose reshaped. The corner where Willy Schneider's big brown house had stood was now occupied by a white block of apartments striped with jutting verandas, and the large garden where they had conducted military manœuvres among the fruit trees and sailed their toy fleets on the ornamental pond was now buried under a cliff of masonry.

Willy had been his best friend – a small, intense, masterful boy, a joyous and persuasive young liar who would commandeer the servants and post them as sentries all over the garden while he planned victorious campaigns against the Nazis from the fortress of his father's summer-house. The Nazis, of course, had won. They caught up with him in Vienna, after the *Anschluss*, and he had disappeared with his family into some nameless mass-grave, or into the furnace of an incinerator. Now not a tree, nor a bush, nor a blade of grass that belonged to the small world of Willy Schneider survived here in Berlin, in the street where he was born.

Farther down were the ruins of his own house. He walked leaden-muscled, as though moving against the resistance of a stiff wind. A night shift was working by artificial light on the unfleshed skeleton of a seven-storey structure, but the grounds were still partly buried under a large mound of rubble. Martin clambered over a heap of sand and went in.

Nothing was recognisable among the fragments of stone and pieces of charred timber, but he felt that if he could dig into the ruins with his fingers he would come across some splinter of the past, some tangible evidence that he had once belonged here. It couldn't be possible to obliterate the life of a family so completely.

'Are you looking for something?' A gruff voice asked suspiciously.

'I used to live here.' Martin spoke without reflection in German for the first time since he'd arrived in Berlin.

'It's a funny time to come visiting.'

'Is it any of your business?'

The man lit a cigarette and tossed the spent match over his shoulder. 'I'm the foreman on this job,' he protested. 'Only doing my duty.'

Martin picked up a piece of carved stone. 'It could have come from the wall outside my room,' he said in a flat, conversational voice, handling the fragment as though it were a remote historical relic.

'I know how you feel. Used to have a nice little house myself, in Reinickendorf. Went through the bombing without a scratch, then a Russian shell got it in '45. Lucky my wife was away at the time.' The foreman waved towards the new building. 'It's going to be quite a place. Designed by the best Swedish architect. You should come back in a month, we'll have it done by then. Mind you, it must have been a pretty big house before. How many floors did it have?'

The shape of the long, dim library with its french windows looking on to the garden came suddenly into his mind. From floor to ceiling the shelves were stacked with the history, the culture, the traditions of Germany. A marble bust of Schiller held silent converse with a bronze Goethe across the polished oak floor.

The library had cast a hushed spell over the rest of the house; for Martin home really began on the top floor where he and his sister Lise occupied adjoining rooms with a distant view of the Grunewald through the trees and Nanny within earshot, ready to produce liniment and medicines at the first sign of a winter chill. And it was from the window of his sister's room that his mother fell the day Lise's belongings arrived in a small bundle through the mail and they were officially notified of her death. They told people his mother had had a heart attack. It was her last request. She would not bear the disgrace of suicide.

'It had three storeys,' Martin said. He dropped the lump of carved stone on to the rubble and began walking away, swept by a sudden desolate recollection of grief.

Frau Goetz opened the door to them in a flowered kimono, her face crumpled with sleep and wisps of dyed yellow hair escaping from under her nightcap. She looked like a bedraggled canary and was terribly, terribly embarrassed at being brought out of bed.

'Hugo, why didn't you let me know you'd be so late?' she asked reproachfully, clutching her kimono at the neck. 'What will Mr Stone think of me like this?'

Martin was far too conscious of his own discomfort to think of her at all. The handles of his heavy suitcases were cutting into his fingers, but he managed a polite smile.

'You're so vain! You know bloody well you're a fascinating bitch,' Hugo growled, grinning amiably. 'Frau Goetz is an old friend,' he explained. 'She was quite the worst dancer on the Berlin stage.' He sang in a flat un-melodious voice: '*I flutter round your candle till I singe my wings…* Remember that, my boulevard butterfly?'

The little woman seemed to enjoy the badinage and blushed like a young girl in love. '*Lieber Gott*, you are a wicked man!' she protested shrilly, and tottered away on her high-heeled mules to lead them to Martin's room. She went around it switching on several dim lights to show the place off to its full advantage.

'Thank you, it's fine,' Martin said, too tired to pretend more enthusiasm.

'You spik Sherman, Mr Stone?'

Hugo patted her rump patronisingly. 'Better than you, *mein Liebchen*,' he laughed. 'You ought to recognise a Prussian gentleman when you see one.' Humming cheerfully, he pulled the curtains apart to see the view from the window. The room overlooked a partly cleared bombed site and a long vista of ill-lit streets. On the other side of the road a dim red sign advertised a *Spiel-Casino* and beside it a portico faced with peeling stucco led into the courtyard of a half-ruined building.

'A nice, cosy desolation,' Hugo commented to Martin. 'This is the suicide room. When I was staying here in 1952 a man named Muller stepped off the window-sill. Couldn't stand any more of Frau Goetz's coffee.' He wrenched open the door leading to the balcony and displaced a collection of rolled newspapers that had been stuffed into the frame to keep out draughts.

'*Ach! Um Gotteswillen!*' Frau Goetz screamed, scurrying over to replace them.

At last Martin was left alone with his silence. He laid himself fully dressed on the wide divan and smoked cigarette after cigarette as the experiences of the day revolved, fragmentary and disturbing, in his mind. Now, with his vitality at a low ebb, he was ready to confess that he'd been wrong when he told himself that

Germany could no longer make him suffer. England, after all, had not cured him. All these years he had lived with an incomplete identity, a portion of his mind numbed by shock. Now it was painfully reviving. Here at the sick heart of Europe he could feel once more the poisons moving in the blood stream, the familiar throbbing of the diseased night.

He lay for a long time deeply listening to all the small noises of darkness. Shadowy memories swam through his subconscious like monstrous fish in the deep of the sea; and though he tossed from side to side to elude them he knew it was impossible. He himself was the pursuer, trapped in his own flesh, his own imagination, preparing his own pitfalls. He lay with his eyes wide open adrift in the inexhaustible night and, gradually, by imperceptible stages of transition, the past drew him unresisting into the depths of nightmare.

… He was sitting in the back of the Mercedes. The late afternoon sky was heavy and overcast. His mother sat beside him looking as she did on the day she died. Perhaps she always looked like that – he couldn't remember; but with an immediate clarity he recalled the perfume she used, an odour of crushed gardenias, the erect, soldierly back of the grey-uniformed chauffeur, the steady soporific vibration of the engine, and an insidious sense of foreboding, as if they were being secretly followed.

Both an actor and a spectator in the drama, he could see himself sitting stiffly on the edge of the seat, dressed in a tweed jacket and knickerbockers, his eyes wide and childish, his hair neatly parted and plastered down, with one hand limp in his mother's lap. They were going out on a shopping expedition and had stopped at his father's office in the Friedrichstrasse where the family's banking business was situated. Now they were travelling along the Kurfürstendamm, the road looking as it did in old photographs – durable, mellow, and prosperous. The five spires of the Kaiser-Wilhelm-Gedächtniskirche, still intact, slowly heeled over as he squinted up at them. He was immensely conscious of being an eight-year-old dwarf in a world of giants.

His mother turned her head very slowly towards him. Her voice was disembodied, an echo. 'I'm going into Braun's to pick up my dress,' she said. 'Wait for me. Afterwards we'll have coffee in Kranzler's.'

She tapped at the window and the chauffeur brought the car to a halt. Martin watched her cross the pavement and enter the dress shop, then he took a pocket-knife out of his jacket and played with it silently. Suddenly he became aware of a curious alteration in the heartbeats of the city. Its throbbing diminished, then accelerated, as lorries loaded with Brownshirts raced along with klaxons blaring. The Brownshirts leaped on to the pavements and hurried into cafés, restaurants, and shops. They reappeared dragging frightened men in their wake, men of all ages and all sizes to whom fear had given a common expression so that they looked oddly like brothers.

A seismic upheaval began in his stomach. 'Manfred, why are they taking those men away?' He spoke reluctantly, afraid of the answer.

The chauffeur opened a newspaper and held it spread out in front of his face. Across the top of the page in ugly black capitals was the heading: '*Reich Diplomat Ermordet*.' He kept his face hidden in the paper. 'It was done by a Jew,' the chauffeur muttered.

The boy looked stealthily at the knife in his hand and wiped away a red trace of rust on to his trousers. His limbs began to tremble violently and he was afraid he might disgrace himself by crying, or worse.

Two Nazis appeared in the doorway of a café struggling with a screaming middle-aged man who could have been a prosperous business-man. Now his jacket was half-ripped from his body, the front of his trousers had been torn, exposing his limp genitals, and his respectable face was wracked by an insane fear. '*Ich bin nicht schuldig!*' he screamed. '*Ich bin nicht schuldig!*' One of the Nazis punched him in the stomach and his body folded in half like a doll that had been bled of its sawdust. People turned away from the sight, shocked and ashamed, and a woman broke into hysterical laughter. A group of Brownshirts slouched by, their jack-boots clattering. One of them peered into the car and grinned into the staring eyes of the boy. They were no longer the eyes of a child. '*Heil Hitler,*' he yelled.

The chauffeur kept the newspaper in front of his face. In the window of a restaurant a diner could be seen delicately wiping his lips with a napkin. In the cinemas crowds watched fascinated as shadows on the screen imitated life. The whole diffuse movement of the world entered the boy's nightmare – the darkening planet pricked with needles of light, the myriad people living their myriad ordinary lives, the peaceful growth of plants, the peaceful coming to birth, the dying of the old and the sick... And the world turning bad because of one man's pain on the pavement of a Berlin street.

Suddenly, as if he'd been guilty of a fatal oversight, he remembered his mother. Wrenching the car door open, he ran into the dressmaker's shop. The assistants were courteously preoccupied with their customers' needs, showing bolts of cloth, discussing the choice of styles, measuring ladies for garments. Martin looked from one woman to another. All that confronted him was a group of strangers and his own reflection staring back from a series of polished mirrors. His mother was not in the shop. He stood there and died.

Over the years he died that particular death many times, the dream always ending before his mother's return from the fitting-room where she had been hiding. His imagination never granted him the mercy of that reprieve. It left the small boy staring with dry-eyed horror at his lonely reflection until he drowned in a slumber too profound for dreams.

As the last flicker of consciousness was extinguished, he knew that this time it would be different. When he opened his eyes again it would not be to the Cockney voice of the milkman singing among the clattering bottles, the muted growl of traffic along Finchley Road, and the folded English newspaper thrust through the letter-box. He would not join the taciturn morning crowds, with their ordinary, kindly, incurious English faces, and arrive at the office, where he worked as an accountant, to find his secretary immersed in the mild insanities of her favourite women's weekly and already talking about brewing tea. This time he would wake in Germany.

Someone was playing Mozart over and over in an adjoining room. Dusty shafts of sunlight penetrated the thick olive-green curtains and he got up, surprised to find himself still fully dressed. It was not late, still some minutes before nine, but as he pulled open the curtains the tide of the day's activities seemed well advanced. Leather-jacketed men cycled briskly through the streets, some towing small carts laden with goods; the ubiquitous trucks filled with rubble rolled in procession to the great dumps in the old city centre, now a wasteland between the Western and Eastern sectors; women were already returning from the markets with heavy shopping-baskets, and the sound of children reciting lessons came from a nearby school.

The night had not refreshed him. His body felt stale with travel sweat, and the taste of yesterday was thick and dry on his tongue. Pleasantly anticipating a hot bath and a change of linen, he began to unpack his cases, distracted by the unfamiliar noises in the apartment which, by their insistent intimacy, gave him the feeling that he was unwillingly becoming involved in the life of a family of strangers.

The pianist had stopped practising Mozart and now seemed to be performing a complicated experiment with a tuning instrument from which he produced a series of high, bell-like notes. The telephone rang several times and resulted in muffled, semi-intelligible conversations. A woman's voice, probably Frau Goetz's could be heard volubly amidst the clatter of coffee cups.

There was a knock at the door, and a tall, emaciated man, elegantly clad in a boldly striped yellow and black dressing-gown, entered and introduced himself as the occupant of the next room, Klaus Richter. He was about thirty-five, with a high bald crown fringed by fluffy fair hair. An actor, he volunteered with a hint of a bow, gesturing with a well-kept hand that displayed a large-cut emerald on its fourth finger.

'Are you the person who plays the piano?' Martin asked when he had completed his own introduction.

'Ah! That is our music professor, Hokoyama. A Japanese specialist in Mozart. Charming, don't you agree?' Herr Richter smiled a trifle grimly. Perhaps Mozart had become a monotonous pleasure. 'I myself do not perform on an instrument,' he continued in a deep, mellifluous voice that suggested he was no mean performer on the most flexible musical instrument of all.

He explained that he'd come on a social errand for Frau Goetz. Apparently it was a tradition of the establishment that new guests took coffee with her on the morning after their arrival or at the first suitable occasion.

With the same inflexible politeness with which the invitation was tendered, Martin made his apologies; he was planning to have a bath just then but he would be happy to take advantage of the hospitality some other time.

Herr Richter smiled pityingly. 'Unfortunately, between eight-thirty and nine-thirty the bathroom is always occupied by Herr Goldberg,' he said. Excessively solemn, he beckoned Martin into the corridor and put his finger to his lips. A loud sound of gargling came from the bathroom, followed by a distinct belch and the noise of someone trumpeting into a handkerchief. Herr Goldberg seemed to be clearing all his orifices at the same time.

'Surely he doesn't have to take a whole hour,' Martin protested mildly.

'One must assume that his toilet is rather elaborate. You may as well join us for breakfast.'

Frau Goetz was already seated behind the coffee-pot in the sitting-room crowded with old-fashioned mahogany furniture and an incongruous assembly of objects that included primitive African carvings, Christian reliquaries, night-club posters, nineteenth-century oleographs, and brass candelabra that looked like Birmingham Oriental. In the daylight she was a delicate blue-eyed doll, slightly faded and withered in appearance as if she had aged on a neglected shelf of some toy shop. Her dyed yellow hair was piled in a Gothic erection on top of her head, creating a startling effect of elongation, as though her skinny neck and small face had at some stage been stretched in an attempt to separate them from the rest of her body. She was heavily and expertly painted.

'Ah, Mr Stone, come and sit here!' she exclaimed patting a cushion on the divan invitingly. As he sat down she inspected him critically and, he felt, accusingly. 'You did not sleep well,' she said, plying him with coffee and creamy cakes.

Martin mumbled a denial, uncomfortably aware of Herr Richter, who reclined on the other side of the table smiling a subtle, brilliant smile that seemed to conceal a mocking amusement. 'One in every five was a Nazi of some kind,' Hugo had said. What about Richter?

The actor conversed with the fluency of a man who had always taken it for granted that people expected him to be entertaining, as if that was how he paid for any hospitality he received. But Martin suspected his glibness for another reason. Behind the façade of effeminate mannerisms and sharp Berliner wit he thought he detected the corrupt cynicism of someone with few scruples, a man who could easily have been a Nazi.

Yet it was infuriating that he should feel this curiosity about Richter's past. Why should he give a damn about the fellow? There were eighty million Germans, each with his own degree of guilt. To condemn them collectively or to probe each individual one encountered was to succumb to paranoia. The only way to preserve one's sanity was to cultivate indifference.

With a determined effort he turned away and concentrated

his attention on Frau Goetz, who was now complaining about Herr Goldberg. She could not understand his lack of consideration for the other guests – especially as he had been in a concentration camp, she added inconsequentially. 'In Buchenwald I learned to make my toilet in a cup full of cabbage water in five minutes,' she insisted warmly.

'You were in Buchenwald?' Martin asked in surprise. She didn't look like a Jewess.

Richter confirmed the fact on her behalf.

'Three years,' he said. His thin, thespian features expressed an appropriate sympathy.

Frau Goetz went to the sideboard and rummaged in a drawer. She returned with a photograph of a group of women surrounded by American soldiers. The women were looking out of the picture with the glazed indifference of people who had gone so far beyond suffering that they were too numbed to register either hope or despair. The contrast between their etiolated, skeletal faces and those of the vigorous, well-fed youngsters in uniform was profoundly shocking. It was as if the soldiers had taken a party of corpses into custody; as if, like Lazarus, the women had risen from the dead, vanguard of a terrible army come to haunt the living with the unforgettable accusation of their staring, lustreless, dead eyes.

But if Frau Goetz was conscious of the macabre quality of the photograph she gave no indication of it. 'That's me,' she said, pointing to a scarecrow in the centre of the group with as much pride as if it were a picture of her class at high school. A fond reminiscent smile touched her lips. 'They used to call me Snowflake. It was very silly. That one on the end, she was my best friend, Clara, a really nice person.' Unable to resist the impulse to boast, she added: 'Her husband was an important magistrate. He died in Auschwitz. Clara knew the very moment he breathed his last because that was when the first message came to her from the Other Side.'

Frau Goetz sipped her coffee abstractedly. 'I will never forget that day as long as I live,' she said in a calm quiet voice. 'We were on a burial party and Clara was very tired – the work was so heavy. She had been coughing for weeks, but she'd tried to hide her illness because if they found out they sent you away. Suddenly I noticed she was trembling: "It's Otto," she said, "he's on the Other Side." I could hardly hear what she was saying, she spoke so faintly. There was a strange look in her face. "The Beast will die soon," she said. "Otto has told me." Three weeks later the war was over.'

Richter, who had listened with evident boredom, cleared his throat ostentatiously. 'It was a miracle,' he declared, extracting a cigarette from a thin silver case and lighting it. 'A miracle, Frau Goetz!'

She nodded her head solemnly. 'Yes,' she agreed. 'A miracle. Clara and I still correspond. She lives in Israel now. Herr Goldberg came to me on her recommendation.'

The telephone in the hall rang. She returned the photograph to the sideboard and went to answer it. 'Professor Hokoyama, it's for you!' they heard her call.

Richter relaxed in his chair and blew a reflective stream of smoke towards the ceiling. 'A remarkable woman, Frau Goetz. Did you know she was a cabaret artiste when she was young?'

Martin nodded.

'I don't remember her myself,' the actor went on. 'They say she was pretty – and very, very gay. She had more guts than most of us, too. People hid in her flat for years.'

'So she's not a Jewess?'

'A Jewess? No, but she had a Jewish lover who was some sort of Communist. Hid him from the Gestapo until he got out of the country. Later, hiding Jews became a habit with her. In 1942 the S.S. raided her flat and found a woman and three children locked up in a cupboard in her bedroom.' Richter smiled slightly. 'A regular Jew-sty, they called it.'

The moment it was said he became uncomfortably aware of his tactlessness. 'Their own swinish choice of language,' he explained hurriedly. 'I wouldn't like you to think——'

'Of course not.' Martin examined the end of his cigarette with meticulous care.

Rather lamely, Richter said: 'Anyway, Buchenwald changed her.'

'It would be remarkable if it hadn't.'

Martin's eye was caught by a faded theatrical photograph in a dim corner of the room. He got up to examine it. 'Please go on,' he urged. 'In what way was she changed?'

The picture showed a chocolate-box blonde dressed in the style of the twenties, smiling coyly up at a man in a double-breasted checked jacket once the fashionable attire of juvenile leads in musical comedy. They appeared to have been photographed while singing a duet. The man was young, with cynically intelligent features. A wayward lock of hair had fallen across his forehead, giving his handsome face an appearance of dissipation. The girl was unmistakably Frau Goetz, but it took a moment or two before he recognised her partner as Hugo Krantz.

'She became religious,' Richter was saying. 'Someone converted her to the doctrine of Jehovah's Witnesses. For a woman who loved pleasure so much it was quite a conversion. Now the only pleasure she seems to allow herself is an occasional little coffee party as an agreeable way of passing the time while waiting for the world to come to an inevitably bad end.'

'She could be right,' Martin commented pessimistically.

In the corridor Frau Goetz was having a minor altercation with Herr Goldberg. Her thin voice sniped at him through the bathroom door, provoking an angry rumbling of verbal artillery. It occurred to Martin that Goldberg's attitude was not different in kind from his own. Over-insistently, he was asserting his rights; the occupation of the bathroom vindicated his humanity. It may have begun when he was carted off like a diseased animal to the concentration camp to be systematically tortured and degraded. Soon the inevitable deterioration of personality would have set in. Then, after the concentration camp, the D.P. camp: the body rotting in its own filth, subjected to periodic delousing not for its own sake but to protect privileged members of society from the danger of epidemics. For a man who had been deloused for years, to be inside a locked bathroom with unlimited hot water and a sweet-smelling cake of soap was to be in a beautiful temple dedicated to the worship of the human body.

Nor should one overlook the rôle of the bathroom in the metaphysics of the concentration camp. The bathroom was the ultimate mystery, the holy of holies. The wretched inmates, having endured every vileness and indignity, were finally lined up to be cleansed before a building clearly marked *Baderaum*. They stripped off their rags which were meticulously listed before fumigation, then, naked as the newborn and the dead, filed into the bathroom where jets hissed until the suffocating bodies stuck together with their own juices. Later, the corpses were hosed with water to un-glue them, so they underwent their cleansing after all.

Perhaps Goldberg had been a bath attendant in the concentration camp, hosing, shovelling, working with a fanatic dedication to the ritual of the Bathroom in order to preserve his own miserable existence. And he must have dreamed of his elevation from acolyte to high priest, of the day when he would enter the bath chamber to celebrate its ritual in his own way and emerge, finally, sweetened, purified, and reborn.

Martin felt that he understood Herr Goldberg: he almost loved him.

But towards Frau Goetz, now that he knew about her past, he felt a deep personal sense of gratitude, as though she had saved his own life. Because of her he even managed to think of Germany with brief compassion. Wasn't there an old Jewish legend that as long as twelve saintly men existed God would not destroy the world?

The high heels of the saintly woman could be heard tip-tapping angrily along the corridor. 'He makes me so mad!' she complained shrilly as she burst into the room. Two uneven red patches glowed on her cheeks. 'Do you know what he's doing now? He's washing his shirts, if you please! I have guests waiting for a bath and he's doing his laundry!'

Making sure the door was open so that her voice would carry to Goldberg's ears, she screamed: 'It's the behaviour of a monster! What normal person shuts himself up in the bathroom for half a day? It's not kindly, it's not considerate, it's not neighbourly!'

They all listened for the effect of this pronouncement, then a series of loud bangs on a galvanised tub made a hideous racket throughout the apartment.

'*Lieber Gott!*' Frau Goetz wailed in alarm. 'That man's gone raving mad!'

Richter adopted an expression of commiseration. 'He's making your life miserable, darling,' he suggested, protruding a sly tongue from the corner of his mouth and winking broadly at Martin. 'Why don't you tell him to pack his bags and go?'

'What am I, a Nazi?' she snapped. 'I only want to come to a reasonable understanding about the bathroom. A reasonable understanding,' she repeated vehemently. Suddenly she grabbed hold of the cumbersome old-fashioned radio and staggered out of the room with it, swaying from the waist like an over-burdened ant. They heard her knocking against the walls of the corridor as she carried it to the bathroom and deposited it on the floor outside.

The noise of a large orchestra performing at full volume erupted deafeningly, setting up a perilous vibration among the crockery in the china cupboard. Goldberg's outraged voice could barely be heard above the din.

'It's not anti-Semitism at all,' Frau Goetz was yelling as she returned to the sitting-room. 'Mr Stone, you haven't finished your coffee yet. Please sit down. There's no need to get upset.'

'Really, I must——' he began.

She interrupted him at once. 'No, no! You are my guest and I won't have you disturbed. Just take no notice of Herr Goldberg.'

A small Japanese came in, smiling with anxious determination. 'Frau Goetz, it's very difficult for me to practise,' he said timidly.

'I understand the inconvenience, Professor Hokoyama. But it won't be for long.' She introduced the professor to Martin, the pleasantries being conducted in loud voices as between people who are hard of hearing. 'Now, do join us for a nice cup of coffee,' she said sociably.

The Japanese put his hand to his ear. 'I'm sorry, what did you say?'

'A nice cup of coffee,' Frau Goetz repeated at the top of her voice.

'Ah, coffee!' Professor Hokoyama smiled painfully. 'Some other time,' he murmured, and withdrew with a polite bow.

The rest of them sat around the table tortured by an exuberant flourish of brass instruments. It would be Wagner, Martin thought grimly. On the other hand, a less bellicose composer would not have provided such suitable siege music.

Then, abruptly, the noise stopped. Somebody had switched off the radio. With astonishing agility Frau Goetz leaped off her chair and rushed to the bathroom just as the more lethargic Goldberg was about to lock himself in again.

'The bath is now free, Mr Stone,' she called, inserting her small frame obstinately in the doorway.

'It's not free,' Goldberg bellowed.

But it was by no means accidental that Frau Goetz had survived incarceration in Buchenwald. Her determination was indomitable.

'If you do not leave at once, I shall get into the bath myself,' she threatened, staring at him with brilliant, angry eyes.

As Martin came down the corridor, the defeated Goldberg marched along, his dressing-gown flapping around his skinny legs.

'*Guten Morgen, mein Herr,*' Martin said affably.

'Good morning.' Goldberg strode past with a curt nod of the head. He paused for a moment before entering his room. 'Anti-Semites!' he hissed contemptuously.

The atmosphere in the apartment settled down to a humdrum, peaceful domesticity. There was a clatter of crockery being washed up in the kitchen; doors banged; voices sounded obscurely through the plaster walls; the Japanese resumed his playing of Mozart. Martin lay steeped voluptuously in hot water to the chin. As the fatigue of the previous night soaked out of his resilient body he experienced an unexpected, unreasoning optimism. Towelling himself vigorously after the bath, he recalled an old nursery rhyme:

'*Es war einmal ein Mann*
Der hatte einen Schwamm;
Der Schwamm war ihm zu nass
Da ging er auf das Gras;
Das Gras war ihm zu grün
Da ging er nach Berlin…'

The rhyme, emerging out of a corner of the remote and forgotten past, reminded him of somebody whose existence had long since passed out of his mind, a Silesian girl with dark gentle eyes and a deep soft bosom who had nursed him when he was very small. She was his first love. Her clear young voice reciting the childish words returned so vividly that he could almost imagine it came from an adjoining room, communicating an ineffable feeling of happiness.

The fragile mood disintegrated abruptly. Frau Goetz was calling him to the telephone. He dressed hurriedly and went into the hall to answer it. At the other end of the wire Hugo sounded peeved at having been kept waiting.

'I've just spoken to my lawyer,' he said. 'He'll see you tomorrow afternoon at his office. Three-thirty. I'll send Heinz Dieter along to pick you up in the car and take you there.' Grudgingly he added: 'Are you settling in all right?'

'Yes,' Martin replied. 'Everything's fine.'

Hugo continued the conversation with an aimless persistence, as if he were preparing the way for a difficult confession. But whatever it was, he finally hung up without making it.

2

Hugo liked to take his time about getting up, reading the mail and the morning newspapers in bed, the first raw whisky warming his belly, the juicy stub of the first cigar in his mouth, the unpredictable day waiting quietly until he was ready for it. *Live every single day as if it were your last*: that was just about all the philosophy he could crumb together after fifty-odd years of experience, the ideas of twenty philosophers knocking noisily around in his head till he'd stopped listening. In the end one could be sure of nothing, so live the day out, gut it, suck it dry, extract the last drop of flavour, carry it all with you into the dark that closed under the eyelids. And if it lay nightmarish and indigestible on the brain, that was a dimension of experience, too.

He could see himself in the mirror on the wall opposite the bed, a stranded whale in bright silk pyjamas, blubbery flesh, thin straggly hair, paunchy eyes that looked back at him knowingly, without pity. The old machine was still functioning, he told himself with sardonic satisfaction, recalling how frequently he'd thought death had got him, its bony hand squeezing his over-ripe heart, or clawing among his tangled intestines. Each time it had been a playful rehearsal, a reminder that his number might come up at any moment – spread-eagled on the grass under the life-hot sun, or chewing a mouthful of succulent meat, or in the drawn-out, ecstatic moment when the hot lava of sex poured through his shuddering body…

The way he sometimes looked at it, all his life for the last twenty years was an unearned bonus. It was mere chance that he hadn't gone the way of the others: with a lunatic arbitrariness they took the gifted, the good, and the strong along with the imbecile, the tainted, the diseased. Among the millions there had been genius enough, actual or in the seed, to remake the world brick by brick, song by song, more splendid than it had ever been. Hugo Krantz, peddler of smart lyrics, good-time boy of the mad Berlin twenties, had got away. They had beaten him up and treated him like a piece of *Dreck*, but in the end the only thing they had taken from him that mattered was his talent, so lacking in robustness that it couldn't survive even a change of climate. Since then he'd lived seven to eight thousand days, each one different, each worth while for its own sake, for things seen, things tasted, things understood. He'd enjoyed the basic necessities – sex, food, and shelter – with all the refinements his temperament demanded. Wasn't that something? Something for nothing, you might say, but something all the same?

He thought of the past with masochistic pleasure, the common vice of the victim more compelling than any passion. Ridiculous not to acknowledge it. No one was immune from the desire to relive his punishment, to sit in comfort in a soft chair and recall with self-pity the arrogant cruelty of his persecutors. That was what he'd tried to explain to Martin Stone. It was meeting Martin again that had set the process in motion: reviving the memory of old Silberstein himself, able, shrewd, benevolent, a banker with civilised tastes in whose home he'd first mingled with politicians and prima donnas, the celebrated and powerful; and the old, crazy nocturnal Berlin with its introverts, its wide boys, its erratic dreamers, who used up one another for pleasure and stimulation; the sadistic Berlin of Max and Moritz, Fritz Lang and 'Metropolis', throbbing with a diseased energy, the pus of hatred already beginning to erupt; the Berlin, above all, of Putzi, the capricious, who loved and betrayed as if the whole thing were merely a divertissement arranged for his private amusement.

And the thoughts of Putzi brought him inevitably back to the night when they dragged him down to the cellars of the Brown House and flogged him under the glaring lights until the skin hung in ragged strips from his shoulders. Yes, he confessed, he was a Jewish pig, he was the most disgusting degenerate in the world for debauching the Aryan nobleman, the blue-blooded whore, Peter von Schlesinger. Yes, yes, yes – as they sprayed him with vermin killer and urinated in his face – thinking then that he would trade an eternity of pleasure for one quick bullet in the brain.

His lawyer paid a fortune in bribes to get him released, but he came out maimed. His jokes no longer made fun with bright malice, they snarled with bitterness; the smile in his pen had turned into a fixed grimace of hatred. And that was that. Putzi had become Ernst Roehm's lover and had, no doubt, learned to be amused by the pornographic monstrosities in Streicher's *Der Stürmer*. In a way it was Putzi, not Germany, who had destroyed his talent, since it was for Putzi that it had shone.

After the Roehm purge, Hugo had heard, von Schlesinger acquired an entirely different personality. He escaped into hetero-sexuality and marriage, became a staff officer in the Waffen S.S., fought recklessly on the Russian front with an S.S. Panzer division, and was decorated in the field. Later he suffered a wound in his beautiful thigh and was withdrawn from the front to take over security duties in the vast prison camp at Lamsdorf, Stalag VIIIB. But one night, after a drunken carousal, he shot a Canadian soldier in cold blood and was court-martialled. The last heard of him was in the battle for Budapest during the German retreat. He was presumed killed in action.

But the presumption was not enough for Hugo. For years he had sought to have it verified. Through a series of newspaper advertisements he had traced thirty-two survivors of von Schlesinger's unit. None of them was able to give much useful information – only that their formation had been scattered, most of its members being killed and some taken prisoner. Hugo hadn't bothered to advertise now for months. It seemed pretty useless. Putzi was almost certainly dead. Suddenly he decided to try again, just once more.

Heinz Dieter brought in the breakfast-tray. Wearing a garish checked dressing-gown with embroidered initials on the breast pocket, he looked like a prize-fighter who makes up in sartorial aggression what he lacks in violence. Heavy-eyed and weary, he set the tray down on the bedside table and collapsed into a chair with a prolonged yawn like a groan.

'You'll shag yourself to death,' Hugo told him brutally. 'Who was it last night? That nympho, Elsa?'

Heinz Dieter swallowed a reviving draught of black coffee and lit a cigarette. His mouth curved into a small smile. He was proud of his prowess as a Don Juan and enjoyed describing his adventures in minute detail, as if the experience were incomplete until it had been shared with Hugo. 'She was an absolute werewolf last night.' He grinned reminiscently and bared his chest to show the teeth marks where his flesh had been bitten. Hugo stared at the livid bruises on the smooth white skin, instantly visualising a girl's hungry red mouth, her widespread, straining thighs. He always thought of their sex as a wound, a mutilation.

'What do you expect, a medal?' he growled, and complained about the coffee, the eggs, the dryness of the toast, with tyrannical fussiness.

'I won't tell you anything if you don't want me to,' Heinz Dieter protested mulishly, like a child.

Hugo could barely restrain himself from digging his fingers into the big solid muscles and shaking him until his teeth rattled.

'How will I be able to live?' he said with mock dismay. Then, vindictively: 'Run the bath, Great Lover.'

Immersed in hot scented water, he began to think of the trivial incident with some remorse. Heinz Dieter was tidying the bedroom, banging rather excessively to advertise his resentment. For some time now the boy had been showing signs of nervous irritability. Had he put one of his girls in the family way, or picked up a disease, or got into debt through gambling? He'd been in various kinds of trouble before – a boy like that usually was. But whether it was money or women, Hugo had always fixed things for him. Sometimes they quarrelled, like the occasion when a pair of gold cuff-links had disappeared from the dressing-table; but he'd forgiven the boy when he produced a new leather wallet, a birthday gift bought with the proceeds of the theft. He was very touched that Heinz Dieter should remember his birthday. It was just like that kind of kid to steal from you with one hand and give you something with the other – your five-hundred-mark cuff-links for a wallet that would be expensive at fifty.

He felt responsible for Heinz Dieter with an indescribable mixture of guilt and tenderness, as one would for a child whom one had accidentally crippled. For all the tough, guttersnipe shrewdness, Heinz Dieter was at the mercy of anybody clever enough to make use of him. The sort of youth who would have committed unspeakable atrocities for Hitler with a wide-eyed innocence, he had the dangerous vulnerability of anybody who couldn't live without the affection of a master.

Perhaps I'm his Hitler, Hugo thought with cruel self-accusing elation, staring into the mirror with dislike as he knotted his tie. Here in his dressing-room he was confronted from all angles by an obesity which neither skilful tailoring nor the most expensive textiles could mitigate. A fat, coarse-grained, powerful, gluttonous man. His hands squeezed the knot of the tie a fraction too tight, making the neck veins swell and tingeing the skin of the face with a hint of purple. Loosening the knot, he gazed meditatively into his own face, the right eye's cynicism pitying the left eye's fear. There were too many mirrors: what could one do to the repulsive stranger in the glass but hate him?

I wonder if my life could have been different? he asked himself. As a small boy he had gone to the great synagogue in the Fasanenstrasse with his father, dwarfed by big fleshy men in glossy hats and prayer shawls whose voices droned a dead language through a hot city summer morning, making a noise like bees buzzing around the deaf face of God. And he used to think that to be a Jew was to be born with a weighted sack on one's back, a sack stuffed full of duties, prohibitions, sorrows, injustices – as if one were chosen to be the Lord's pack-horse with no hope of any reward but punishment.

When he was older he thought he'd shrugged off the sack. You didn't have to be a Jew, they were saying in Berlin during the 1920s. It was easy enough to have some holy water sprinkled on your face. But baptism was something he couldn't stomach, a form of intellectual cowardice. There was a sufficient choice of labels; you could change them as easily as changing your shirt. Everybody was having fun trying on new creeds to see if the styles became them. But what it amounted to was simply that you wanted to escape from the Jewish fate. The sky of Europe was beginning to turn the colour of persecution; you didn't want to be martyred for an intolerable antiquity, for a two-thousand-year-old crucifixion, for the shape of your nose, the loss of your foreskin.

In the end, there was nothing you could do about it. If you were born a Jew in Europe you carried death inside you from the cradle. You were destined to die at the same time as your grandfather. Were you as strong as a young bull, you would live no longer than the tubercular, the cancerous, the cretinous. Your horoscope might predict good or ill fortune, journeys by water, news of a friend, strange meetings. What did it matter? Individual destiny was overruled, and stamped in invisible letters across the configurations of the planets were the words: Cancelled – Jew.

Coming down the stairs to the richly appointed drawing-room where he worked, he was not too preoccupied to notice that Heinz Dieter moved hastily away from the desk, pretending to be interested in something occurring in the street below. One of the drawers in the desk was slightly open. Hugo lowered himself into the powder-blue leather swivel chair and pushed the drawer shut.

'Shall I get you a drink?' the young German volunteered brightly, watching him with an air of strained deference.

Hugo trimmed and lit a cigar, letting the smoke filter gently from the corner of his thick rubbery mouth. He wanted to say: 'Relax, Heinzi, don't look so worried. I'll take care of you.' Instead, he said in a soft, sarcastic tone: 'Were you reading my diary or looking for money?'

'Diary? Money?' the youth repeated, as if the words were without meaning. 'Ach! What's the matter with you today? Why are you picking arguments?'

'You're not denying you opened the drawer?'

Heinz Dieter gave him a rigid, almost comical stare of outraged dignity. Then he collapsed into sullenness, kicking the carpet with his toe. 'I've got money. I've been saving,' he said unwillingly. 'You must have left the drawer open.'

Hugo ground the newly lit cigar into the ash-tray. If it wasn't money it must have been the diary. He drew out the thick, leather-covered notebook and flicked through its pages. The entries were elaborately cryptic, inscribed not only in German, but also in English, French, even occasionally in Greek and Latin. It would be of little use to anyone, even if they succeeded in deciphering it. All that the snooper could possibly discover were private reflections, some erotica, and some carefully disguised references to acquaintances. The dialogue of a certain kind of loneliness.

What perplexed him was Heinz Dieter's unexpected interest in the diary. The boy was certainly not the soul of honesty. Loose cash, cigarettes, small valuables left lying around were there to pocket if he felt he needed them. But what possible motive could he have for prying into the diary? That sort of curiosity didn't fit in with his character at all. Perhaps, after all, he was mistaken. Perhaps the desk had been carelessly left open.

Almost reassured, he replaced the book and took out his bunch of keys to lock the drawer. One key was missing. Heinz Deiter bent down suddenly and picked up something from the floor. 'Are you looking for this?' he asked, his face red. 'You must have dropped it yesterday.' It was the missing key. Hugo felt a sickening surge of dismay. 'Thanks,' he said, looking away.

So the day steadily disintegrated. He interviewed a few salesmen, inspected fabrics, ordered new stocks of perfume, discussed business with the manageress of his shop, checked a few investments; lunched at Schlichter's with the theatre critic, Brauner, who tried to flatter him into believing that the whole Berlin theatre was waiting impatiently for him to write a new satirical revue, a suggestion that gave him the sort of discomfort a one-armed man feels when he imagines an ache in the wrist of his amputated arm; wasted an hour in the afternoon at an exhibition of macabre paintings by a young artist for whose Teutonic romanticism he was not just then in the mood, then played roulette in the *Spiel-Casino* in which he held a twenty-five per cent interest. And all the time the thought of Heinz Dieter, the diary, the morning's bickering, but, above all, the ache of the past, weighed dully on his brain like a persistent migraine.

During dinner he drank a great deal, as he always did when dining alone, then joined a party at the Opera for Verdi's 'Otello'. Desdemona in fine voice but ugly as a whore with her carrot-red wig, white face, and thick, middle-aged body. He snored through the strangling scene, dreaming that he wrestled with a white, formless, suffocating mist, cruel and treacherous as Iago.

Afterwards he took Klinger, the publisher, and his lawyer, Gustav Ulrich, with their wives, to the Maison de France. Mellowed by several brandies, Hugo lectured them sentimentally on the need for reconciliation between the Germans and the victims of the Nazis, and soon tears were glistening in everybody's eyes, Klinger's wife being especially tearful and her pink, pigeon-plump bosom quivering with emotion.

Near them some English journalists were putting away whiskies quickly and with determination, probably homesick for polished mahogany, brass-and-ivory beer pumps, the dull thwack of the leather ball against wood, and the spatter of hand-clapping as batsmen strolled peacefully to and from the pavilion. Their colourless English voices brought to mind wet Portsmouth pubs filled with sailors, sea mist and black-out behind the windows, the beery choruses, the posters: *Careless Talk Costs Lives*. Hugo was moved by an unexpected happy nostalgia and declined an invitation from Klinger to join the rest of them at a late party.

He felt the need to be solitary for a while. Outside the Maison de France the street tilted gently to and fro with a sleepy insistent rhythm. He strolled along the pavement savouring the drifting odours of boiled sausages from a nearby street kiosk, watching the stout people in restaurants eating sauerkraut and pickled pork and schnitzel, and the big, shrewd-eyed blondes swinging their broad bottoms as they paraded hopefully past the pavement tables of cafés. Drunk or sober, how he enjoyed the sheer gluttony of the Berlin street!

When he got home an hour or two later, he looked in Heinz Dieter's room, hoping for a reconciliation. But the boy was already asleep.

The advertisement appeared on Monday morning. On Wednesday at breakfast Hugo found a crumpled dirty white envelope among his correspondence. He put all the other letters carefully aside and opened it. Although it bore a West Berlin postmark, the address inside was that of a street in Friedrichshain, East Berlin. The letter said: 'Referring to your advertisement, I was in the S.S. Panzer-division Feldherrnhalle, 1st Squadron. I was taken prisoner and sent to Russia. Have been back now twelve months and would be glad to meet an old comrade. Yours in anticipation, Karl Gross.'

Even after thirty-two failures, Hugo felt the familiar stirring of excitement. He hurried through his meal and an hour later drove across the city boundary into Alexanderplatz. A few hundred yards from the address he parked his car and walked the rest of the way down a street pitted with stagnant puddles of rain water.

The place was above a leather workshop. He passed through a flagstoned passage, and on the second floor found a piece of white cardboard nailed to a door. It read: 'K. Gross, Carpenter and Handyman.'

A thin, gaunt man, his face deeply seamed by sickness and hunger, answered his knock. Hugo showed him the letter. 'Are you Herr Gross?' he asked.

The man looked at him for a few seconds before replying. 'Come in,' he said, leading the way into a shabby room with an unmade bed in the corner. The damp, stained wallpaper, the bare floor-boards, the few sticks of rickety furniture testified to the poverty of the occupant. 'Sit down.' Gross pointed to the bed. 'Worse than the army,' he added with a crooked attempt at a smile. 'I can't say I recognise your face, Herr...'

'Keller,' Hugo intervened hurriedly. 'I'm trying to find out about an old friend.' He offered his cigar-case to placate the other's mistrust.

Gross lit the cigar and smoked hungrily for a while, scrutinising the good cloth of Hugo's suit, the well-polished hand-made shoes, the expensive gold wrist-watch. 'You weren't in the division yourself then?'

'No, I was not.'

The man nodded his head slowly, as if the answer had confirmed his suspicions. 'I'm disappointed, Herr Keller,' he said gruffly. 'I was thinking maybe I'd meet an old comrade, and maybe he'd have done all right for himself. You understand, I've spent years in Siberia. My health isn't so good. An old comrade, he might appreciate that, Herr Keller.'

He smiled briefly and painfully, exposing a mouthful of decayed teeth. It was rather ghastly, a grimacing parody of amiability.

'I'm prepared to pay for information,' Hugo explained, averting his eyes. 'I'm interested in news about an officer. Von Schlesinger. Does the name mean anything to you?'

'Von Schlesinger?' Gross began to move about the room in restless excitement. 'That's a strange coincidence.' He spoke rapidly, in an almost inaudible undertone. 'When I read that advertisement it made me think of all the old comrades – Schtoller and Jurgens and Friedmann and Walter and the others – thinking how they died, some of them, the unlucky ones, raving mad with pain, and I thought to myself wouldn't it be funny if——' He broke off abruptly and said: 'You did say von Schlesinger?'

'Yes, you knew him then?'

Gross puffed at his cigar feverishly. '*Sturmbannführer*, tall, very blond, bad limp. Does that sound like the man? About thirty, thirty-two. Good-looking fellow, too good-looking maybe.

Used to smell nice. Funny, even in the shit and the muck he smelled like he was covered with flowers.'

Used to smell nice! The absurd detail brought Putzi sharply into focus again, vividly recalling his sensual addiction to perfume. That and the fine gold chain he liked to wear on his right wrist. Hugo kept the excitement out of his voice with difficulty. 'That's the man,' he confirmed quietly. 'You describe him very well.'

'Just a minute,' Gross said. He took a worn leather wallet out of his pocket and extracted some well-thumbed snapshots. He selected one and passed it over. Three healthy, good-looking German soldiers standing by a staff car smiled cheerfully out of the picture. It was just possible to recognise Gross, the seamed face filled out, the bloodshot eyes clear and young. Putzi was unmistakable. Nothing about him was changed: slender, tall, arrogantly mocking and beautiful, there was a suggestion of masquerade about his appearance, as if the business of war were a high-spirited piece of fun and he was getting the most out of it. One hand rested possessively in an unmilitary gesture on the shoulder of the third man in the snapshot, a tough, rugged-looking corporal.

Hugo laid the snapshot face down on the table. It affected him with uncomfortable violence. 'What can you tell me?' he asked shakily.

'About him? Anything you want to know. I was his orderly, I knew him inside out.' A reminiscent, lop-sided smile passed over the sick features. 'A fine officer, Herr Keller. Had guts. One of the best, I tell you. You'd be proud of him, sir.' He began to talk eagerly of the vicissitudes of the retreat, the strafing and the artillery barrages, with men dying all the way from the bitter snows of Russia to the corpse-congested streets of Budapest.

Hugo listened patiently and without comment. In relation to Putzi the recital seemed unreal. In the old days he'd shrunk from violence like a girl: even a cut on the finger would fill him with dismay. *Sturmbannführer* von Schlesinger, heroically marshalling his men under murderous fire, was another creature entirely. It gave Hugo the strange feeling that he was pursuing the wrong man.

Finally he interrupted the flow of reminiscence. A cold, calm, final question: 'Was he killed?'

'Killed?' Gross spoke stupidly, his staring eyes watering with weak tears. 'I've seen thousands of them die. I'm not squeamish, but I can't bear to think about it. That boy there in the photograph, the one with me and the commander, he was my pal. Would you like me to tell you about him? As lovely a boy as you could wish to meet. Came from Stuttgart. Wasn't a day he didn't write to his mother——'

'I'm only interested in von Schlesinger. You say you were his orderly. Did you see him die, or did you see his body?'

'Why are you asking me this?' Gross asked fearfully, pressing his hand against his forehead. 'I don't understand.' He walked to the window and peered evasively out at the shabby street. 'He was reported dead. If he came through you'd have heard by now. All these years, do you think I can remember the name of every corpse I've seen?'

'I'm only asking you to remember what happened to one man, your own officer.'

The German came back to the centre of the room. 'I don't trust you, Herr Keller,' he said in a strained, suppressed voice. 'I don't think you were the commander's friend at all.'

Hugo's heart was beating unevenly. He felt slightly giddy, as if he'd smoked too much, trembling on the brink of a deeply unpleasant discovery. Flatly he said: 'He wasn't killed, was he? Von Schlesinger is alive, and you know it.'

'Why do you question me like this?' Gross shouted. 'You've got no right to come here cross-examining me. You're not a comrade, not a comrade at all!' His voice broke hysterically. 'You fat profiteer! I bet you sat on your fat arse in some funk-hole while good Germans were killed. Get out! Get out!'

Shocked and afraid, Hugo went to the door, but before he could open it the man clutched his arm.

'I'm sorry, Herr Keller. Forgive me, I'm sick. My nerves – I've had a terrible time.' His sour breath filled Hugo's nostrils as he lifted his sallow, tortured face in a gesture of entreaty. 'I can tell you what you want to know. A hundred Westmarks, that's all I want. I'm starving. I haven't eaten for days.'

Hugo counted out the money and deposited it on the table. The price was surely too trivial to buy a death.

'It can't do any harm now. The commander was good to me. He used to joke a lot. You were his friend, Herr Keller, there's no harm in telling you.' Gross paused, vainly expecting a word of reassurance, then continued haltingly. 'The Russians had crossed the bridges into Buda. They weren't taking many prisoners. Officers especially, they shot them on sight. Three of us were left alive in a slit trench near the fortress – the Major, my pal Wolfgang Sommer, and me. Wolfgang got a grenade splinter in the head. The Major changed clothes with him. He thought he'd stand more chance as a corporal.'

'So he was taken prisoner.'

'I don't know. We separated. The Reds kept me around for days on burial fatigues, but some of the other men were sent back to the rear right away.'

'Didn't you hear anything in the prison camps in Russia?'

'You've no idea, Herr Keller, there were so many of us.'

Hugo stared at Gross, wondering even then whether he was telling the truth. Wolfgang Sommer. He wouldn't forget the name. After all these years…Downstairs in the street he stood for a while dazedly inhaling the sharp astringent air as if he had emerged after months from a windowless room. Somewhere, at that moment, his enemy was alive. And wherever he was, whatever he was doing, he made the world a different place.

On the way back to the car Hugo found himself peering into the face of every passing stranger.

Late that evening he was drinking alone in Charlie's Night Club. It was raining heavily outside. A man came in shaking the rain off his hat and stood in the doorway looking around as if he couldn't make up his mind whether or not to stay. Hugo put him down as a tourist right away, noting the stranger's wide-eyed astonishment as the club's exotic attraction, a young Negro pansy, wiggled coquettishly past fluttering his mauve-painted eyelids.

The newcomer pushed a fifty-groschen piece into the juke-box and selected a Sinatra record before strolling over to the bar. Hugo was aware of being sized up. Did he speak English? he was asked. Certainly. The stranger was relieved: his German wasn't too hot.

'Quite a place,' he said, nodding unobtrusively towards the young Negro. 'I bet she-he is an ex-G.I. I've seen the same in Harlem. The gown must have cost a fortune.'

It was one of Krantz's exclusive models, but Hugo saw no point in saying so.

'Have a drink,' he offered politely.

'Thanks. Can you trust the bourbon here?'

He assured the stranger that the liquor in Charlie's was up to the necessary international standards, and so were the prices. 'We Americans are kinda spoiled,' the latter apologised. 'The name, incidentally, is Mel Kane.' He held out a broad square palm and exerted a crushing handshake.

'You've got a place in the Kurfürstendamm. I passed it today,' Kane said when Hugo introduced himself. His attention wandered to the young Negro again. 'Say, doesn't he look like Eartha Kitt! It's the most marvellous female impersonation I've ever seen.'

'Would you like to be introduced?' Hugo asked, assuming that Kane's interest was an indication that he wanted to become acquainted with the boy.

'No, thanks. Not my sort of fun.' Still watching the Negro's arch and graceful posturing, he grinned with the complacency of a man who regards heterosexuality as a mark of superiority. 'Mind you, with someone like that in the dark it would be hard to make out just what you'd got hold of.'

Soon Kane was talking freely, too freely, about himself. It wasn't his first trip to Berlin. He'd been there for some months during the Airlift. With the U.S. forces. What branch? A perceptible hesitation, then a strictly *entre-nous* wink of the eye. Air Force Intelligence. He'd specialised in languages at Harvard. After enlistment, when they discovered he knew Russian, they whipped him into Intelligence so fast he hadn't time to catch his breath. Now he worked for this San Francisco paper. Well…

actually, he was a free lance, but he had a contract. What stories was he covering? Oh, anything and everything. He pretty well had *carte blanche*. Something might blow up in East Berlin and he'd be there to report it.

Hugo heard all this with considerable scepticism. With its post-war reputation, Berlin attracted visitors who sought to make themselves sound more mysterious than they actually were. Any moment now the man would give himself away by some stupid discrepancy. Sure enough, he did. He began to tell an amusing story about his experience in ordering breakfast a few weeks before on arrival in Germany. 'My vocabulary didn't go much further than *ja* and *nein*, so you can imagine what a mess I got into trying to get them to bring me ham and eggs.' But if he specialised in languages at Harvard, and if he had spent some months in Berlin during the Airlift, how was it that he could only manage *ja* and *nein* on this present visit?

There was a certain fascination for Hugo in inveigling Kane into contradictory admissions.

'Do you cable your paper very often?' he asked innocently.

'Oh, I try to,' Kane replied with an equally naïve earnestness, 'but it's very expensive.'

What sort of journalist could he be if he'd never heard of collect facilities? And what sort of newspaper could it be that sent a foreign correspondent to Europe at some considerable expense, but did not make the usual cable arrangements at the comparatively negligible press rates?

'Of course, it's possible that you're not a newspaper-man at all,' Hugo commented slyly. 'You could even be a secret agent. There are plenty of them in Berlin, working for the Americans, the Russians, the British, the French, even for all of them at the same time.'

Kane sipped his drink in embarrassed silence, studying the white leatherette walls of the bar with abstracted concentration. 'This bourbon is pretty good,' he remarked eventually, and, without a change of tone: 'If I were an agent, I'd be a damned funny one. I talk too much.'

When Hugo drove away from Charlie's a short while later, a cruising taxi remained obstinately reflected in his driving mirror, dawdling, accelerating, turning corners in his wake as if its engine were synchronised with his own. In the next few days he thought he glimpsed Kane several times. Then, lunching at Schlichter's, he glanced up from his newspaper to see him sitting at the next table.

'This place is a village,' Kane remarked. 'You keep running into the same people.'

Hugo examined him with deliberate care, conducting a re-assessment. The American was about thirty-five, his pale phlegmatic face puffily disfigured around the small grey-glass eyes. The drab, ill-made suit concealed a powerful physique. There was something awkward yet assertive about him. Somehow, it was less easy now to think of him as a tourist.

'Have you picked up any good stories for your newspaper?' Hugo's sour smile masked a lurking uneasiness.

Kane examined his blunt finger-tips. 'I'm on to one, I think.' He took out of his pocket a folded copy of the *Telegraf*. 'I've been studying newspaper ads. That's where you find it all – comedy, heartbreak, romance, despair.'

'A charming American sentiment,' Hugo said dryly.

'Take this, for instance,' Kane went on, ignoring the sarcasm. '"Widow, forty-two, still attractive, comfortable pension, seeks friendship with cultured gentleman. Two daughters, seventeen and nineteen. Prepared to invest in sound business." There's an obvious story in that. A colonel's lady, perhaps, widow of a Nazi war hero. What a prospect for some smart operator! I'm almost tempted.'

'She won't be short of candidates.'

'That's for certain,' Kane agreed. His eyes scanned the column and were caught by another advertisement. It had been heavily underlined. 'This one's interesting. Have you heard of the S.S. Panzer-division Feldherrnhalle?'

Hugo poured a glass of wine, controlling the steadiness of his hand with difficulty. 'I'm not an expert on the German Army, I'm afraid,' he replied coldly.

Kane stuffed the newspaper back into his pocket. He stood up and donned a black leather overcoat, adjusting the snap brim of his hat as if it were the peak of a helmet. '*Auf Wiederschauen*,' he said, walking heavily away with a policeman's tread.

Hugo sat for so long without touching his food that the waiter became rather concerned. Schlichter's was noted for the excellence of its fare, and Herr Krantz was a valued customer.

'It is not satisfactory?' he asked anxiously.

With an irritable gesture Hugo waved him away. He was thinking back to the first meeting with Kane. Looked at in a certain light, the man had deliberately advertised himself as an American agent by his flimsy journalistic front and too-ready disclosures of his service in military counterespionage. But a genuine American spy would have created a much more convincing impression as a newspaper correspondent. In fact, he would probably be a newspaper-man with a well-known by-line. Who, then, would deliberately set out to create the impression that he was a secret agent of the State Department? A practical joker? A poseur? Kane did not fit into such reassuring categories.

Fear groped in Hugo's body like a dull spasm of pain. Supposing, just supposing, the man was not an American at all, but an English-speaking German, or Pole, or even… a Russian? There were Russians who had so perfected their American accents by listening to tape-recorders that their authenticity would not be challenged anywhere, certainly not outside America.

He recalled a meeting with a young Soviet interpreter who had accompanied a trade delegation to the Leipzig Fair. A fattish fellow, freckled and open-faced, with a crew cut and a Brooklyn accent you could hit with a baseball bat. The Russian had been eager to talk about the poor whites of central California, conditions in the Chicago stock-yards, the degeneracy of Hollywood film stars and Boston millionaires, and about the gang wars. He had acquired a highly coloured picture of America from the novels of Steinbeck, Upton Sinclair, and Scott Fitzgerald…

Yes, despite the improbabilities, Kane could be a Soviet agent. Thinking of the flat, puffy face, the small grey eyes buried in flesh, the almost Oriental impassivity, Hugo was sure of it. Not even a Russian face: Central Asian. One saw men like him in news-reels walking heavily behind Gromyko towards a plane, their suits specially tailored to conceal the pistol holster under the left armpit. But there was nothing criminal about advertising in a newspaper, he assured himself uneasily. His interest in Putzi might be morbid, but it wasn't against the law.

Of course, a series of advertisements seeking contact with former members of an S.S. group might justifiably be suspected as originating from a Nazi, but even that was scarcely an offence in Germany nowadays. Far from it, since Hitler men again held high office in the country. It would be a strange irony if he, Hugo Krantz, the ex-refugee, were an item on the budget of the M.B.G. or the State Department, suspected perhaps of organising a neo-Nazi movement.

The thought was so ridiculous that he was convinced he had made a melodrama of an insignificant incident. Kane was merely just another busy-body, a low-grade journalist hoping to unearth a sensational story. Yet the uneasiness persisted, and when he got back to the office he quietly transferred a half litre of brandy from the bottle to his stomach.

Heinz Dieter looked at him solicitously. 'Got a migraine, Hugo?' he asked, anxious to be friends again.

'No, Heinzi, just a bit of a headache. Fetch me the eau-de-Cologne.'

While the young German was out of the room he began to check through the telephone directory, looking for a name. There was no Wolfgang Sommer.

3

Martin stirred restlessly in his chair by the window. It was now dark, and the pallid street lamps shed an acid-yellow glow on the pavements of the long grey street. He lit a cigarette and let the spent match fall to the floor. A day, a night, and a day had passed since he had come and he was still abnormally stirred, the way a man might be if he experienced a strange shock that awakened in him areas of feeling of whose existence he had been oblivious. He'd thought of himself as someone with strong moral convictions but moderate feelings – in that sense, strictly English. Now he seemed complex and neurotic, a tangle of exposed nerves, a loose bundle of untidy passions precariously concealed beneath the neat exterior of conformity, which itself had become something of a habit. When he first put on the uniform of an English schoolboy, he'd studied the movements, the graces, the way of speech of his fellows and learned to reproduce them with some accuracy. One admired image had followed another, until he'd lost himself somewhere in the multiplicity of impersonations.

In this, he now recognised, he had a slender affinity with Hugo. Hugo's Hampstead Bohemia had been a convincing pastiche, a clever literary fabrication. The writers, the painters, the mild left-wing intellectuals had rehearsed the conversation pieces of their time while Hugo moved among them dispensing drinks and epigrams with stylish ease. He was queer, of course, but never scandalously, and Marion had lovers. But that, too, among the moneyed, the mannered, the people of talent and sensibility, would be regarded with indulgence. Hugo, the cultivated refugee, one thought, not even guessing at the mockery with which the rôle was sustained and the appalling sham of it all.

The sound of Mozart came through the walls as the Japanese professor performed his evening exercises, and suddenly Martin revolted at the boredom of his solitary reflections. He got up and switched on all the lights. It would be a good thing when he'd got his restitution claim started and went home. He'd lie back on his own divan and play the Dave Brubeck records and maybe bring a girl in. Only the old man would be next door, coughing insistently. It was worrying, the way he refused to see a doctor. 'Can they stop you dying?' he'd say. 'Give me a game of chess. That's a better cure,' and while they played he'd comment with an ironic detachment on the latest news about Germany. 'They can't wait to give them nuclear armaments. You see that Messer's a big man in Bonn now? If anyone deserved to be hanged in Spandau it's that Nazi. They're all gentlemen again. Any day they'll make Krupp a freeman of the City of London...'

When the restitution award came through he'd send the old man away for a couple of months to the sunshine. Maybe to Israel – plenty of his old friends over there. One was even a Cabinet Minister.

Frau Goetz came in with coffee and biscuits, smelling strongly of violets and schnapps. Clearly she was not always equal to her austere religious principles.

'I'm worried about you, Mr Stone,' she announced with a husky laugh. It was easy to guess that her voice had once been roughened on burlesque ribaldry. 'A young fellow shouldn't be sitting alone in his room on an evening like this.' She darted a quick, birdlike glance at the uncurtained window, probably remembering that a guest had once chosen that way to make a sudden exit. 'It's all right for me – I've got my memories. But you should be enjoying yourself, then you'll have something to think about when you're old.'

'Frau Goetz, you're not in the least bit old,' he protested dutifully. She patted the elaborate coiffure of her dyed yellow hair with bashful pleasure. 'I've always said Englishmen are gentlemen. Hugo can say what he likes about you being a Prussian, but it's the upbringing that counts, Mr Stone. Would you find a young German sitting alone in his room when he could be out drinking or dancing or gambling? The good times, that's all everybody seems to want here. They couldn't care less that they're damned.' The thought seemed to give her considerable satisfaction, but rather inconsistently she went on: 'Get yourself a girl, Mr Stone. There are plenty of lively, pretty young things in Berlin who'd be glad to meet a young English gentleman.'

'Thank you for the coffee, Frau Goetz,' Martin said.

But now she was listening to Professor Hokoyama's piano-playing, tilting her small head towards the music and briefly closing her blue-veined eyelids in concentration.

'Charming!' she announced. 'He plays that passage rather well, I think,' and, with an abrupt characteristic restlessness, tottered unsteadily to the door on her stilted heels. 'Mustn't gossip any more,' she chided herself severely. 'There's so much to do.'

Alone again in the emptiness of the room, the coffee, too, tasted of loneliness, a bitter sediment on the tongue. And the thought of girls Frau Goetz had planted began to germinate. Blonde girls, plump as Rhine maidens, their pork-nourished flesh heavy with sensuality. An imaginary encounter began to form in his mind. He could see the girl as clearly as if she stood before him, well-built and pretty in a cow-like way; full, pouting mouth and sleepy eyes; a soft, yielding, sex-ripe body. About eighteen. He asked her to dance. A faint smell of perspiration clung to her warm flesh, not disagreeably...

It was too ridiculously adolescent. Auto-eroticism in a Berlin pension. The humiliation drove him out to walk the cold, treacherous streets until his blood recovered its frigid enmity.

Next day, shortly after three in the afternoon, Heinz Dieter Schulz called in the car to take him to the lawyer's office. It was one of those bright, frosty days with early spring sunshine that gives Berlin an atmosphere of optimism and vigour, when the blood bubbles like Rhine champagne and dreams of mad-March greatness haunt the city like echoes of a Wagnerian crescendo. But all the way to his destination, Martin shivered with cold and depression, replying in monosyllables to his companion's affable chatter.

He was thinking of his father back in London, probably spending the early afternoon sitting in his favourite café in Finchley Road with his regular cronies, meditatively fitting his half cigarettes into the amber holder and immersed in refugee gossip. He had begun composing a letter to the old man in his mind when Heinz Dieter braked the car and announced their arrival.

Gustav Ulrich and Partners, Hugo's lawyers, were on the second floor of a large commercial bank in the Kantstrasse. They had all the paraphernalia of a prosperous practice. A well-groomed receptionist seated at a daffodil-yellow desk interrogated him with practised charm. 'You have an appointment with Herr Gustav Ulrich *himself*?' she queried respectfully. Herr Ulrich reserved his personal attentions only for important clients, her manner implied. Consulting a green morocco diary engraved with gilt lettering, she confirmed that Martin was expected at three-thirty. He was five minutes too early and correctness decreed that he should be announced punctually, neither too early nor too late.

'I hope you won't mind waiting a few minutes,' she said, directing him to a room with opaque walls of corrugated glass which smelled of lavender floor polish and disinfectant air-conditioning. A low metal and ebonite table was covered with German industrial magazines and a selection of newspapers. He sat down despondently and glanced with bored disinterest through a highly technical article on electronics. A slight nervous sickness had settled on his stomach as it did when waiting his turn at the dentist's.

Punctually at three-thirty a secretary brought him to Gustav Ulrich's private office. The lawyer was a good-looking man of about fifty with a pink, plump, priestly face and fine silver hair brushed carefully over a bald spot on his crown. He rose for the usual handshaking formalities.

'Sit down, Mr Stone,' he said, speaking English in a gentle voice with only a slight accent. 'Mr Krantz has given me some idea of your claim. Cigarette?' He proffered a thin gold case politely, watching Martin with the intent, kindly expression of a doctor examining a sick patient.

Hugo had told him that the young man was difficult: his family had suffered badly, of course. But even without that warning he would have known right away that here was an awkward client. The undisguised hostility with which Stone observed him; the perfunctory, reluctant handshake; the wariness with which he seated himself on the other side of the desk, as if confronting an enemy. Ulrich had experienced it too frequently with Jews to fail to recognise it. At first he'd also felt an awkwardness, although God could be his witness that he'd never personally harmed a Jew in his life. Now he no longer felt so involved. One handled them as gently as possible – they bruised easily – and got their claims settled as quickly as could be managed; and, in a small way, helped to undo some of the harm the Nazis had inflicted on them.

Martin pushed a portfolio of documents across the desk. They had been sorted out from a dusty collection of papers his father had preserved in an old cardboard box – family birth certificates, faded deeds of sale, official letters, financial statements, insurance policies: meagre evidence that the House of Silberstein had once existed with its commercial offices, its mansion, cars, servants, and rich bank deposits, its art collection, library, and silver plate – result of the business acumen and industry that had transformed a small money-lending concern into a flourishing bank. Two hundred years of history reduced to a bundle of musty paper… On the basis of this, the cash reckoning between the House of Silberstein and the heirs of the Third Reich would be made.

But only the cash reckoning. You could scan the documents in vain and find nothing about Lise. If you searched assiduously enough you might find the name written in some official record, some medical file, perhaps. Lise Silberstein, Jewess, aged fifteen;

diagnosis: melancholia; deceased 12 February, 1938. Effects duly returned to next of kin, postage collect. Even so laconic an entry would, in the light of events, seem overloaded with tragedy; but when one such case history was multiplied by millions it became a mute cipher in a column of statistics. Death had even been robbed of its tragic poetry, reduced to the language of industrial output.

At this moment, sitting in the office of a German lawyer making a claim for compensation for his family's property, Martin felt it was his duty to recall Lise. The one person who carried her image intact was his father, and when he died she would go unremembered, her pale child face with its great sad eyes fading from Martin's mind like a portrait sketched on misted glass. Only retrospectively did he love Lise. Several years older, she had teased and persecuted him, jealous of the special affection their mother had bestowed on him. In fact, he remembered feeling relieved when she fell into the melancholy silence broken by storms of weeping which frightened his parents. Nowadays, Martin supposed, such mental conditions would be cured by shock treatment. The Nazis, however, had their own system of pathology. They sent a peremptory order that Lise should be brought to a hospital for sterilisation. His parents tried to bribe the doctors into issuing certificates that the girl was not mentally unsound; they went to lawyers. One day the police called and took Lise away. All the family's inquiries were rebuffed: they were never able to find where the authorities had sent her. And then one morning the mail-truck delivered a small parcel. It contained the clothes Lise had gone away in, a fluffy toy dog from which in her sickness she refused to be separated, her tooth-brush and comb, and a handful of hairpins which fastened her long brown hair. The postman asked for the few groschen postage the parcel cost, as regulations demanded. The next mail delivery officially notified the family that Lise was dead, and that same day his mother killed herself. Weeks later they heard that Lise died in a very special German institute. Experiments on her fifteen-year-old Jewish body had provided scientists with useful data on the treatment of diseases contracted by soldiers on the battlefield. She had made her sacrifice for the Fatherland.

Yes, Martin reflected as the lawyer examined the documents, there could be no cash reckoning for Lise. Nor for Uncle Franz, who walked into his garden after the Nazis confiscated his publishing house and blew his brains out by the lily-pond; nor for Uncle Heinrich, who once commanded an artillery battalion and revered Hindenburg, but locked himself up in the kitchen of his eight-room apartment on Unter den Linden with his wife and four children, turned on the gas, and died ridiculously in full-dress uniform with his campaign medals and the Iron Cross pinned to his chest.

He screwed his eyelids up against the bright, thin sunshine that shone obliquely through the window and was reflected upon the polished desk. In the street below it glittered on the chrome and enamel of luxury cars parked along the centre of the road. In all the offices of the Kantstrasse clerks coped briskly with the intricate problems of finance. It was any bright functional day in Berlin. Business as usual. Business regardless.

Meticulously Herr Ulrich was examining the documents, making notes in a small neat hand on a writing-pad. Once the telephone rang. 'I do not wish to be interrupted,' he said curtly, and returned to his reading, one finger pressed against his right ear-drum as if to aid concentration. Finally he closed the portfolio.

'Yes, these will be extremely useful,' he commented thought-fully. 'We'll have to do a lot of research, though. The problem in these claims is to establish fairly precisely what is involved. In this case, you are only concerned with obtaining compensation for material assets, I believe.'

Martin said: 'There are limits to restitution.' He looked at Ulrich with undisguised hatred, not so much because he was German, but because they were accomplices.

'Quite so,' the lawyer agreed uncomfortably. Yet he detected only the bitterness, not the hatred. During the Hitler period he occupied a minor post in the legal department of the Finance Ministry. Had he joined the Party he might have earned prom-otion, but religious scruples prevented him. He was a good Catholic, and although many other Catholics had not found it inconsistent with their principles to join the Nazis, for him there had been only one Führer, the Pope. So he had only a limited sense of guilt. It would not occur to him that anybody, even a Jew, should actively hate him.

'Well, Mr Stone, let us hope we will get your claim through without much delay,' he went on. 'A good deal of money is involved and some of the details may be rather complicated, but you can rely on me to do my best.' He smiled with a great deal of charm. It usually worked rather well. 'Shall we drink to our success?'

'Thank you, I'd rather not,' Martin said, rising abruptly. 'You don't need me any more just now, do you?'

The rebuff surprised Ulrich unpleasantly. He felt an unusual anxiety to explain himself, to break down the young Jew's hostility.

'There is one thing I would like you to understand, Mr Stone,' he said with quiet insistence. 'I give much personal attention to restitution cases. Many of them are small matters – a man claims for a little shop, or a government pension, or loss of earning power because of illness contracted as a result of ill-treatment. What I want to say is that it isn't just a matter of business for me. There are many people in Germany who feel ashamed.' His voice hesitated and then continued almost inaudibly, as if he were speaking to himself: 'Perhaps we could have done more. It's difficult for a man to be a hero in cold blood.'

Martin averted his eyes. It was not for him to understand. 'As far as I'm concerned, Herr Ulrich,' he said harshly, 'this is strictly a matter of business. I'd like you to handle it in that spirit. Your commission, I believe, is ten per cent. That is quite satisfactory to me.'

'I'm sorry. You seem to have misinterpreted——'

'Please, let's not discuss it.'

Ulrich shook his head in discouragement. He prided himself on being a patient man, but at that moment he was tempted to give up. The Silberstein case would be profitable, but he was not short of business and man did not live by bread alone. Yet one must keep trying; the task of conciliation was never easy. He thought: A nation must also do penance. It must stand in the confessional of the world and say: I have sinned. The individual may not have been personally guilty, but there was a corporate guilt. Every German who loved his country must atone. That, today, was patriotism.

With an almost physical distress, he said: 'I quite understand, Mr Stone,' half extending his hand in a forlorn gesture of friendship. But Martin had already turned away.

Heinz Dieter Schulz was chatting gaily with the blonde receptionist, perched familiarly on the edge of her desk swinging his leg so that part of a hairy muscular calf showed above his transparent nylon sock.

'I got fed up waiting in the car,' he explained nonchalantly, 'so I came up to see Hilde. See you Saturday at Resi's,' he told the girl. 'Put on your prettiest dress and don't come with the boy friend. I don't like competition.'

He strolled away with a slight swagger of his broad shoulders, hands negligently thrust into the pockets of his stylishly cut duffle coat. Martin followed behind, as if to emphasise the merely arbitrary connection between them, observing with dislike the loose, assured grace of Heinz Dieter's walk, the cropped head shining yellow as corn stubble, the too-tight light-coloured trousers that showed the movement of the buttocks.

With a mocking, exaggerated politeness, the young German held the car door open for him, then, tossing a half-smoked cigarette out of the window, drove off with an impressive roar of acceleration.

'If you're not in a hurry, we could stop somewhere for a beer or coffee,' he suggested amiably.

In more congenial company Martin might have felt like getting drunk. He needed not so much the stimulation of alcohol as the illusion of detachment that it gave, the feeling that everything could be brought to a ridiculously easy solution.

'It'll do you good,' the young German persisted with an amused, sidelong glance. 'You look as if you've had a rough night. I know a place where the company's pretty lively.' He hooted loudly at a pretty girl crossing the road.

'Does she suit you?' he asked with a wink. 'She suits me.' Nudging Martin with his elbow, he said: 'I bet you're married.'

'I'm not.'

'Got a girl?'

'Nobody special,' Martin said patiently, staring out the window.

'Me, I'm crazy about girls.' He stated the fact with pride, as though it were a talent. 'I've got two kids already, you know. They're over on the other side, in the East. But the woman is no good. Skinny.' Taking both hands off the wheel, he described a curve in the air. 'I like them like that.'

Martin said dryly: 'Girls are no good if you're dead. You want to watch your driving.'

'Scared you, eh?' the youth exclaimed gleefully. 'Don't worry, your number's not been called yet. Me, I don't care. Enjoy life while you've got it. You're *kaput* for a long time.'

His frank hedonism provoked less mistrust in Martin than the moral ambiguities of such educated Germans as Ulrich. He reflected that Heinz Dieter would have been no more than nine or ten at the end of the war. Probably picked up crusts by trading cigarettes and precociously pandering to the vices of Russian and American soldiers. There was something in him of the preternaturally experienced juvenile, understanding nothing beyond sensuality and untroubled by such incomprehensible abstractions as guilt or innocence. Physical survival and physical gratification were the only things that mattered for many of his generation.

They were back in the Kurfürstendamm. Although it was still broad daylight, the neon lights burned palely, an intimation of the garish inevitable night. They stopped in front of a large café. The legend 'Old Vienna' was written in glowing red filament above the doorway, but the same stolid Germans sat at small tables on the glass-covered terrace staring with unblinking curiosity at the continual pavement promenade. Inside, a gleaming Gaggia sizzling aromatic steam was enthroned behind a horse-shoe bar crowded with young men and girls in sweaters, duffle coats, and jeans. Small tables distributed round the walls were mainly occupied by older men attracted by the erotic stimulation of the young. The interior was neo-Cosmopolitan rather than Old Viennese.

Heinz Dieter walked in as if he owned a substantial part of the establishment. He waved to several people, stopped to whisper in the ear of a teen-aged girl, staring boldly at the plump bulges in her bright red sweater, then led Martin over to an unoccupied table. 'Not bad here, eh?' he said, sniffing the atmosphere sensually.

Martin did not reply. He had just seen Goldberg sitting up at the bar beside a group of chattering youngsters, defiantly reading a Hebrew newspaper. A waitress served him a cup of coffee. 'The sugar!' Goldberg demanded in a loud, brusque voice. She looked at him oddly as he spread his elbows on the counter and held the newspaper prominently in front of his face, still fighting the battle of the bathroom. Martin got up and walked over. 'Herr Goldberg,' he said, extending his hand. Goldberg turned his head bullishly, ignoring the proffered handshake. 'I'm your neighbour, remember?'

'Yes, you are from London.' The suspicious look was cautiously relaxed.

'That's right.' Martin smiled foolishly. There seemed nothing to say; he couldn't very well explain that his purpose in accosting Goldberg was merely an affirmation of solidarity. 'Is that an Israeli newspaper?'

'*Ha'aretz*,' Goldberg said. 'I have it mailed to me every day.' Moved by an unexpected impulse, he offered to lend it.

'I'm sorry, I don't read Hebrew.'

'You should,' Goldberg boomed, addressing the whole of Berlin, Germany, the world. 'Every Jew should know Hebrew. Have you ever been to Israel?'

'Not yet.' Martin was reluctant to confess that it had never occurred to him to go there.

His companion looked at him sternly. 'How can you be a Jew and not go to Israel? You should see what we are doing there. We are making a paradise. We are showing everybody what freedom means. We have a wonderful army. Even an English newspaper had to say the Israelis have the best infantry in the world.' He stared round as if challenging anyone to contradict the assertion; no one seemed interested in doing so.

'Yes,' Martin said. 'Yes, I know.'

Mollified, Goldberg asked: 'You are here to make a compensation claim? Look, my friend, if you have any difficulties, come to me.' He bent forward and tapped the side of his nose confidentially. 'I know their law inside out, don't worry.' The smile had finally broken through the desperate defences. It was almost triumphant. 'What they did to me, I won't even tell you. But one thing they couldn't take away. I was a doctor of German law. They could draw out your teeth, they could tear out your limbs, they could murder your children, but as long as you were alive they couldn't take away what you had in your brain.'

'Of course not,' Martin agreed soothingly. He saw his own image distorted in a crazy mirror. '*Auf Wiederschauen*, Herr Goldberg.'

Goldberg rustled his newspaper vigorously and turned away. '*Shalom!*' he said.

Heinz Dieter was glancing round restlessly. 'It didn't take you long to meet an acquaintance,' he commented. A small girl in skin-tight jeans strolled past hippily. 'Evelin!' he exclaimed, 'I haven't seen you in weeks. Meet my friend, Martin.' The girl freed herself from the detaining grasp and acknowledged the introduction coldly.

'See what I mean about the company?' Heinz Dieter remarked unabashed. 'What a sugar! She looks French, don't you agree?'

She also looked like any girl one might see sipping Coca-Cola in a Brooklyn drug-store, or bouncing with sweaty concentration to guitar music in a Kensington or Chelsea coffee-bar. Mass culture had succeeded in rubbing out national differences. A generation before, these Germans would have sat around in brown shirts singing full-throated Hitler Jugend lieder; now they looked like fraternity and sorority members of some American university that had opened branches in all the West European capitals, wearing snappy clothes labelled 'Fifth Avenue' or 'Hollywood Special' or 'Palm Beach'. Perhaps it was reassuring; Martin didn't know. But thinking of the older people sitting out on the pavement terrace, he did not believe that the imitative characteristics of the young could have more than a transient effect.

Heinz Dieter pressed his forearm in a gesture that was ingratiatingly intimate. 'You do like it here?' he pleaded. 'It's a good place to make friends.' He spoke loudly to make himself heard. Near-by, an elderly man sat resting his chin on his clasped hands, staring through the blue smoke at the laughing groups of youngsters. There were others also who were excluded from companionship by age or shyness. It was a good place to be lonely in, too.

The young German's restless glance slipped constantly towards the door, as if he were expecting somebody. Martin watched the signals of tension with dispassionate interest: the muscle spasmodically moving in the cheek, the teeth biting the lower lip, the eyes watchful and apprehensive. Whoever it was had arrived. Probably a girl.

But it wasn't a girl, after all. It was a man of about thirty-five wearing a black leather coat.

'I'm glad you were able to come,' he said to Heinz Dieter, speaking German with a clumsy foreign accent. He sat down and adjusted the table carefully with broad freckled hands that looked as if they had frequently served as weapons. 'The name is Kane, Mel Kane,' he told Martin with a keen glance. 'I'm an American.'

Martin introduced himself in English. He couldn't bear to be mistaken for a German even for a moment.

Kane carefully committed him to memory. 'What brings you to Berlin, business or pleasure?' he inquired, adding: 'You mustn't mind me being nosey. It's my profession. I'm with a San Francisco paper.'

'My presence in Berlin won't be of any interest to your readers,' Martin said dryly.

The American subjected him to a long deliberate stare. 'Maybe you're right,' he said. 'But I like to check on the possibilities.' He switched his attention to Heinz Dieter, who uneasily drummed the table with his finger-tips, unable to follow the conversation. The youth immediately lit a fresh cigarette. Kane said softly, reverting to German: 'How is Herr Krantz? Is he doing any interesting business?'

Heinz Dieter flickered a warning glance at him. 'I don't know much about his business. I'm only his secretary,' he said with an uneasy laugh. He looked at his wrist-watch and rose abruptly. 'I'll have to get along now. Can I have a word with you, Mel?' The American followed him and they spoke quietly together for a few minutes. Then Heinz Dieter shook hands with them both and slouched out.

Kane watched him all the way to the door. 'That's a messed-up generation,' he murmured, as if reflecting aloud. 'They're the real casualties of the German defeat. I wonder what will happen to a kid like that?'

Martin remembered the wise guy shrewdness, the 'you're *kaput* for a long time.' 'I'd say he's a born survivor.'

'I'm not so sure. He's going nowhere pretty fast. But you couldn't care less, could you?' Kane said ironically. 'That's the trouble with the world, nobody cares about the next man. I've got a theory, Martin – may I call you Martin? – everybody you meet, even if you only brush past them on a street corner, changes your life a little. We can't afford not to care.'

It was a sentiment straight out of one of those little 'How To Be' books some people swallowed like pep pills, but it was not a formula for Martin. If there had been any point in doing so he would have explained that here, in Germany, he wanted to avoid having feelings about people. More than anything else he wished to be indifferent, neither to hate, nor love, nor understand; against all reason, all moral platitudes, he craved for an impossible invulnerability.

'You're like a lot of people,' Kane persisted. 'You can't forget what the Germans did. You can't forgive.'

'What right have I to forgive?' Martin stared into the neutral grey-glass eyes with bitter ferocity. 'Am I God?' The phrase emerged with blasphemous violence. His glance ranged over the soiled coffee-cups, the ash-tray spilling cigarette ends, the sticky grains of sugar adhering to the surface of the table. What was happening to him? He used to be superstitiously tidy. Everything should be kept in its proper place and, without being religious, he'd felt there was a proper place for God. The name a dry whisper among the cloisters, a thin sweet smell of piety emerging from the pages of hymn books, an intimation of wrath vibrating in the resonance of a synagogue chant.

'I'm sorry,' he apologised awkwardly, 'I didn't mean to be quite so emphatic.'

Kane eyed him curiously. 'I'm the one who should be sorry. I seem to have touched a nerve.'

Across the other side of the café Goldberg was watching them over his newspaper.

After a while Kane left. Martin went into the street and bought a copy of the illustrated weekly, *Der Spiegel*, at a corner newspaper kiosk. Pale twilight spread its anæmia along the Kurfürsten-damm and a chill wind searched the interstices of his clothing. He crossed the road into Kranzler's, where a hundred childhood excursions had ended with coffee and sticky pastries. A woman who might have been his mother sat near the window, nested in furs, staring out at the people parading along the pavement with a gaze that was bereaved and melancholy. A cold finger of misery touched him. The rich fragrance of pastry, the conviviality of music, laughter, and conversation that used to exhilarate him as a child, now flowed through him with a cloying, disagreeable warmth. Burdened by a weight of inertia and lassitude, he turned the pages of the magazine, idly absorbing gossip about film actresses and their wealthy lovers.

At the next table two men were talking, one an American with a pale, rubbery, pool-room face and a big lazy body, the other thin, with big scolded eyes and a soft voice speaking in awkwardly accented English.

'My leg is getting every day worse,' the thin man was complaining, shifting in his seat as if in pain.

'Would you believe it,' the American ruminated, 'once I could've picked up a piece of the Kurfürstendamm, near Karlsruhestrasse, for a coupla hundred dollars? Me, Joe Soap, wouldn't look at it. Today it's worth more than a plot on Broadway.' He picked thoughtfully at his stained teeth with a broken matchstick and stared at the girls lingering over *cappuccinos* on high stools at the bar, looking them over with a deep, melancholy knowingness as if they were discarded mistresses whose sexuality now bored him. 'That,' he said emphatically, 'was one helluva time. Every American guy had twenty t'irty dames on a string. I heard of one fella set out to make a different one every day for a year.'

'If I could prove it started to go bad in Buchenwald, maybe I could have a bigger pension. But for everything here you must use a bit of *blat*,' the thin man went on pessimistically, employing the Russian word for wangling.

'I'm on pension too,' the American said. 'I convert it into marks. It goes much further here than in New York.' He leaned back and massaged his stomach with both hands. 'Got into the habit of living soft in the U.S. Army. In them days you could buy up Europe with soap and cigarettes.'

Martin was eavesdropping reluctantly. There was nothing he could do about it anyway, for the voices of his neighbours carried clearly to his ears. The American's remark made him recall a few months he'd spent in Italy at the end of the war. The soldiers with their skinny, docile girls, bright and feverish and little more than children. Everywhere the flesh markets, people trading their bodies for the swill off their conquerors' plates. But the worst memory of all, burned with acid into his mind, was of a hot afternoon on a beach near Naples. The bright sun on the dazzling sea and a girl-child walking slowly along the foreshore collecting seaweed. Near-by a middle-aged British officer, well-polished leather gleaming, sat at the wheel of a jeep. He smiled at the child and called her over. What's your name, little girl? How old are you? Do you go to school? With a kindly indulgence the officer put the child on his knee and gave her a piece of chocolate. Then, furtively, his hand began to explore under her skirt...

Martin felt a stab of acute, deeply physical bitterness, and with a terrible longing imagined a world in which all the morally diseased, the sadistic anti-Semites, the perverts, the child-seducers, were herded together into a great reserve and one bright avenging bomb falling from the clean blue of the sky. So intense was the feeling that when he looked round the café it seemed strangely unreal. He felt stifled, as if the sterile, machine-conditioned air was poorly oxygenised. Abruptly he got up and left.

On the pavement of the Augsbergerstrasse he drank in the squalor of the red-light district with a deep, slow excitement. Night sprawled drunkenly over this part of the city. The strident music of juke-boxes issued from the bars which trafficked in sex and alcohol. A girl with a pallid, garish face swayed towards him, the odour of her corrupt, perfumed flesh teasing his nostrils. An image flashed through his mind of himself following her through the dark streets to her room, watching her strip off her clothes, her nude body bluish-white in the small light of a naked electric bulb, writhing in a joyless embrace. Then the body was no longer writhing sexually – it was in the throes of death. Death was in the air.

'*Kommen Sie mit*,' the woman said. She tilted her white defenceless face towards him, the eyes wide open with a public professional stare.

His fists were clenched in the pockets of his coat and a tremor passed through him like a chill current of electricity. With a feeling of inexplicable panic he hurried away, but the brief incident had aroused him to a smouldering uneasy lust, and the night streets were now filled with the scented corruption the girl had breathed into his face. Whenever he passed a woman he was conscious of the silken rustle of her limbs under her dress, her warm polluted flesh drowsy with sensuality.

He called a taxi and, staring out at the cold, glittering, unfriendly city, realised that there was nowhere in particular to go.

'Can you take me somewhere where there's dancing?' he asked the taxi driver. 'Not too expensive.'

The man considered briefly. 'You don't want one of them tourist joints,' he said. 'They'll soak you for the cabaret. I know just the place.'

He drove for about twenty minutes across the central ruins of the city towards its shabby northern perimeter and pulled up outside a beer hall in a street of dark buildings. *Tanzplatz*, it proclaimed in red neon light, an oasis of noise in the midst of a desolate silence.

The place was crowded and smoky, resounding to the music of a thumping accordion band. Shabby youths from near-by East Berlin jigged on the dance floor with girls in shapeless dresses, their thin bodies still marked by the years of deprivation. Marx's *Lumpenproletariat*: Orwell's proles. A swill of beer under their belts, a belch of syncopation and a quick lay under the iron struts of the railway bridge near-by, and they would endure the intolerable almost indefinitely.

Seated in an obscure corner of the bar facing a fly-blown advertisement showing a fat, jolly man drinking a Pilsner, his attention was attracted by a young German who gazed with drunken affection at a small, prim little girl of about eight. A railway-man's peaked cap was pushed back on the man's curly hair and his expression was one of bland, fuddled innocence and amiability.

'How much money you got?' he asked the child.

She looked at him with wide-eyed seriousness and held out a handful of small coins.

'*Liebchen*, buy your father a drink,' he wheedled.

The girl shook her head.

'You don't love your papa?' the young German asked, baffled and shy.

She played with her money and did not answer. Gently the man stroked her hair.

'Lend it to me, baby. I'll pay you back on pay-day. Papa's thirsty.'

She seemed to give the proposition grave consideration for a few moments, then, pursing her lips obstinately, pushed the hand in which she clutched the money into the pocket of her dress. Her father smiled helplessly and looked across at Martin.

'She doesn't trust me,' he explained.

Martin said: 'I'll buy you a drink if you take that child home and put her to bed.'

The young German shook his head stupidly. 'She likes it here. Don't you, baby girl?' He patted her encouragingly on her thin shoulder-blades and the child smiled up at him with a precocious, protective tenderness. 'The music is pretty, no?'

'Yes, Papa.' She put her head to one side and listened.

'This is no place for kids,' Martin insisted severely.

'*Warum?*' The German gazed at him with mild, stupid blue eyes. '*Warum?*' Someone laughed. He turned and grinned into the faces of two women who sat near-by.

'The little girl's all right,' one of them said in English, her lips parted in an amiable dentured smile. 'You *Frankreich?*'

'No.' Martin stared coldly at her pendulant breasts under the thin blouse and back into her face.

'*Americaner?*' the woman persisted.

Her friend tapped the empty glass in front of her. '*Lädig,*' she said. 'You buy us a cognac?'

Martin shrugged and turned his back.

'He thinks we're a couple of whores,' one of the women began in a quiet voice. 'What do you think of these Americans? Every German girl's a whore to them.' The tone became shrill. 'They treat everyone like muck. We're decent women, do you hear, you bastard? Decent women!'

Her companion said: 'My husband would break his jaw if he was alive.'

'Swine!' the first woman screamed, arresting attention throughout the bar. 'Swine! Treating us like muck because our men were killed.'

People drifted over from the dance floor and crowded round. The barman wiped his bare arms on a grimy towel and came over to investigate the disturbance, but the accordionists continued to squeeze their instruments with apparent indifference, as though violence were part of the boring pattern of their lives.

'What's going on?' the barman demanded. He was a big, phlegmatic fellow cushioned in fat.

Several people began shouting at once. A small middle-aged man bent his face close. 'You know why you won the war? Because we were fighting the Communists. We bled our guts for you!' Tears of rage were in his eyes.

'Shut up, everybody!' the barman bellowed, bringing the flat of his hand down hard on the table, making a glass jump off and splinter on the floor. He sized Martin up carefully with an eye expert at detecting trouble-makers and seemed to come to a favourable decision.

'Don't provoke the customers,' he warned the women, who stood up with an air of being offended and left.

The dancers wandered back to the floor reluctantly, still hoping that they would not be deprived of a promising bit of fun, and Martin ordered a bottle of wine and began drinking it quietly. He felt strangely exhilarated by the incident. His conduct had been out of character, but back in London he would never even have come to such a place, it would be inconsistent with his orderly existence. Here he was close to a world of subterranean violence;

far from being frightened, he found it challenging. For perhaps the first time in his life he felt perilously free.

Humming to the music, he strolled between the tables looking for someone to dance with. Most of the women were unprepossessing, their hair crimped and their knobby faces uniformly dusted with pink powder. But sitting alone near the accordion band, dark and self-contained as a gipsy, was a big shapely girl with coarse black hair hanging to her shoulders. She met his glance frankly and stood up to dance, moving stiffly away but without apparent resentment when his thighs importunately pressed against hers, as if the liberty were customary.

After the dance he joined her at her table. Her manner was neither discouraging nor inviting. She seemed to accept his presence as indifferently as she might regard a stranger seated at her side on a bus, and this remoteness lent the girl a suggestion of mystery, of strangeness that enhanced his physical awareness of her. She was far from beautiful. Her skin had the coarseness of her type, and her soft, olive-black eyes were too small. The hands playing with the stem of her glass were big, with damaged, work-roughened fingers. When she noticed him looking at them she concealed them on her lap.

'No,' she said in answer to his question, 'I haven't been here before.'

'You don't look like the others. Why did you come?'

'Just curiosity. This place has a bad reputation. I was interested.'

'There are pleasanter places with equally bad reputations,' Martin pointed out. 'Why this one?'

She looked at him with slow amusement. 'I could ask you the same thing.'

'I'm a foreigner. A taxi driver brought me.'

'You don't sound like a foreigner. Your German's too good.'

'I was born here.'

'Yes, that would explain it,' she agreed as though she understood perfectly. 'Actually, you remind me of someone I once knew.'

He was immediately on the defensive, hating the idea of being identified with some German, yet curiosity impelled him to probe. 'Anyone interesting?' he asked casually.

Her smile was sudden, warm, and sensual. 'I don't know you well enough to tell you.'

'It's not important,' he said. 'I can live without knowing,' staring with hostility into her dark-ringed dispassionate eyes. The girl returned his gaze with a bland kind of innocence. His enmity simply roused no response and was consequently defeated.

They danced again several times and gradually she let him hold her close, but although her moist lips were parted and she shut her eyes as if in sensual contemplation of his embrace, he had the curious impression that she was even more remote and indifferent to him than the first time they danced.

Then she glanced at her wrist-watch and said firmly: 'I must go now.'

Martin's eyes encountered her again; it was like reading a strange book in a half-apprehended language. There was certainly an intangible bond between them, something more than a casual physical attraction. At least, the wine, the music, the strange evil mood of the evening combined to make him believe it. It would be safer to let her go with a smile and an ironic remark. *Good-bye, thanks for the company. I can pay you one compliment. I almost forgot you were German.* An abrupt act of will, and it would be as easy as that to preserve his hatred chaste and whole.

He stood irresolutely, creating a tension that in itself held them in an unwilling relationship.

'May I see you home?' he said, adding, 'I need some fresh air,' as if it were necessary to devise a motive, no matter how flimsy, to justify himself.

'I don't even know your name.' She had a full sensual mouth and large, even teeth. Her smile almost made her beautiful. 'Mine's Karin Paulus.'

'Martin Stone,' he replied, examining her with uneasy suspicion. The exposed nerve throbbed again. A name with associations. The siege of Stalingrad. But even for the remotest relation of a field-marshal she was shabbily dressed, a cheap tweed coat over a thick black sweater, clumsy, ill-made shoes, cheap stockings.

They walked in silence for a few minutes, their horizontal shadows intermingling on the pavement. Away from the dark side streets, walking in a brightly lit thoroughfare with traffic manœuvring along the congested roadway, he felt lonely again, wondering what forbidden adventure he was blundering into. It was still not too late to be safe.

Karin paused at a shop window, admiring the clothes with no sense of awkwardness at being in the company of a stranger. The glass offered a ghostly reflection of the street behind, but their own figures looked ordinary, as if they belonged together. She stepped away slightly to study a svelte white dress worn by a dummy whose blank face was painted to resemble a well-known film star. Her hip touched him briefly, the warmth of flesh penetrating through the layers of dress, and again he experienced the fatal attraction of the forbidden. They were taboo to each other. Even this arbitrary stirring of desire was drugged and compulsive with guilt. Love between them would be like an act of miscegenation.

'Where do you live?' he asked unevenly.

'In the East Sector. You needn't come if you don't want to.'

'I'm curious,' he said. 'I haven't seen it yet.'

'It's just a place for the poor. If you've seen slums you've seen East Berlin.' For the first time she spoke crossly, detecting a non-existent condescension in his attitude.

'All right,' Martin said. 'Let's go.'

He sat by her side in the Underground feeling conspicuous. The train was crowded with people coming home from cinemas, restaurants, late factory shifts, the strain of the day shadowing their faces with fatigue. It reminded him of the evening crowds herded on the London Tube, off their guard, their brisk morning guise awry; how the stamp of the granite city was on their faces as they rustled their evening papers and lethargically imbibed their chewed-up pre-digested mass culture. It was a time of day when a man's history could be read at a glance, the disappointments, the insecurity, the humbleness, the defeat that lay at the core of each one's life.

And these seemed no different. They stared with the same dull eyes at the small newsprint, reading the same titillating stories of catastrophe, murder, lust with an uncritical weariness, as if that was how the world was and there was nothing to be done about it. Even though he told himself it was his duty, he could not condemn them and soon began to feel almost one of them, an indistinguishable cipher in a great multitude travelling far below the pavements of Berlin. It gave him a strange sensation of drowning. One could surrender to it and it could even be pleasant.

At Wittenbergplatz they changed trains, joining a crowd perceptibly bleaker, shabbier, more work-weary. The absence of Western newspapers was a reminder that these were East Berliners forbidden by decree to bring 'capitalist' literature across the Sector boundary. Karin bought some cigarettes and choco-lates at a kiosk and carefully concealed them inside her coat. 'For my sister-in-law,' she whispered.

At Potsdamerplatz two uniformed policemen entered the compartment and stood by the door like warders shepherding a party of convicts. A dwarf-like woman with a big satchel full of Communist papers and magazines walked through the train, flourishing the *Tägliches Rundschau* in people's faces. Karin bought a copy. Smiling at Martin as if they had a secret understanding, she passed it over to him. He turned the pages, noting the familiar non-language of Communist cliché. His glance travelled stealthily to the policemen by the door, to their high leather boots, the heavy buckled belts, the jutting arrogance of their peaked caps. They made him feel that his very existence had a dubious legality. It was much easier to hate Germans in uniform.

Karin touched his arm to distract his attention. He was so near that he could see the gold-brown flecks in her black eyes, the faint down beaded with minute bubbles of perspiration above her upper lip.

'I'm becoming curious about you,' she admitted. 'Aren't you curious about me?'

Of course he was. He wanted to know so many things: what she did, thought, felt, how she earned her living, who her parents were – but, above all, he wanted to know what lay in her past. She was the first German to emerge out of the crowd and make human contact with him. It was important that he should know. But what? When it all happened she was a child, one of the millions throughout the Continent whose dark, pitiful eyes stared with absolute, uncomprehending innocence at the corpses swinging on the lamp-posts, the looming shadow of the rapist, the pillars of smoke by day and the pillars of fire by night. There were times when all one could say about the young was that some were more unlucky than others.

'I'm nearly twenty-five. I work as a seamstress in a West Berlin factory and I try to write in my spare time. I share two rooms and a kitchen with my brother and my sister-in-law.' Her slow, attractive smile came again. 'I believe I'm not very pretty.'

'You're wrong,' Martin said. He took out a cigarette and lit it to cover his embarrassment. Compliments never came easily to him. The press of passengers on the cramped seat forced them into a disturbing propinquity. A faint aphrodisiac scent of cosmetics teased his senses.

'What about you?' she asked in a low voice.

He hesitated before abandoning his anonymity; even his name was, after all, a concealment. 'I'm thirty-one,' he said eventually. 'I work in an accountant's office. I live with my father.' The train rattled noisily into a station, almost drowning his final disclosure.

'I'm a Jew,' he said.

Karin remained still and silent, her hands restling limply on her lap, until the train moved on with a jerk so that the bodies of strap-hangers jolted backward and forward with the lifeless docility of dolls. She was pushed close against his side. She said absolutely nothing.

The train entered the long tunnel with a hollow roar and a grinding of metallic wheels. The lights in the carriage momentarily failed and he sat in the darkness, briefly alone, thinking: Why didn't she say something, anything? What does it mean to her? And then he felt the gentle pressure of her knee, felt it with an overwhelming embarrassment.

They left the train at a station a long way down Stalinallee, where the brand-new massive apartment houses, like the façades of a giant row of super-cinemas, petered out into a wilderness of rubble and rusted coils of wire. In the early twilight the long straight avenue, pride of the East German Communist bureaucracy, looked gloomy and inhumanly forbidding, as though it must be inhabited by industrial units rather than by people. All down the length of the semi-deserted road loudspeakers were relaying an interminable exhortation, the grating, mechanised voice pursuing them as they turned into a derelict side street fitfully illuminated by the dim lights of a *Drogerie* and *Bäckerei* that spilled over cobbled pavements.

Karin walked rapidly through the network of dreary streets slightly apart from him, as though now it was compromising to be seen in his company. There was an oppressive silence between them; everybody in the neighbourhood seemed to converse in undertones and even the children out late with their parents walked quietly, as if trained never to raise their voices.

Soon even the loudspeakers could no longer be heard, only the distant rumble of traffic, the eerie, isolated clatter of feet on the pavements, thin voices sounding behind doors. 'This way,'

Karin said. 'It's not far now,' leading him like a blind man deeper into a maze.

A blue light shone on the sign 'Wühlischerplatz'. In the centre of the square there was a brownish plot of grass with three deserted park benches. A road on the far side led down to the railway sidings. Few people were about. A boy in short leather trousers rolled an iron hoop along the pavement. A woman with broad hips and a pursed, money-wise face, her fat arms mottled with red, stood outside a greengrocer's polishing apples as though they were prized household gods. An elderly man in a dark, faded, well-brushed suit, wearing steel-rimmed glasses and a celluloid collar, patiently scoured a heap of rubble between two buildings for scraps of metal or timber which he collected in a sack.

Martin shivered slightly. It was not, as Karin had said, like any other slum. It lacked vulgarity, the noise and over-spilling vitality, the profuse, untidy, over-ripe garbage-strewn squalor of slum life in Whitechapel, the Gorbals, or the *bassi* in Naples. The poverty had a picked-to-the-bone frugality; he couldn't help pitying anyone who lived there.

A man came out of a tall crumbling tenement with a bag of tools in his hand. '*Guten Abend*, Fräulein,' he greeted Karin, staring with fixed curiosity at Martin.

'*Guten Abend*, Herr Meisner,' she replied, and walked into the dark passageway. She pressed a time switch by the door and a feeble light came on, illuminating the narrow stairway. When they reached the second landing she asked him to wait, as she wanted her brother's permission before bringing him into the flat.

Martin heard her ascend three flights of stairs. A bell rang faintly, voices exchanged greetings, a door closed. The automatic light switched itself off, leaving him in pitch darkness. His fingers fumbled along the wall and encountered two switches, but he was reluctant to press either in case he rang somebody's bell. Instead he struck a match and peered at his wrist-watch. He'd been waiting five minutes.

The light went on again and someone climbed slowly and painfully up the creaking stairs. It was the elderly man with the celluloid collar, his sack on his shoulders, his face deeply indented by chronic undernourishment, who bobbed his head in a gesture that contained the lifetime's ingrained servility of a minor official of strictly stratified bureaucracy. A few moments later a thick-set man in shirt-sleeves with a sanitary bucket came out of one of the apartments on the landing. Casting a suspicious glance at the stranger, he locked the door behind him before carrying the bucket downstairs, to reappear sometime later with a surly-looking companion who scrutinised Martin without a word before the two men re-entered the apartment. A brief glimpse of dilapidated furnishings and bare, worn linoleum was revealed as the door slammed shut. The time switch shut off the light again. The sound of trucks being shunted in the railway yard jarred the silence.

With a growing uneasiness Martin struck another match and consulted his watch. He had been waiting nearly ten minutes. An obstinate curiosity prevented him from leaving. Standing in the darkness with his senses straining, he heard all the small sounds of the claustrophobic tenement, the muted grumble of voices, the mewing of a cat, feet padding across a floor, a door opening and shutting. Now he was teased by a melodramatic idea. Had he fallen into the clutches of a Communist Lorelei who had lured him into the East and was even now making contact with the secret police?

The door of the near-by apartment was suddenly opened. 'Why are you waiting here? Is there anything you want?' a voice demanded gruffly. It was the surly-looking man, perhaps the janitor of the building.

Martin said: 'I'm waiting for a friend.' An instinctive caution prevented him from divulging who the friend was.

The man looked him up and down suspiciously, probably assessing his status and politics by the quality of his clothes. Whatever the value judgement, the result was unfavourable.

'You can't hang around here,' he growled. 'It makes people uncomfortable to have a stranger standing outside their door in the dark.'

It is easy to feel guilty. Martin told himself he should never have come in the first place. If a policeman did appear on the scene, what sort of excuse would he give for following a girl he'd picked up in a café all the way to her home in East Berlin? Curiosity, he'd probably plead. Lust, they'd certainly say. There was an ingredient of truth in both arguments. But now he was being seen off the premises, and there was justice in that, too.

The man stood at the head of the stairs watching him until he reached the door. Outside, the street had grown gloomier with advancing darkness. As he reached the square again he heard someone running after him; the secret policeman was wearing high heels, by the sound of it.

It was Karin. 'I'm terribly sorry I kept you waiting so long,' she apologised breathlessly.

'Not at all.' His voice was heavy with sarcasm. 'It gave me a chance to get to know your charming neighbours.'

'My brother was afraid to let you come in. He's got a job in a night bar here, and he's not a Party member. People talk. It can be dangerous.'

'That's quite all right,' Martin cut in sharply. 'I don't want to get anyone into trouble.'

He walked on quickly so that she had difficulty in keeping pace.

'I'll see you back to West Berlin,' she said. 'You might get lost.'

'I don't think so. All I have to do is get to Stalinallee and follow my nose.'

Karin laughed. 'You have an unfriendly temperament,' she chided. 'You must have been a spoiled child.'

'Very spoiled.' He smiled back at her, suddenly conscious that he was being humoured and liking it. She had changed her clothes, he noticed. Instead of her thick sweater she now wore a green silk blouse and ear-rings that glittered in the dim light of the street lamps. Not insensible of the compliment, he slackened his pace, but when she slipped her hand into his arm the familiarity of the gesture shocked him.

Karin accompanied him all the way back to the Kurfürsten-damm, even leaving the Underground to see him up to the street. The artificial stimulation of brightness and noise, here in the heart of the city, was like an elating drug. The loud-mouthed garish night ran at its high tide, filling up gambling casinos, night clubs, and bars, jingling the money in spendthrift pockets, blatantly advertising its easy pleasures.

'Let's have some fun,' Martin suggested recklessly.

Karin shook her head. 'I have work to do. I bring some from the factory to earn extra money.'

Now that she was about to leave, he hated the thought of the continuing loneliness stretching ahead day after day.

'Perhaps we'll meet again,' he suggested hesitantly, certain that the morrow would make it impossible.

With a promptness that surprised him, she said: 'Thursday. Eight in the evening. I'll meet you here, at this very spot.'

Walking back to the pension, so preoccupied that he almost forgot where he was, a thought came violently and unbidden to his mind. 'For God's sake! What does it matter?' he heard himself say.

4

Frau Ulrich was discreetly flirting with Brauner, the theatre critic, Hugo noticed with detached amusement. She was a woman whom it was difficult to associate with the untidiness of adultery, a severe, slender lady of declining beauty whose firm, controlled gestures expressed an unostentatious authority.

'Herr Brauner is sometimes harsh in his judgements,' she reproved him in a low, thrilling voice, holding his glance a precise fraction of a moment longer than was strictly necessary.

'Not at all.' He wagged his big, loquacious head playfully and ran his fingers through his untidy hair in a harassed, little-boy gesture. 'I simply don't see anything in the German theatre but a barren display of technique. Just tell me one important new play that has been written here since the nineteen-thirties. Even Brecht became merely a producer, capable only of re-deploying his early masterpieces. And now he's dead, there's nothing.'

'There you are,' Frau Ulrich said roguishly. 'He hasn't a good thing to say about us.'

Gustav Ulrich smiled at his wife indulgently. 'But he's right, my dear. We haven't a single creative playwright of our own. Everything nowadays is translation – Sartre, Eliot, Tennessee Williams, Arthur Miller, Ustinov...'

'Germany will have to find its way back to the spirit of the *Aufklärung*, the Enlightenment,' Brauner insisted. 'One must try to recapture that optimistic view of history you found in men like Leibnitz, Pufendorf, or, better still, Lessing.' He gazed with burning passion into Frau Ulrich's eyes.

'Ah, but it's precisely in that enlightened rationalism that the trouble started,' the lady's husband protested, engaging in an intellectual duel with his rival. 'The German character is fundamentally religious and authoritarian. The *Aufklärung*, by bringing God into question, began a process which was bound in time to create a secular tyranny. What do you think, Hugo?'

Hugo puffed contemplatively at one of Ulrich's excellent cigars and waved the question away. 'You feed your guests too well, Gustav. I'm not capable of metaphysics on a full stomach.'

The conversation, of course, bored him, and he had too many other preoccupations to be diverted for long by Brauner's flirtation with the willing Frau Ulrich.

'You need more coffee, my dear man,' that lady decided briskly, summoning the maid. The girl's starched cap and apron were part of the careful blend of traditional and modern the Ulrichs cultivated so successfully. From the glass-and-concrete Swedish villa to the English Rolls and the old-world servants in the domestic wing, they conscientiously set a standard of correctness for Germany's new professional aristocracy.

Hugo regarded it all with wry approval. If things had gone differently he might well have adopted a similar mode of life. It suited the middle-aged German temperament, the sensual passion for food and comfort tempered by a *bürgherliche* dignity. Such a pattern of living might even have included a Frau Ulrich.

These things could be more neatly arranged in Germany than anywhere else.

'Another thing that puzzles me,' Brauner said, frowning thoughtfully, 'is the way our talent for satirical revue has dried up. Today Berlin cabaret consists of seminudes and American wisecracks. It is as though we can find nothing to be intelligently funny about. You should do something about that, Hugo.' He persisted in the pretence that Hugo's reputation was contemporary, in the curious belief that it was subtle flattery.

Gustav Ulrich smiled appreciatively. 'Ah, you are right! A Krantz satire! It would be like old times again.'

'No Krantz satires any more,' Hugo grunted. They were beginning to tread on dangerous ground. In Germany one talked about the past, if at all, with circumspection. He hoped he'd been sufficiently discouraging, but Frau Ulrich chose to treat him as she might a gifted pianist who has to be coaxed to play.

'You're just being mulish, Hugo,' she chided. 'After all, I was much too young to be allowed to see your wicked revues and it's not kind of you to deny me the satisfaction of enjoying one in my sophisticated middle age.'

He patted her hand across the coffee-table. 'Darling, you're just a chicken. Don't ask me to shock you.'

'Yes, yes! Do shock me!'

Behind the playfulness there was a hint of cruelty. It could be read in the level provocative gaze of her brilliant cat-green eyes, her thin-lipped smile. He was tempted to defeat her in the easiest way possible, to say: 'The wit you ask for died in the concentration camp. That irony, that sharp destructive humour, wasn't German at all, it was Berlin-Jewish. And it will be at least a hundred years before Jews will be able to really laugh in Berlin again.'

'Brauner,' Hugo said, 'would you care to shock the lady?'

The theatre critic went bright pink with embarrassment and laughed guiltily, like a schoolboy discovered kissing a housemaid. Gustav Ulrich chivalrously decided to change the subject.

'By the way, Hugo, it looks as if we're going to have quite a lot of difficulty with your friend's restitution claim,' he said. 'It's not easy to assess the value of a banking concern with its complicated financial dealings, particularly after the lapse of some twenty years. It could take two or three years' research to get all the figures we need. Of course, I'll get Mr Stone a provisional award.' With some hesitation he added: 'I wish he weren't quite so bitter. It would be easier to work with him.'

The subject hadn't been changed after all. Its course merely had been deflected. It was the sort of thing that happened frequently. One erected a careful barrier against the past – perhaps, as in the present instance, a façade of polite, intelligent, after-dinner talk. You moved in a circumscribed conversational area as well plotted as a path through a swamp. But the pressure of the past was irresistible, like a wall of floodwater seeping through the cracks in a dam. And once the leakage began, one seemed helpless to prevent it.

'I understand, of course, how he feels,' Ulrich continued. 'His family – I've gone into it – it was a very tragic affair. Several relatives committed suicide in a single week. I would like so much to help him.'

'You should ask him over to dinner some time, Gustav,' Frau Ulrich suggested, no doubt convinced that hospitality in a civilised German house, in the company of cultured German people, would be effective.

'I would like to, my dear, but I don't think he would come.'

She smoothed the silk of her dress over her knees and avoided looking at Hugo. 'It's a pity,' she said, thin-voiced and strained.

The silence that followed seemed interminably prolonged. Hugo slowly exhaled cigar smoke and stared through the enormous window that formed a glass wall of the room into the smouldering darkness of the garden. A thin moon shone through the black leaves like the gleam in the iris of a supernatural eye. It gave one the feeling of being under observation.

There was nothing he could say, nothing anyone could say, that would not be an intolerable banality.

It was left to Brauner, with his congenital tactlessness, to prove it.

'I hope no one will misunderstand me,' he said carefully. 'I am not excusing anything. But I think, sometimes, that one consolation can be derived from the Jewish martyrdom. Nothing like that can ever happen to any people again.'

Soon afterwards Hugo left. Only when he was alone could he trust himself to speak. 'You ass, Brauner!' he muttered to the empty street. 'It was the most useless martyrdom in history!'

Bonn came on the line as quickly as though it were a suburb of Berlin, speaking in the efficient, formal tones of a Foreign Office civil servant.

'War prisoners? We have a special department for that question. Just a moment, I'll put you through.'

Hugo listened to the click-click-click as the connection was made and absent-mindedly doodled on his desk blotter. Wolfgang

Sommer. An enigmatic name, half brutish, half delicate, a name that conjured up an image of someone stocky and muscular, with red hair growing on square capable hands, but a soft musical voice and a smile of sunny charm. Not Putzi at all. Once again he was conscious of the unreality of his quest; it was a search for a ghost, an invisible man who threw no shadow. It was incipient madness. Even if Putzi had temporarily assumed the identity of a dead corporal, was there any reason to believe he would not quickly have adopted a more suitable pseudonym?

A voice came on the line, heavy, glutinous, and given to impressive pauses. Hugo put a face to it easily: square, with two plump chins, a bristly cropped head polished and bald on the crown, and two tiny gimlet eyes peering through thickly bevelled glasses.

'*Ja, mein Herr*,' it said curtly as he outlined his request, and a briskly punctuated: '*Ja... ja... ja!*' to indicate that there was no need to linger over explanations. But finally it was a stalemate. This was not a matter for the Foreign Office. In any case, such things could not be discussed over the telephone. Perhaps the police could be of assistance, or the Red Cross. Good-bye.

It was but the latest of several blind alleys. The first had been the Red Cross. The woman in charge of their prisoner-of-war records had treated him with distressing sympathy, as if he were an anxious relative. She went to great trouble to consult her lists and, yes, had actually located a Wolfgang Sommer. His name had been given by a returning prisoner whom they interrogated. She showed him the entry: 241563 Sommer, Wolfgang, S.S. Panzer-division Feldherrnhalle. Prisoner at Vorkuta. Transferred February, 1946. New destination unknown.

It had seemed a promising lead, but the Red Cross woman was discouraging. If after so many years there was no further record of a prisoner, neither of his place of detention or release, it would suggest… She shook her iron-grey head pessimistically. Many of the soldiers had not been well treated, numbers had died. Yet while there's hope, there's life, she said with a sympathetic smile, usually finding that the mild jest was appreciated.

The police were considerably less helpful. They questioned him, he thought, correctly but suspiciously, pointing out that even if they could find the missing man, he might not choose to have his whereabouts disclosed to Herr Krantz. Not every prisoner of war who was repatriated rushed to make himself known to his relatives, even less to his friends.

Heinz Dieter, who didn't really know what Hugo was after, only that he was interested in tracing an old acquaintance who'd served in the army, came home one day with an ex-serviceman's magazine, *Wiking-Ruf,* which published a 'search service' in its back pages. Hugo consulted library files of the journal, looking through copy after copy filled with photographs of young men in uniform posing with stern expressions of patriotism and martial vigour. Most of them looked touchingly juvenile and defenceless, an astonishing number seemed to wear spectacles, and it was difficult to believe that these self-conscious boys had been the 'invincible' German Army that once terrorised the world. Now most of them were dead, Waffen S.S., Hitler Jugend, and all, and it was useless to think of them with bitterness.

He had to tell himself that Putzi was different, as indeed he was. Not because he'd become a Nazi; not because of the beatings in the cellar of the Brown House, but because once he'd been deeply loved. It was the act of betrayal that made him different. The others had a generic guilt, but it was not possible to hate each one of a million men, except as a religion or an ideology. So he shut the file copies of *Wiking-Ruf* with its pictures of dead boys and looked elsewhere for Putzi.

The idea came to him suddenly the next morning. Heinz Dieter had brought in the breakfast-tray and sat on the side of the bed boasting about a new girl he'd found. She was on holiday from Stuttgart.

Hugo lay in the rumpled bedclothes dragging on the first cigar of the day, listening to the young man's eager voice above the faint vibration of traffic in the Kurfürstendamm, and wondering: Stuttgart? What's the significance of Stuttgart? The name had some association that was important.

He thought of the Rhine, and the heavy, vine-scented country-side, and the timber barges floating down with trees from the Black Forest, and slow Württemberg peasants coming into market and going home, flushed with beer, the money jingling in the pockets of their *Lederhosen*; and the other side of the picture, the factories, busily adding to the greatest prosperity Germany had ever known. Stuttgart.

Then he remembered Gross, the sick man in East Berlin. 'Shall I tell you about Wolfgang Sommer? He was my pal, came from Stuttgart. A good boy who wrote to his mother regularly.' So in Stuttgart there was a woman who loved Wolfgang Sommer. She would not have spent the last thirteen or fourteen years without trying to find out what had happened to her son. If anybody in Germany knew where the so-called Wolfgang Sommer was now it was the mother of the soldier killed by a shell splinter in Budapest. And the man in East Berlin might well know the address of that woman. If so, he would probably be ready to sell it for a hundred Westmarks.

The Lufthansa plane taxied gently to the runway and swung round for the take-off. As it mounted and circled the Tempelhof he fancied he could see his car nosing along the slender ribbon of road on its way back to the city. He had a moment of anxiety for Heinz Dieter, hoping he wouldn't get into mischief during his absence, then became absorbed in the sickening upheaval taking place in his stomach. Flying disagreed with him. He leaned back against the head cushion and half closed his eyes, wincing as the aircraft bumped through a series of air pockets. An elderly woman was counting the beads on her rosary, soundlessly invoking God to neutralise the perilous emptiness of space.

God had never come out of the darkness for him, even as a child vivid with terror. A brown stain on the nursery ceiling, an old man shuffling by as the street turned blue and cold with dusk, the shriek of a distant train in the night, a moth beating its wings against a dark window – God had become all that was deformed by strangeness. So began the need for human warmth, the narcotic craving for love. And the vulnerability, the inevitable betrayals.

The plane slid into a white wall of cloud. Hugo bent his head and held the stiff paper bag to his lips, overcome with revulsion at his infirmity. Then, feeling slightly better, he looked out of the port-hole as they broke through to the sunlight and skimmed high above the green Bavarian fields, beginning to enjoy the flight now that it was almost too late.

Soon they were over Frankfurt, its cubic towers, sharp roofs, and acres of glass glinting like Eldorado. He liked Frankfurt. Perhaps on the way back he'd stay there overnight.

From Frankfurt he went on by train. It pulled into Stuttgart early in the afternoon and a ten-minute ride by taxi brought him to his destination. It was a whitewashed cottage just outside the town with an idyllic, picture-postcard view of the River Necker gleaming through a row of poplars. The other, smiling face of Germany that looked out of the holiday posters in the travel agencies of the world. A strange place to come looking for Putzi.

A group of children playing in a near-by field ran over eagerly and stared with solemn excitement as Hugo paid off the taxi-driver. They crowded to the gate as he walked up the flagged pathway to the cottage door and gently rapped the gleaming brass knocker. He waved to them half playfully, half in dismissal, but they did not budge until the door was opened by an old woman dressed plainly in black who shooed at them severely before turning her attention to the caller. An elderly cat came and rubbed its moulting fur against his trouser leg.

'Frau Herta Sommer?' Hugo queried politely.

She had a narrow wrinkled face with a prominent nose and small sharp eyes. A few strong white hairs sprouted from her chin. By the hurried scampering of feet behind him, he guessed she might be the local witch.

'Herta! She's been buried three years,' the old woman said, asthmatic but decisive. 'I'm her elder sister, Rosa. Are you from the government?'

Hugo disclaimed the honour, looking beyond her into the dim interior that smelled of cooking, wax polish, and boiling linen. He explained that he was in Stuttgart on business and had called on behalf of a friend, Kurt Gross, who'd served with her nephew during the war.

The old woman nodded her head several times. 'I'm doing my washing,' she said doubtfully. 'Well, you'd better come in.'

The cat followed them into a small parlour and crept stealthily on to his knees as he sat down. He stroked it with distaste and it purred wheezily, as if it shared its mistress's asthma. A large carved pendulum clock ticked creakily.

'She's taken to you,' Frau Sommer remarked with satisfaction. 'She likes stout people.' Hugo unobtrusively scratched himself, beginning to itch. 'A nice animal,' he said, shifting his knees under the detestable cat's weight.

'Oh yes,' she agreed. 'I can't stand dogs, though. Dirty creatures.'

'About my friend, Herr Gross——'

The old woman got up and excused herself. She had to stir the washing in the boiler. When she returned a few minutes later it was with a bottle of wine and two glasses and an expression of determined hospitality. But for some reason she left the bottle unopened.

'Yes, Herta took a bad turn and died three years last March,' she said, nodding her head quite briskly. 'You government gentlemen were told at the time because of the pension. You've just forgotten. We always keep to the regulations in this household.'

'Frau Sommer, I'm not——'

'Oh yes, we do our duty,' she continued with a definite hint of reproof. 'I remember when the dear Kaiser came to Stuttgart, and Reichsmarschall Göring – that was a few years later – we took the children along to the parades. And all the men fought for the Fatherland.'

Hugo glanced round at the faded pictures on the walls of the respectable, dark little room. There were enough military gentlemen there to man at least a platoon, and Wilhelm II commanded them all in a Prussian helmet from a garishly tinted print fringed with a border of rosebuds.

'I suppose,' he suggested tentatively, 'you were all proud of Wolfgang.' Surreptitiously, he pushed the cat off his knees.

The old lady was not a good listener. 'Yes,' she said, 'we didn't draw Herta's pension, not after the funeral, although we missed it. But those were the regulations and we just had to manage.'

'Is there someone living with you here?'

This time she heard. 'Oh no! There's only me. We live quite alone here. There's Herta's girl, Frieda, but she married an American soldier. And Franz keeps the butcher's shop. All the cousins, too. Oh yes, we were a big family, the Stuttgart Krafts. You government gentlemen would know, we had so many relations.'

'Frau Sommer, could you please tell me——'

'Oh no, not Frau Sommer. That was Herta. I'm Rosa, her elder sister.' She smiled with a shy, touching embarrassment. 'I never got married, really. Herta was a pretty girl. You should have seen her when she was twenty. A gentleman from Hamburg with a motor-car wanted to marry her.'

The cat cunningly crept on the table and jumped on Hugo's knees again, then immediately began to lick its paws. He felt near to defeat. Had he come all the way from Berlin to listen to the ruminations of this amicable but senile old woman?

'Can you please give me some news about your nephew Wolfgang? Wolfgang – Herta's son.'

She nodded vigorously and silently for a few moments. 'Well, she did, she did,' she exclaimed, obviously engaged in an inner monologue.

'She did what?'

'Whatever was best for the boy, of course. He was just like his father. Did you know Herr Sommer? Oh, he was clever. A man like that, all the thinking must have hurt his head just to keep it in. But a terrible temper first thing in the morning when he was leaving for the leatherwork.'

'A pity,' Hugo said patiently, resigned to the possibility that the information he sought would not be forthcoming. 'So Wolfgang was like his father?'

'Oh yes, he was a serious boy, all right. Worked hard at school and looked fine in his brown uniform. The dear Führer would have been proud of him, the way he went marching off to fight the Bolshevik Jews.'

'They don't say that any more,' he told her gravely.

'Oh, I'm silly. I forgot. Frau Posner, who made the dresses, would be glad.' She looked at him sharply and shrewdly, holding her gnomish head to one side. 'They killed her, you know. I don't care what they say. Sent her to one of those places and killed her, Frau Posner.'

The pendulum clock groaned like a living thing and struck the hour. The cat scratched a bare patch behind its ear. Hugo looked at his watch and said something about having to go soon. The old woman just kept nodding her head.

'Herta cried,' she said at last. 'Every time one of those letters came. He was a beautiful writer, the boy. And then not a word, with all the bombs falling day and night. And him, they say, a prisoner of the Bolshevik J—— oh, excuse me, I nearly forgot again.'

'Don't you hear from Wolfgang now?'

'He ought to be ashamed, that scoundrel. Like his father.' She shuffled into the kitchen to stir the washing, muttering crossly under her breath. The cat snored gently, curled up against the warmth of Hugo's stomach. He stood up abruptly and it dropped to the floor with a squeal of fright just as the old woman returned.

'You'll get your milk,' she snapped at the animal. She was crying. Feeble tears trickled down her wrinkled cheeks and a strange quavering whine of grief seemed to force its way out of her pursed mouth. She clutched Hugo's jacket fiercely and pleaded: 'Tell him to come home. His Aunt Rosa wants him.'

'Yes,' he said miserably, trying to disengage himself. 'Yes.'

'I'm old. They laugh at me here, the children. Tell the boy. How long can I wait?'

The hand on his coat was thin as a bird's claw. The flesh had altogether shrunk, exposing the big swollen veins and arthritic joints. It moved him indescribably, more than the loneliness, the bereavement, the misery and neglect of old age. He disengaged himself gently.

'All right,' he promised gruffly. 'I'll do my best. Don't worry, Mother.'

The wine stood on the table with the two glasses, as if ready for a celebration, symbolically untouched. That was how it had to be. Hugo put on his overcoat. 'Good-bye,' he said.

She lifted the hem of her black apron and wiped her eyes.

'He'll want a picture,' she said, and tottered unsteadily to the heavy mahogany sideboard to wrestle with a stiff drawer that seemed to have been shut for years. She came back with the family album and produced a photograph of herself with a younger, middle-aged woman, both of them standing pinched and unsmiling on either side of a luxurious, gruesomely vital fern, the sere and the green. The younger woman wore some medals on the front of her dress, probably a dead husband's war decorations. Hugo guessed she must be Herta. He took the photograph and prepared to put it in his wallet, but an official-looking letter lying face upwards in the album attracted his attention. He read it surreptitiously and a wave of dizziness overcame him.

It was to Frau Herta Sommer from the Ministry of the Interior. 'We have reliable information that your son, 241563 Sommer, Wolfgang, corporal in the S.S. Panzer-division Feldherrnhalle, was released from imprisonment by the authorities of the U.S.S.R. in February, 1946, for special training. He was repatriated to East Germany on 10 June, 1949. We understand that he is employed in the East German administration in the Soviet Sector of Berlin.'

His heart was beating with spasmodic irregularity, the shock of physical infirmity overwhelming everything else, so that his first thought was not that he'd found what he'd come for, but that he must see his doctor, have a cardiogram taken, ration his consumption of alcohol.

The old woman bent down and picked up the cat. 'Say goodbye to the government gentleman,' she said. 'He's going to bring our Wolfgang home.'

Hugo closed the door and walked down the path slowly, overwhelmed by the weight of his own flesh; and the children came scampering across the field, vivid with mischief, singing:

'The witch's man, the witch's man!', their cruel, innocent laughter ringing in the sunlight.

He didn't stay overnight in Frankfurt. During the journey from Stuttgart he'd fallen into a dull, heavy slumber troubled by dreams in which the train, the passengers, the hoarse cries of porters trundling packages to and from the freight cars at passing stations were disconnected threads of a nightmare that he was back in wartime England on the way to internment in the Isle of Wight.

The memory of that episode only returned to him nowadays in dreams. The British had not at first made any distinction between Jewish refugees and ordinary German nationals resident in Britain, but bundled them together into hastily prepared huts with an obtuseness not even explained by the initial confusion which followed the outbreak of war. Mostly, the Jews had regarded it as yet another infliction refugees must endure, but the Germans immediately organised themselves into a disciplined body and behaved as if the internment camp were a Nazi state in miniature.

One young German, however, had gone out of his way to express his sympathy for Jews. A philosophy student at Cambridge, he'd acquired the rather outmoded ideas of Fabian socialism and, when the German Embassy ordered its nationals to leave for home, contrived a sudden vacation in a remote village in the Scottish Highlands. He told Hugo that Hitler would be defeated in six months, Germany's underground socialist movement would reestablish political democracy, and totalitarian tyranny would pass out of the blood stream of Europe like a short-lived virulent fever.

Then one night the young man was savagely beaten up in the camp latrine and taken to the hospital. The Germans claimed the outrage had been committed by Jews and demanded that group punishment be inflicted on them; but no one was in doubt that the assault had been committed by camp Nazis as a warning that fraternisation with Jews would be harshly punished.

At this distance of time Hugo could not even remember what the young German student had looked like, but in the long nightmare his face was Heinz Dieter's. Ten minutes out of Frankfurt he opened his smarting eyes and fumbled for a cigar. Perspiration had turned the collar of his shirt limp and his limbs were leaden with fatigue. The image of Heinzi's face grotesquely distorted by bruises remained and he made up his mind to get back to Berlin without delay.

It was just before midnight when the plane landed at Tempel-hof. He took a taxi into town, relaxing at last as the familiar streets sped by and the extrovert noise and brightness of the Kurfürstendamm distracted his mind from the events of the long, tormenting day. It would be good to lie in a hot scented bath, with the radio making a reassuring noise and a large, neat brandy as a stimulating sedative.

The sounds that came from his apartment were, therefore, a disconcerting surprise. Harsh, frenetic chords of jazz competed with laughter and the thump-thump of energetic dancing. Heinz Dieter was having a party. Of course, he hadn't been expected back that night.

Hugo hesitated with his key in the door, vaguely and unreasonably irritated. It sounded like the sort of party that could go on all night, so there was little point in taking himself off for a couple of hours until the kids had had their fun. Damn it all! It was his house and he felt tired. They'd just have to clear out!

He stepped inside the door quietly and surveyed the scene from the hall. About a dozen boys and girls were distributed about the place, some dancing to the phonograph, others embracing on the couches. Heinz Dieter was not in evidence; he'd probably gone into his own room to make love to a girl in privacy.

The air was thick with tobacco smoke, and broken glasses lay in small puddles of spilled drink on the top of the cocktail bar. A youth with a cigarette in his mouth and a girl in tight jeans waved an inebriated greeting. The noise was hideous.

He stood there feeling embarrassed, an unwanted, uninvited guest. A tall, thin girl with hollow rouged cheeks, who lay on a divan indifferently submitting to the caresses of an amorous young man, looked over her partner's shoulder at him and made some laughing comment. The young man hurriedly jumped off the divan.

'Hello, Hugo,' he grinned sheepishly, not bothering to intro-duce his companion. 'Can I get you a drink?'

He was a good-looking youth of about twenty with thick brown hair carefully barbered to fall in a wave on his forehead, and there was a heavy-lidded expression of cynicism on his smoothly shaved face. Even if Hugo had not recognised him as one of the boys from Bobby's Bar, the manner of the male prostitute was unmistakable. Heinz Dieter knew he disliked having people like that in the house.

'Where's Heinzi?' he asked shortly. The youth winked and gestured towards the bedroom. 'He's having fun,' he said. 'A girl from Stuttgart. Some smasher!'

Hugo controlled his anger. 'I'll have to turn you all out,' he said impassively. 'I'm rather tired.' With an attitude of complete indifference he walked between the dancing couples and poured himself a stiff brandy, sipping it with strained concentration, as if carefully testing its flavour. A primitive African carving had been knocked askew on the mantelpiece. He picked it up and examined it minutely for damage before replacing it in its proper position. The boy from Bobby's Bar went round whispering to his friends, who stopped to stare at Hugo without resentment or embarrassment, but with an insulting incuriosity.

The telephone started to ring, and he strolled the length of the room to answer it. 'Yes,' he said curtly.

A distant voice speaking in strongly accented German asked for Heinz Dieter.

'Who wants him?' he demanded, aware that they were all listening. 'Hello, are you still there?' The line clicked dead. He put the receiver back, vaguely troubled. The voice had not been unfamiliar; it was one he'd heard before somewhere. And suddenly he knew. Kane. He'd not recognised it immediately because whenever he'd met the man they had conversed in English.

'All right, everybody,' he shouted. 'The party's over. Good night!'

The youngsters filed out, leaving the gramophone blaring away. He was alone in the empty, littered room, with cigarette stubs ground out on the carpet, cushions thrown about on the floor, the stale smell of spilled alcohol. A strident female voice was singing:

'Be a natural, kissable baby,
Lovin' ain't no sin.
You gotta shake those blues, baby,
Right outa ya skin.'

He shut the noise off angrily. In a moment Heinz Dieter appeared, his hair and clothing disordered, shading his eyes against the light.

'Where's everybody———?' he began, and then, open-mouthed, noticed Hugo. 'You back already? I expected you tomorrow.'

'That's quite obvious,' Hugo said acidly. 'If your girl friend can spare you for half an hour, you'd better clear up the mess.'

'Hugo, I'm sorry———'

'Please, Heinzi, shut up! I'm too damned tired. Tell me in the morning. By the way, somebody called you.' He was not too tired to catch the fleeting expression of alarm that passed over the young man's face.

'Did they leave a message?'

'No, just a name,' he lied, watching the other carefully. 'Kame, or Kale, or something.'

'Never heard of it,' Heinz Dieter said. He smiled with convincing charm. 'Must be someone who wanted to crash the party. Sorry about the mess, Hugo. I'll tidy it as good as new. The girl's going, anyway.'

Hugo went up to bed thoughtfully. Perhaps it hadn't been Kane. After all, a voice on the telephone. One imagined things. The day had been too much for him. Tomorrow he'd see his doctor.

'Breathe out... breathe in...' the doctor commanded, listening intently to his stethoscope.

Hugo shivered as the metal tip of the instrument moved searchingly over his chest. Now that he was actually submitting to examination the procedure bored him. He did not need a doctor to tell him he was a poor physical specimen, that his heart, lungs, liver, kidneys, blood pressure were all in some measure defective. He'd abused his body too long to expect it to remain undamaged. It was a battered old machine, and he didn't ask more of it than it should keep on functioning and not break down on him altogether.

The doctor motioned him to a chair. 'Sit there and make yourself comfortable, Herr Krantz,' he said. He was a small, precise man, a Swiss specialist, who gave the impression of being totally absorbed in the detection of disease, devoting to the task a concentration of skill and energy that had earned him a European reputation. With brisk economical movements he adjusted the cardiogram equipment, then sat down to study the readings, making notes on an impressive-looking chart.

'I'm still alive, I hope,' Hugo said sardonically.

'I think so,' the doctor replied with a wintry smile. 'What is more important, I hope we can keep you that way.'

'For how long?'

'That is not exactly a scientific question, Herr Krantz. But I see no reason why you should not enjoy the same expectation of life as any other man of your age. But we had better discuss that after you have dressed.'

Fully clothed again, Hugo asked permission to smoke. He needed a cigar badly, having abstained during the day out of an obscure impulse to cheat the verdict of the examination, for he'd really been afraid that his heart was bad and that if he maintained his usual heavy consumption of cigars the cardiogram would confirm his fears. Now it seemed there had been nothing to worry about.

The doctor leaned back in his swivel chair and placed his antiseptic finger-tips together in a judicious gesture.

'This flutter you sometimes feel, this breathlessness, it is not a result of disease. Your heart is fundamentally sound. But I must tell you, the heart is not an organ you can afford to over-tax.'

'Certainly not,' Hugo agreed, resigning himself to the inevitable lecture on the need for moderation. That was what one paid for, anyway.

'You are overloading your heart by about twenty kilograms,' the doctor went on severely. 'That in itself can shorten your life by ten years. Tell me, Herr Krantz, can you remember the last time you went for a long walk?'

'It must be five years, at least. When I lived in London I sometimes walked across Hampstead Heath. But I never allowed it to become a vice.'

The doctor permitted himself a ghost of a smile as an act of courtesy, but tapped the chart impatiently with the back of his pen.

'If you want to remain an active man you will have to change your ideas. Go on as you are doing and you will damage your body beyond repair. Not only your heart, but other vulnerable organs too. Do you know what your greatest danger is, Herr Krantz? Not cancer, not heart disease, not tuberculosis. Over-indulgence, the malady of prosperity. So I do not propose to prescribe drugs for your condition, but self-discipline. You will eat meat sparingly, fruit and salads in abundance, according to the diet I'll give you. It would be better if you did not drink and smoke at all, but you may have three cigars a day and no more than one glass of alcohol, preferably in the evening.'

Hugo listened carefully, took a last puff on his cigar, and stubbed it out in the ash-tray. Self-discipline? The man sounded like a Prussian general sentencing a defaulter. But the advice was sound, of course. If he hadn't wanted to hear it he shouldn't have come in the first place. It wouldn't hurt him to try the treatment. Not quite so drastically as the doctor ordered, though – he wasn't dying, after all.

'Doctor, if you insist, I'll drink nothing but soda-water from now on', he said cheerfully.

But abstemiousness was not in his nature, and he saw no point in practising self-deception. Quite apart from anything else, the situation called for a celebration; one wasn't reprieved every day. It would be soon enough to start being a good boy tomorrow.

That evening he called up several friends and collected a party for dinner. They drove out to a small lake-side restaurant and ate enormously – oysters, grilled turbot, chicken, champagne – singing boisterously to an old-fashioned Bavarian orchestra and lapsing into tearful sentimentality like a group of middle-aged survivors of a student *Brüderschaft* enjoying a drunken reunion. Then, about midnight, staggering under the influence of good drink and giggling stupidly when one or another broke wind to relieve the congestion in his over-full stomach, they piled into their cars and went off to Charlie's Night Club for a boisterous nightcap that turned into a regular orgy of brandy-swilling, back-slapping, and smutty storytelling until about two o'clock in the morning.

Then, suddenly, in the abrupt way it always happened, Hugo was too tired to put up with it any longer. The alcoholic vitality had drained away, leaving him depressed and disenchanted. He waved a weary farewell to his companions and left. The street outside Charlie's was cool and quiet, soothing to his flushed face and throbbing head. And then, at his elbow, there was Kane. Kane of the black leather coat, the sour, one-sided obstinate grin and cold oyster-grey eyes.

Hugo said: 'Don't you get tired of following me about, you bastard?' He gripped the man's leather lapels and rocked slightly on his heels. 'You're lucky I don't take you seriously,' he went on softly, breathing brandy fumes into Kane's face.

'I wish you would.' Kane pulled his coat free, his voice neutral, carefully concealing any trace of dislike or resentment. 'It could save a lot of trouble. Tell me, strictly off the record, why are you interested in a man named Sommer?'

'This will surprise you.' Hugo smiled at some private joke. 'Who's Sommer?'

'You know,' replied Kane patiently. He lit a cigarette, shielding the match against the wind, his putty-coloured face still expressionless. 'You've been chasing him hard enough, haven't you?'

'If you don't stop following me around, I'll ask for police protection.'

'I don't think you will. We understand each other. All I want is background.'

'For your paper in San Francisco?'

'That's right,' said Kane. 'I've also got to make a living.'

Hugo looked him up and down, from the crown of his snap-brimmed hat to his heavy crepe-soled shoes, with frowning malignance. 'What sort of American are you?' he asked. 'Who are you fooling?'

'What sort of Jew are you?' Kane countered.

'A bad Jew, a reluctant Jew, a Jew-hating Jew, a Nazi-manufactured Jew, a Jewish louse,' Hugo told him gravely. 'Now I've confessed, you confess. We'll give each other absolution.'

The tight mouth closed into its one-sided enigmatic grin. 'I'm an American American. Any other ideas you've got about me are cock-eyed. What about Sommer?'

'You annoy me,' said Hugo, walking unsteadily towards his car.

Kane followed him and put his foot in the door. 'A little bit of information, Mr Krantz, that's all I'm asking. You're in a delicate position. I know how you make your money, and I know your hobbies – all of them.'

Hugo started the car and revved the engine loudly, then drove off with a jerk.

'If you don't talk, I know someone who will,' Kane called after him, but Hugo hardly heard. He was still preoccupied with the first threat. The significance of the second only penetrated some moments later.

They all thought the same way, he reflected savagely. You could always put the screw on a queer. But it wasn't so easy here in Berlin, the great European Sodom. Not like London, with its clandestine parties of sailors, its schoolboy jokes and pansy actors. He wasn't afraid. Not after the furtive assignations in Soho, Bayswater, Chelsea, afraid of detection, afraid of blackmail and ostracism, the boys as cruel and capricious as women; not after the anonymous telephone calls and Marion screaming: 'God! it can't be true! You're not a pervert! You couldn't be so disgusting…' understanding, for the first time, their morbid, lacerating relationship. All those years, controlling his disgust when they lay side by side in bed, her female body pressed full length against him; and while it happened he would hold desperately to the image of Putzi, trying to make the sterile embrace tolerable by evoking the memory of the lean, lithe grace of a boy's neat body.

He could still see Kane in the driving-mirror, faceless and diminished, a spider disappearing into the dark crevices of the street. Kane, the pseudo-American, the phony journalist, with his cruel, Central Asian features and obstinate ubiquity. He drove entirely by reflex, fear groping in his body like a sharp spasm of pain. What had Kane called out as the car moved off? About knowing somebody who'd talk? Heinzi, he thought instantly, the name knocking at his heart. The disarranged papers, the open drawer, the key on the floor. The shamefaced 'Are you looking for this?' Another treachery? The worst? God, no!

The thought made him feel so weak he stopped the car and leaned his head against the wheel. Now he saw Heinz Dieter's recent nervousness as a confirmation of guilt, a feeling of uneasiness that he might be found out. He recalled the sullen repudiation of the accusation that he'd been looking for money. 'I've got money. I've been saving.' How could he possibly have passed that over? Was there anybody in Berlin more spendthrift, throwing around whatever cash he had in his pocket to impress some girl, buying fancy ties, gambling in the casinos? If he had money, it was because someone had been giving it to him. Payment, perhaps, for information received.

Hugo experienced a dreary sense of despair. Had he ever, in his whole life, been anything but lonely? In all his relationships, had there been one single genuine friendship? His father had always been remote, caught up in the fretful difficulties of a near-bankrupt fur factory, puzzled by the strangeness of his only son, and slowly, bitterly reconciling himself to the fact that he had fathered a man not like other men. His mother and older sister? They had fussed over him, indulged him, protected him like a piece of fragile china; one or the other would wait outside the school to take him home even when he was fourteen. As he grew older, he'd begun to make his own society. There were many people he thought of as friends then, some of them women, but mostly they were youngsters like himself who were just beginning to adjust themselves to their abnormalities and were beginning to explore with guilty delight the secret, forbidden emotional experiences of their outsider's world.

In those early years he had felt liberated from loneliness. The discovery that there were many people like himself, among them the handsomest, most gifted, and most sensitive of young men, had given him a wonderful sense of belonging to a high-spirited élite. They seemed a band of youthful hedonists, filled with a frolicking exuberance in which passion was often no more than an intense interlude. There were a few with whom he thought he experienced a deep and secret understanding, who shared his own emotional idiom, whom he had really loved – Putzi von Schlesinger particularly, despite the ingeniously devised torments that in themselves were part of his mocking love game. But there had always been the betrayals, the small treacheries, and he always had been hurt. Even these emotional friendships had gradually become fewer and the commercial transactions more frequent; the grimaces of disgust in the dark, and in the morning the averted look, the cash payment. Loneliness.

But then he found Heinz Dieter. He was weak, not particularly intelligent, and frequently silly and vain. There was no rational explanation for the immensely protective tenderness he felt for the boy. He recalled their first meeting – how many years ago? Four, five? He'd come out of the Charlottenburg station, and there, in the doorway of a bombed-out building, an American sergeant was beating up a ragged scarecrow of about sixteen. 'Little bastard!' the sergeant shouted in an outraged voice. 'Try to lift my wallet, would you, you dirty little kraut?' Hugo had intervened. 'I got a good mind to turn him over to the cops,' the American said. 'These brats gotta learn a few morals.' The boy cringed against the wall, watching them closely from under the shelter of his forearm. The soldier buttoned his wallet securely inside his tunic. 'For Chris-sake, let him go,' he growled disgustedly. 'The bastard'll hang one day.'

The boy was waiting for Hugo down the street. 'Give us a few groschen,' he wheedled. 'Got a smoke to spare?' He had big, candid blue eyes in a half-starved face. Though his skinny body shivered under its ragged clothing, he brushed a few specks of dust from Hugo's coat with practised coquetry. 'How about a sausage?' he suggested desperately.

Hugo took him to a little back-street restaurant. He gave his name as Schulz, Heinz Dieter Schulz, from Dresden, snapping at the food like a ravenous dog and pocketing the meat bones to gnaw later. The story he told between mouthfuls was the usual pitiful one.

When the Russians came he was eleven. His father, an unemployed teacher, had lost a leg in the war and the boy was the main support of the family. The Russian soldiers were stupid, he confessed with an engaging grin. He stole from them, sold them *kaput* watches, found them girls, slept with them. If he didn't bring home enough his father beat him. He was thrashed for minor infractions of discipline at home. One day Heinz Dieter picked up a meat knife and pushed it into his father's stomach. It didn't wound him badly, apparently, because the knife was blunt, but the boy got frightened and ran away. He was then fourteen. What about his mother? Wouldn't she worry about him? No, she didn't seem to care what happened to any of them: she was sleeping with a Russian corporal.

The boy was a natural charmer, smiling with ready candour, touching Hugo's hand with an intimate gesture that was yet gravely respectful, looking deeply and trustfully into his eyes. Hugo took him home, washed him, bought him clothes, educated him in the basic civilities, pulled strings to obtain documents that enabled him to reside lawfully in West Berlin. As time passed and the flesh grew on the thin bones he began to experience a deep parental affection for Heinz Dieter quite novel in his life. It was almost like that of a mother who delighted in her son's masculinity and was both jealous and proud of his prowess with girls. Lately they'd even joked about the time when he would marry and his children would call Hugo 'Grandfather', although for Hugo the joke was a wry one. He couldn't endure the thought of Heinz Dieter domesticated, someone's husband, enclosed by the jealous, possessive affections of some female. To wake up at night and know that Heinz Dieter was not asleep in the next room would be to feel loneliness beating its bat wings in the dark.

Heinz Dieter was all the blond, careless boys he had ever loved, the trusted friend, the son he would never have. He was his entire complex of intimate human relationships – his family, his tender world, his suffering.

Could it have been all self-deception? he asked himself. All the time of trust, the years shared, did it all mean nothing? No, surely it was impossible! What, in fact, had happened? He had bickered with the boy, found some papers disarranged, a drawer open, a key missing, And on the basis of these he jumped to the conclusion that Heinzi was selling him out. Put like that he could see it as utterly absurd. There could be any number of explanations. His spirits soared at the thought. You're getting old and crusty, he chided himself gaily. There's nothing to worry about at all.

He started the engine and felt confidence surging through him as the car gathered speed. He'd look in at the apartment and see if Heinzi was there. If so, they'd go out and have fun. Maybe even do what they joked about so often, pick up a couple of girls. He'd play the polished middle-aged seducer just to make Heinzi laugh. His eyes glowed with amusement at the thought.

But Heinz Dieter wasn't at home. Hugo switched on the lights and walked restlessly round the apartment's elegant emptiness. His own presence, bulky as it was, didn't make the place seem less deserted. It was as though he were a ghost returning to the room of his death, and the room, the furniture, the pictures on the wall no longer recognised him. They waited passively for another tenant.

On an impulse he went into Heinz Dieter's room. It was disarranged. The boy must have had a girl in again and they'd left the bed rumpled. Cigarette ends were stubbed out on the bed-side table. He stooped to pick up a chiffon handkerchief from the floor and a gust of cloying perfume turned him slightly sick. Among the photographs of girls on the dressing-table was an enlarged snapshot of himself and Heinz Dieter taken the summer before when they went off for a month to the Black Forest. He had his arm around Heinzi's shoulders. The recollection of that happiness moved him near to tears, and he stood looking at the picture for some time.

Outside, down below, faintly vibrating against the glass of the window, there was the night throb of the city. Things going on, traffic going somewhere, people talking shrilly above the growling brown-sugar voices of trumpets and the syncopated beat of pianos. He felt as though he were soaring away, immensely alone in a capsule of glass and metal into the emptiness above him. Emptiness to emptiness.

With an effort he poured himself a large brandy, lit a cigar, and switched on the radio, but soon he was returning to Heinzi's room. He began picking things up and putting them away. Then he tidied the bed. Then he looked at the snapshot again for a long time.

5

At first Martin thought he must be mistaken. Could it really be Fred Adler? The last time he'd seen him Fred was a political refugee from some East European Communist republic in an Arts Theatre production of an American political drama. Afterwards they had a drink in the bar and Fred spoke vaguely about going to Australia with a touring company. Two years ago, at least. Now there he was on the terrace of Kempinski's, with a pretty blonde, looking relaxed and happy and altogether at home.

Martin tapped on the plate glass to attract his attention. Fred turned and peered short-sightedly. With the vanity of his profession he preferred myopia to the disfigurement of wearing glasses. Only when Martin came in and stood by the table did he recognise him.

'Hal-*lo*, old chap, what a marvellous surprise,' he exclaimed in his carefully articulated B.B.C. English; then, reverting to German: 'Hedy, darling, this is Martin Stone, an old school friend of mine.'

The girl dimpled and gave him an attractive smile. Her voice when she spoke was clear, rounded, and skilfully produced. An actress.

'How was Australia?' asked Martin.

'Australia?' Fred was puzzled. It took him a moment or two to rediscover the association. 'Oh, *Australia*. You mean the touring idea. I didn't go. Sit down and have a drink.' He signalled the waitress and ordered beer all round. 'Since I saw you last, my boy, I've discovered the advantage of being bilingual. I can play sinister foreigners with broken accents in both English and German.'

Martin grinned wryly. 'There's something rather symbolic there, I suppose. Do you like it?'

'It's a living. It even supplies the funds for a Volkswagen. I do six months in Germany and a couple of months in England, which gives me enough to enjoy the idleness in between. Hedy and I are doing a film together.'

Fred stroked the back of the girl's neck possessively. 'Isn't she cute?' he said proudly. 'You want to watch this child, Martin. She's sexy, she's talented, she speaks four languages, she's got a first-class press agent. In a couple of years she'll be an international star.'

The little actress smiled with pleasure. 'I am really excited,' she admitted. 'Now I am wanted for an Italian film. A German actress must play in foreign films if she is to have prestige in Germany. The Germans have such inferiority complexes.'

Fred patted her approvingly. 'That's right, darling. You've got the idea perfectly.' He took a long appreciative drink of his beer and lifted a quizzical eyebrow. 'To what are you applying your bilingual talents here, Martin?'

'Just business,' Martin replied shortly. He looked at Adler with a certain baffled curiosity, unable to fit his cheerful complacency into the general picture he had of Berlin. They'd attended the same kindergarten here, two small Jewish boys from prosperous homes who had been violently uprooted just when their impressionable young minds had been most vulnerable. Adler had gone into the theatre, always associated with uncommercial experiments in a series of shabby halls and clubs, on the point of getting an important rôle in something, sometime, and materialising occasionally as a minor character written in to enhance the turgid atmosphere in a B film or a television serial. Like other people who shared his predicament, he'd been inclined to sing the refugee blues, ascribing his lack of success to some amorphous prejudice – to the fact that he was a German refugee, or to the 'old boys' network' of theatrical homosexuals which allegedly discriminated against young heterosexual actors. Professional frustration had given him a slightly haggard look of perpetual discontent, but his face had now filled out, his clothes were expensive, and the chronic tensions seemed to have dissolved into a bland self-confidence.

'I gather you like it here,' Martin said.

Fred allowed his gaze to wander tolerantly around the restaurant to the well-groomed businessmen and their wives and beyond, through the glass façade, at the leisurely parade of people on the pavements, the hard, expensive glitter of automobiles.

'It's comfortable,' he admitted. 'At first there was a feeling that things weren't what they seemed, if you know what I mean. As if everybody you met was acting the part of being kind, agreeable, tolerant. Hedy understands, don't you, darling?'

'Oh, yes,' she said, puckering her pretty face into a serious expression. 'The German people want very much to be liked. They try really hard to be nice to foreigners.'

Fred's left eyelid drooped and he exchanged a long, amused look with Martin. 'You see, it's all history now.' He fondled Hedy's arm affectionately. 'She's also Germany, and you can't say she isn't delicious.' He winked again.

Martin smiled into her big flirtatious eyes. She had the natural charmer's talent for agreeably enhancing a man's awareness of his masculinity. Her kind was international. For them men were not democrats or fascists, Jews or Moslems or Catholics. Men were men, to be beguiled, exploited, enjoyed. The Hedys of the world were enemies only in the sex war, brilliant at the strategy of victory through submission.

'If you're doing nothing this evening, how about having dinner with us?' Fred suggested. 'I can probably find someone to make it a foursome.'

'Yes, why don't we make up a party, have dinner, and go back to Freddie's place for dancing?' Hedy proposed vivaciously. She clapped her hands together like an excited little girl. 'We can call up a few friends and have a lot of fun.'

But thinking of the dark, self-contained girl he was meeting, Martin wasn't sure. A seamstress from shabby East Berlin. He couldn't see her at ease in the company of smart young theatre folk. Maybe some other time.

Fred Adler didn't press him. He handed over an engraved visiting card. If Martin changed his mind, he should just come along. There wouldn't be a shortage of drink.

The encounter had stimulated him. He went off whistling cheerfully, in the mood for a gay, careless evening. On an impulse he stopped at a florist's and bought a cellophane-wrapped gardenia, but back in the street with the flower in his hand he felt that it was out of character: florid gestures were not for him, and he stuffed the gardenia into his pocket self-consciously.

Karin was already waiting. She stood in the entrance of the Underground, half-concealed in the shadow of the wall as if afraid of being too conspicuous. She was shabbier than he had expected and the dim fluorescence that filtered up from below made her appear tired and sallow. Inevitably, he compared her with Fred's bright young actress and the comparison moved him both to pity and distaste. It would be easy to sneak off. She would wait ten, fifteen minutes and go home again. Not exactly a gentlemanly action, but to hell with it! Worse things had happened in Berlin.

A wave of people issued from the Underground and for a few seconds he lost sight of Karin. When the crowd had passed he saw that she was being accosted by a man. She moved away, but the stranger followed and touched her arm. Martin felt a quick spasm of anger and crossed the road.

'I'm sorry I'm late,' he apologised. The man lifted his hat in a drunken gesture of mockery and walked unsteadily down the stairs of the station. Martin took the gardenia from his pocket and handed it to her awkwardly as an act of contrition. The encounter with the drunk seemed to have upset her deeply.

'Thank you,' she said in a small voice. 'I'm frightened of men like that.' Her hand was trembling as she fastened the flower to her coat and for the second time that evening, even more powerfully, his masculine protectiveness was evoked. Now her shabbiness stirred him in a different way, making him side with her against the aggressive prosperity of the western city which suddenly seemed tawdry and heartless.

'Forget it,' he said, smiling at her reassuringly. 'I hope you're as hungry as I am,' and they crossed the road with linked arms, like lovers.

They consumed a small banquet in the glittering Berliner Kindl restaurant, pleasantly relaxed by the food and the wine, and Martin didn't even allow it to cross his mind that the waiter who served them might have been a Nazi functionary, or that the same orchestra leader who nodded his head in time to the music only a few feet away had probably waved his baton at concerts arranged as recreation for S.S. troops and concentration camp guards. Afterwards they drank beer seated in an alcove in a smoky pseudo beer cellar in the Steinplatz among beefy middle-aged Germans and their wives, and for all the concern it caused him they might well have been detribalised Polynesians. He was determined to see Berlin with an innocent eye, like a tourist out on a spree enjoying a lucky meeting with a local girl. They danced often, Karin's soft, animal-warm body close to his, her long black hair brushing his cheek in calculated intimacy, and for a while they seemed to inhabit a small world of their own, possessing an absolute invulnerability.

But, of course, it couldn't last. Every time the music stopped and their bodies separated, he was drawn a little more into his own loneliness, until, imperceptibly, it began to reimpose its sterility on the promise of the evening.

Yet when he got back to London he would remember this evening a little sadly, a little regretfully, and not without affection. For a few hours Karin had given him a holiday from his own history. She would be the one person who had come to him unambiguously and he would always be grateful for it.

She smiled and leaned towards him, her bare rounded arms on the table. The green blouse she wore enhanced the warm apricot bloom of her skin, the gloss of her hair, her strangely suppliant eyes. She didn't look German. If it were Rome, or Madrid... But then he would be a different person, an Englishman warmed by a foreign sun, his mind a gallery of sunny Mediterranean pictures, not an ex-German nailed to the past by his memories.

'What are you thinking?' Karin asked.

'Nothing,' he replied evasively, 'nothing,' looking round at the half-empty bar, the spurious elation gone, leaving a dispirited sense of futility.

'You must be thinking of something.'

'I'm thinking a mood,' he said. 'You know the sort of thing. You can play it on a piano. Perhaps you can paint it. But you can't put it into words.'

A middle-aged man and woman got up and danced distractingly between the tables, thick bodies clumsily parodying the rhythm. Martin looked away, fumbling with a packet of cigarettes. It seemed to him that everything about the couple was singularly ugly, their corpulence obscene, and the knowledge that his reaction was morbid made no difference at all.

'Give me a cigarette,' Karin said. She did not wait for him to strike a match, but lifted his hand towards her lips and lit her cigarette from his. The gesture moved him distressingly.

'Now that I know you a little I shall tell you who you remind me of,' she went on. 'His name was Luther. He lived in the flat above us with his grandmother. I was only six and he was eleven, but I loved him. He had long, thin, elegant legs like a stork and a solemn grown-up face. My father said I was not to play with him, but I used to follow him to the park round the corner where he stood alone watching the other children play, always holding a book against his chest. His grandmother had the same habit, only she used to hold a handbag against her coat. Luther would talk to me but he wouldn't play ball or chasing games when I wanted him to. "Why do you always hold that book there?" I asked him once. "Is it your Bible?" He began to walk away. I ran after him and snatched the book out of his hand. There was a yellow star on his jacket.'

'I know the rest of the story,' Martin interrupted. 'Let's not talk about it.'

'I didn't understand,' Karin said, 'honestly I didn't. The people queueing at the Jew shop to buy their rations, pushing desperately for places. People suddenly disappearing overnight and nobody saying anything about it – not in front of the children, anyway. It was like sex, they stopped talking in the middle of a sentence.' Her cigarette burned away unnoticed as she sat isolated by her memories. 'I stood clutching the book and staring at the yellow star. The sun was shining and I wanted to hide from it. I wanted to creep into a cupboard. He didn't cry, or get angry, or go away. He just stood there, blushing, looking at the ground. I was the one who cried.' With unexpected violence she said: 'People say they didn't know what was going on. It's a lie. Everybody knew.'

Martin said: 'I thank you for that confession.' He had to say it. He had the ridiculous feeling that he would cry if he didn't. It seemed to him just then that he'd come all the way to Berlin only to hear this. 'Don't let's get too emotional,' he went on huskily, afraid he was being betrayed by sentimentality. It wasn't as easy as all that. A few drinks, a girl who was a decent human being, a background of pleasant music. One couldn't just capitulate to it. It didn't change a single thing. He remembered Fred Adler's party. Now he had no misgivings about taking her. 'Come on,' he urged, 'this place is getting sleepy.'

Fred lived on the ground floor of an apartment block in Charlottenburg and they found a note pinned to the door. 'We've run out of liquor. Join us in the bar down the road.'

It was long past midnight and the clockwork city was beginning to run down, cars turning homeward to the suburbs, couples saying their quiet good-byes in sheltered doorways, somewhere the nocturnal, marrow-freezing scream of an amorous cat.

'Would you prefer to go home?' Martin asked. 'Everybody will probably be drunk.'

'No,' Karin said. 'No one who lives in an overcrowded flat in East Berlin is ever in a hurry to go home.'

The bar was easy to locate. At two hundred yards they heard the ground throb of drums and followed the sound until it thickened to a rhythmic catarrhal blur. Inside, the usual clouds of stale tobacco made their eyes sting and Fred came over to wring Martin's hand with alcoholic cordiality. He dragged them through the smoke, thrust drinks into their hands, and introduced them to several handsome people who smiled with perfect teeth, made friendly noises, and wandered off into the semi-darkness vaguely preoccupied, as if they had mislaid themselves in some corner. Fred pushed a handful of coins into the garishly-lit juke-box and advanced on Karin with his arms held open in invitation. She hesitated slightly, then moved stiffly into the dance.

'I'll bring her back – if you're lucky,' Fred boomed, impersonating the brute male.

Martin was chagrined to discover that he felt jealous. He retired to the table and saw Hedy sitting on a man's knee. She was very tight, her hair mussed up and her pretty eyes slightly glazed and unfocused. 'Come'n' dance,' she insisted, disengaging herself from the embrace of her partner.

'You've had too much to drink,' Martin said gravely. 'You ought to go to bed.' The whole of her slender, desirable body lay against him and she lifted her face to his with a silly inebriate grin.

'Always thinking of bed, naughty.'

Her head rested sleepily on his chest and he could feel without desire the drugged erotic movement of her round soft limbs. The thought of the other girl, Karin, tormented him. It would have been so simple if he, too, were drunk, needing nothing but a girl, any girl, and one already in his arms. But now it seemed absurd that he could have compared Karin unfavourably with this inconsequential little blonde. He saw Fred near-by bobbing energetically among the dancers.

'Hedy's not feeling very well,' he told him. 'You ought to take her home.'

Fred came over and examined the young actress solemnly. 'She's sozzled, the poor darling,' he said with serious concern. 'I told her not to mix her drinks.'

Martin deposited her firmly in his arms and went off in search of Karin. Fred seemed to have lost her. But she'd only gone to the powder-room and they began to dance together with relief, as if after a long separation, saying little, not noticing that Fred and Hedy and their friends had departed.

When they separated and he noticed how late it was, he wanted to explain that it might be difficult to get a train and that, as taxis didn't accept fares to East Berlin, she would have difficulty in getting home. Instead he kissed her big soft mouth with a sudden reckless desperation.

The strength seemed to go out of her for a moment. 'Let's sit down,' she said quietly, and led him by the hand to a secluded table. 'Give me a cigarette, please.' The flame of the match lit up her damp, dilated eyes. She inhaled deeply and put the cigarette down, her hand trembling. Shakily she commented: 'That was a very public kiss.'

'I'm sorry if I offended you,' Martin said. The dim beer cellar was almost deserted except for a reticent waiter, two men drinking morosely and watching their own reflections in the pink-tinted mirrors behind the bar, and a pair of lovers embracing in an alcove as shadowy and intimate as their own. A squalid place to end a squalid adventure, he told himself, discounting everything but the rebuff.

'You didn't offend me. You don't understand,' Karin said. 'I find you very attractive.'

'Thank you, and I, too. Now we've been so polite, let's close the incident and leave.'

'My God! You're so full of yourself,' she burst out. 'Your feelings are no more important than anyone else's. What do you think I owe you?'

He said, gently: 'This is ridiculous. Just a kiss. Pretend it didn't happen. We only owe each other respect.'

'Yes,' she agreed in a small voice, her face averted. Speaking into the shadows, she went on wretchedly: 'I ought to tell you, I'm afraid of love.'

'So am I sometimes.'

'No, that's not quite right. I'm frightened of men.'

He felt miserable and embarrassed. 'Please don't say any more. I didn't realise.'

'It's my fault,' she persisted. 'You couldn't be expected to guess, the way I've been behaving. But I felt differently about you. I thought it would be possible. But it seems I was wrong. I can't really change.'

So he had stumbled on to some private tragedy. Not only the bombs and shells that made a common disaster; not only the hunger, the squalor, the growing up among ruins, but something shameful and secret that time alone could not cure.

'I must tell you. It was the Russians.'

With a sickening dismay he said: 'No, how could they? You were too young.'

'It happened to younger children.' She told him the story quietly and simply. It was during the end of April, or the beginning of May, 1945. Street fighting was still going on among the ruins. Corpses lay all over the place, the bodies of old men and youths, executed by the S.S. for attempting to escape from Berlin, hung from lamp-posts; people were starving. Her mother cut off Karin's hair and dressed her in an old pair of trousers and a jersey that belonged to her brother. One day rifle-butts hammered on their door. Her father hurriedly locked her in the wardrobe. She crouched in the darkness among the clothes that smelled faintly of mothballs, listening to the heavy, trampling feet of soldiers and the coarse Russian voices exclaiming with excitement over the articles they were plundering. '*Komm, Frau!*' she heard them yell. Her mother began to scream.

Karin said: 'I thought she was being killed.' She lifted the stub of her cigarette to her mouth and drew deeply on it, trying to remain calm. 'I cried and beat my hands on the wardrobe door. A Russian soldier kicked it in and dragged me into the room.

He started to laugh and pinched my cheek in quite a friendly way. My father was standing in a corner, his face to the wall, crying like a child. My mother was lying on the bed surrounded by soldiers with heavy Mongol faces. They were arguing over who was to get at her first. I screamed at them to leave her alone, but the Russian who pulled me out of the wardrobe held me back, talking to me in what seemed a reasonable way, although I couldn't understand what he was saying. He kept on repeating the words "*kulturny choloveik*". I discovered later on that he was telling me he was a cultured person. In the struggle to hold me back, he put his arms around my body. I suppose he could feel that I had breasts, because suddenly he changed altogether. "*Komm, Frau*," he growled, and pushed me away from the other soldiers into our small kitchen. Then he tore my clothes off.'

Martin felt soaked to the bone in horror and filth, but he was held by a morbid, unwilling fascination.

'When the soldier finished with me,' Karin went on, speaking with painful hesitation, 'he picked me up and carried me in his arms back to the other room and offered me naked to the other men. They made noises like wild animals... There were so many of them——' She began trembling violently.

'Why can't I get over it? It was so long ago.' She turned a tormented face towards him, purple shadows circling her eyes like bruises. 'For years I couldn't bear to look even at little boys. I hated my father and brother. But it began to pass and I could sometimes think of falling in love. And then——'

'We're ugly. We're condemned,' Martin told himself bleakly. Twenty centuries of poetry, art, reason, religious aspiration had proved merely an empty gesture. What else could one say of a

society that crucified its God and fed its lusts on the bodies of its
own young? There was no hope but to begin from the beginning,
to re-create the Creation, to become the first Man and the first
Woman. Amen.

'Waiter!' he called. 'Bring a bottle of champagne.'

'There's nothing to celebrate,' Karin said miserably. But something was happening inside him. It hurt like red-hot needles
thrust into the soft flesh, or as if he were being minutely sifted
and reconstituted. Perhaps, in a terrible way, it was love.

'Maybe there is,' he said.

When they came out it was raining hard. The smooth asphalt
streets gleamed with the cold reflection of moonlight and sodium
street lamps. It was after four. Silent as black marble, the city
stretched like a cemetery around them.

'I could walk home, I suppose,' Karin said, shivering. 'But I start
work at seven.'

'Isn't there a café for night workers where we can get some
breakfast?'

'There's nowhere, nowhere at all.'

'You'll have to come to my room,' Martin said. 'You're as safe
as a nun,' he assured her ironically. 'You won't even be late for
work. Come on!'

Seizing her by the hand, he began to run through the rain until
they both became out of breath and started to laugh like children.
In the Kantstrasse a solitary taxi picked them up. They were still
laughing when it delivered them at the door of his lodgings.

The lift came down and ascended again with a noise like a train
uncoupling. 'Ssh!' Martin cautioned as he fumbled his key into
the lock. 'We mustn't wake Frau Goetz.'

Once inside the room they both became painfully self-conscious. Frau Goetz had made up the bed on the large divan and laid out his pyjamas. Martin went round switching on all the lights, exposing the threadbare furnishings, the frugal respectability of the hideous vases, coloured prints, and tasteless bric-à-brac. The lacquered waste-paper basket, decorated with a red cockerel, he discreetly pushed out of sight.

'Do sit down,' he urged her politely, for all the world as if the situation were perfectly ordinary. There was nothing to offer her but cigarettes.

It was so quiet. The silence rang in their ears.

Karin said: 'Why don't you lie down? You look terribly tired.'

It was quite true. An accumulated fatigue had suddenly descended on him. He caught a fugitive glimpse of himself in the mirror looking haggard and ill.

'I've been unlucky for you,' she said compassionately.

'Unlucky?' Martin smiled vaguely and sat down on the end of the bed. His weighted head sank back on the pillow.

She got up quickly, as if she'd come to a sudden decision, and stood looking down at him with an overpowering tenderness. 'I'm sorry,' she said, and knelt at his feet. Then, gently, she removed his shoes, making him feel curiously feeble and helpless as an infant. Sleep was beginning to muffle him in dark swaddling clothes. Karin put out the lights. He did not see her get into bed, but her cold touch on his chest woke him. She was lying by his side naked, one hand protecting her dark groin. 'Don't,' she whispered, as his masculine grip closed on her fingers. 'Please, don't.' But a raging desire stormed through his body. His hot mouth fastened upon her mouth and he forced himself into her nakedness, making her shudder and moan. And soon they were moving violently together in a delirious, exhausting conflict.

When he opened his eyes several hours later, Frau Goetz was knocking discreetly at his door bringing a tray with breakfast. The sun filtering through the drawn curtains and the smell of coffee dispelled the last stale traces of the night.

There was a note on the desk. 'I had to leave for work. I didn't want to wake you. I work at Schmidt's, in Fasanenstrasse. We finish at 5 p.m. I shall wait there outside the factory, if you want to see me again.'

It seemed like an accusation. Martin read and re-read the message as if it were some code for which he had to find the key.

When Frau Goetz came in to collect the breakfast tray she looked at him archly for a moment. 'You had a girl in last night,' she said. 'I heard you coming home. At last you're learning how to live in Berlin, Herr Martin.'

Part Two

6

He stayed in all day, smoking cigarette after cigarette until the ash-trays were choked with stubs, thinking that never in his whole life had he hated a place more than this room with its hideous mahogany wardrobe, its plump old-fashioned chairs with their fraying upholstery, the ugly china vases, statuettes, and paper flowers which, in the short time he'd lived with them had become as drearily familiar as the very furniture of his mind. The suicide room, indeed! Not only because a man had once walked through its window but because of those who had borrowed it for a few nights or a few weeks, killing time, impregnating it with the smell of dead yesterdays and human decay that lingers impalpably in rented rooms.

Frau Goetz, persistently kind, brought sandwiches and coffee. 'Herr Martin, I'm old enough to be your mother,' she scolded him. 'It's not right – sitting in all day hiding away like a sick dog.' Fussily she twitched the folds of the dusty velvet curtains, trying to pull them apart to let in the declining rays of the afternoon sun. 'What is it? Are you depressed about that girl you had in last night?' She came and stood by his chair. Even seated, he was almost as tall as she was.

He smiled unconvincingly. 'I'm not depressed,' he said. 'I like to be alone.'

'You're never alone, young man. Just get that into your head. You can be lonely, but never alone.'

The thought didn't cheer him at all. 'Do you worry so much about all your guests?' he asked, resigned and weary but a little touched by her concern.

'*Ach!* what a stupid question,' she replied in her brisk, bantering, oddly flirtatious voice. 'Women of my age have a soft spot for young fellows. That's one bit of nonsense we never get over.' Patting her brittle yellow hair a trifle complacently, she confessed: 'I was a wicked girl in my time. Mad about good-looking men. But don't think I regret a bit of it. Repentance, maybe, but no regrets. God made us that way along with the birds and the beasts, and if that's the way God made it, it must be holy. So don't you be afraid that anything you tell me would be different from what I've seen with my own eyes.'

Her chatter wasn't all that inconsequential, even if it squared oddly with her supposed conversion to the teachings of Jehovah's Witnesses. Martin was almost tempted to talk to her, just talk on and on about everything – about himself, Germany, his father; even about Lise and the way his mother had died. She would contribute nothing but her bright intense compassion, but it would be good and healing. And afterwards he would go out and wait for Karin, cross the street to her and say: 'It shouldn't have happened. I'm sorry.'

But the impulse to confess was immediately followed by another, darker impulse – to parade his self-disgust and frighten the little woman out of her garrulous kindliness. He would tell her about the tart in the Augsbergerstrasse, how he'd felt a horrible impulse to strangle her, and how he'd picked up this other girl,

Karin, this psychopath with her fear of rape. He would describe the way she shrank from his touch, the raging lust with which he assaulted her rigid body, how she lay quivering when it was all over, and that they'd said nothing to each other, not a word of tenderness, lying apart until sleep blotted them out.

The memory of it made him feel degraded. It was something he mustn't even think about.

'Frau Goetz,' he said emphatically, 'I'm not going to tell you a thing, not a single thing, except that these sandwiches are delicious.'

She fluttered her hands in a gesture half indifferent, half disappointed. 'You don't have to tell me. As if I don't know everything that goes on in this house without being told. You've gone and fallen in love with some girl and she's married.'

Martin guessed that she was upset because he'd denied her his confidences. 'Yes,' he said, 'maybe that's it.'

'I won't have any trouble with husbands here,' she warned him sternly, and marched out of the room with her silly head rigidly erect.

At five he drew the curtains and shut out the daylight. Outside a light drizzle was beginning to fall and a dull congestion of rain clouds drifted low over the roofs. He hoped Karin wouldn't wait too long and get wet. At least she'd anticipated that he might not want to see her again, he argued, and there was no reason why he should. Already it was hard to remember what she looked like – only the black hair spread out on the white pillow and the dark holes of her eyes in her pale expressionless face staring at him in the room's darkness. Looking down at that face, so frightening in its impassivity, it had seemed in the terrible moment of climax that if he could rip it off like a mask there would be nothing behind it, only a void; and the warm belly, the full, firm, swelling breasts, the strong womanly thighs that embraced his body ceased to be human and became the great torso of a goddess, as featureless as eternity.

Except for the note left on the desk, a hair clinging to the pillow, the whole thing might have been a diseased fantasy, a shadow play fitfully cast by the flickering lantern of his imagination. Now, another dead yesterday.

In the morning there was a letter from Gustav Ulrich. The embossed paper crackled with self-importance when he unfolded it. It was so pompous, it invited framing like a diploma. The matter was disguised with stilted phraseology, and even in his letter Ulrich seemed to achieve verbal equivalents to the formal handshake and the stiff respectful head-bobbing, advertising its author's correctness to the last comma. It came as an anti-climax, therefore, to discover that it was merely a request for a meeting to discuss certain unspecified details in connection with his restitution claim. Herr Ulrich would be happy to place himself at his complete disposal should he be kind enough to telephone and arrange an early appointment.

He rang immediately. 'It is good of you to be so prompt,' the lawyer said, smooth and placating. 'Can you spare me a little time on Monday? Say, eleven in the morning?'

'What is it about?' Martin temporised.

'A number of details are involved.' There was a moment of hesitation. 'Some of them may be distressing to you, but, please believe me, it is necessary that we clarify them.'

'Yes, of course. But I'd like to have some idea.'

'Naturally, Mr Stone. First of all – a mere formality – I need to produce a document from your father awarding you power of attorney. You have that, of course?'

The precise, competent voice contained a note of scepticism, Martin thought. Damn him! What right did he have? Anybody might think he was out to swindle his own father! To be quite realistic, on this matter the old man wasn't competent to act; his obsession about German blood money constituted a degree of insanity. If it had to be done, he'd write the power of attorney himself.

'Is that strictly necessary?' he asked coldly.

'I am afraid it is. Unless there are special circumstances.'

'I'll see that you get it.'

'There is another thing,' Ulrich went on. 'Silberstein's was a family bank. Your father owned forty per cent of the stock, your mother twelve, twenty-five per cent was held in trust equally divided between your sister and yourself, and the remaining shares belonged to Heinrich Silberstein. Your uncle, I believe.'

'Yes,' Martin said, 'my uncle.'

The lawyer's voice dropped to an undertone. 'With the exception of yourself and your father, they are all——' he hesitated—'dead?'

'They are dead.' He had not intended to say it so harshly, but the words came out hard and cold like solid pellets of lead.

There was a longish silence at the other end, as if Ulrich were committing this information slowly and painfully to paper. 'It's a question of heirs,' he said eventually.

'There are no heirs.'

'I really am sorry, but I must have the dates and the circumstances.'

'The circumstances I can supply. Dates are another matter.' He knew that irony was unnecessary, that the point didn't need making, but he made it, nevertheless. 'It never occurred to me to keep a diary,' he said. 'I'll have the information ready for you on Monday. Eleven, you said?'

'Yes, eleven. I won't keep you long,' Ulrich said huskily. He sounded as if his throat were parched and constricted. It was probably unjust that this one German should have to bear the main brunt of his hostility. But at least he would be paid for doing so.

'Once we have these details clarified, Mr Stone, there will be no need for you to remain in Berlin if you don't want to. It will be many months before our case can be completed, and should the need arise we can settle things by correspondence.'

Martin re-entered his room thoughtfully and sprawled out on the divan. So his business here was ending. He could go home, to England. Strangely, the idea evoked no emotional resonance: only the inevitable jolt one felt when something stopped. Now that the question of his departure had arisen so concretely, he was more vividly aware of his surroundings than he had ever been. His next-door neighbour's warm baritone rumbled faintly beyond the wall. Since the morning of his arrival he'd exchanged only an occasional word with Richter, but the actor's vocal exercises were almost as constant a feature of the apartment as the piano-playing, the radio, the clatter of crockery, and the shrill ringing of the phone which at intervals punctuated the disorderly orchestra of noise. 'I'll miss it,' Martin realised with surprise. The throaty gargle of water flushing down the waste-pipe indicated that Goldberg was at his daily ablutions. The thought was faintly amusing. He'd miss that, too.

As though he were engaged in a deliberate discipline he repeated the words 'home' and 'England', thinking of the plane arriving at London Airport, the coach journey into the grey, solid, congested city that was calmer and more unhurried than any city he knew. Then the taxi to Swiss Cottage, back among the elderly *émigrés* clinging to the same café tables like old stray dogs who return again and again to some dusty corner, needing the small warmth of a familiar place. The disinherited; they had nothing, not even dignity. The final irony was that they had become ridiculous.

Yes, Martin reflected, staring sardonically at the lofty ceiling yellow with the grime of decades. There's no place like home. A spider, fat with nourishment, disappeared into a nest of cobwebs in the corner. No place.

There's a little no place that's just like home, he hummed, thinking of the second-floor flat with its view of a derelict church and the backside of Swiss Cottage Odeon, and the grimy milk bottles on the doorstep, and the row of bell buttons labelled with good German names – Mrs Schmidt, Mr Klausner, Dr Ollendorf, Dr Schaeffer, Miss Königsberg. Through the dark hall smelling of dry rot, wet mackintoshes, and stale Continental cooking, and up the worn linoleum of the stairs, with a smile for Mrs Klausner, on her way with shopping-bag to buy the day's meagre provisions and sit for an hour in the Cosmo to rest her swollen old legs and stare through the steam of coffee at the incomprehensible, forever foreign, procession of Finchley Road.

Then something went wrong. He could visualise clearly enough his own chocolate-painted front door. But when he opened it he was back in Berlin, in the rented room with Frau Goetz, the mahogany wardrobe, the paper flowers, and the dishevelled divan. The professor was playing Mozart's Piano Concerto. After a while the telephone began ringing again.

He thought: 'I ought to see her before I go. When something like that happens between two people you can't just walk away from it without a single word. God knows, one is still human!'

It was raining outside, an insistent drumming on the window-pane. He put on a plastic raincoat and went bareheaded into the street. The smooth roadway of the Kurfürstendamm glistened black and wet like the back of a whale, and the traffic sped by with a hiss of tyres, spurting drops of water on the legs of passers-by. The air of damp dejection chimed in with his mood, a vacant sense of anti-climax now that a term had been put to his stay in Berlin. But it wasn't that alone. He was actually experiencing regret! At what? At leaving Germany? It didn't make sense: he loathed the place. It was only tolerable the way a deep, persistent ache becomes tolerable. God, no! The only regret he could possibly feel about Germany was that it existed at all, that history had not arranged for Bismarck and Frederick the Great to die of croup in their beastly little cradles in the hope that the four hundred little Germanic states might have survived to prevent the rise of any Hitler.

If he regretted anything at all it was because of Karin. His heart was weighted with an imponderable guilt. One was always responsible for people. You put your hand out in an involuntary gesture of tenderness, and you were lost. Indifference became impossible. He ought to have known better. When you lay with a woman you didn't only penetrate her body, you entered the complex, intimate world of her whole life, and you rose from the bed with the terrible responsibility of knowing too much about a person. It should never have happened between him and a German girl, but it had. Now she was burdened with his dead and he with her guilt. Even if they never saw each other again.

What was it somebody had said the other day? Everybody you meet changes you a little? You're damn right, he thought.

At five o'clock he was outside Schmidt's in Fasanenstrasse. The factory seemed empty. He peered through a scratch in the green-painted window of the ground floor. Rows of idle machines were covered with dust-sheets. The far wall was lined with naked tailor's dummies. Of course, it was Saturday and the factory closed early. A policeman paraded slowly down the street towards him with a sharp expression of vigilance. Martin walked away, reluctant to admit his disappointment.

Well, he thought, I tried.

The long ordeal of an empty evening lay before him. He made his way like other lonely men to the little bars of the Augsbergerstrasse where at least there were garishness, noise, and harlotry to alleviate the crippling boredom. In one of the scruffy bars he recognised Heinz Dieter sitting at a corner table with the American, Kane. The young German was speaking quietly but vehemently, and Kane's head was inclined towards him as if he had some difficulty in hearing properly.

Martin left before they saw him. He was not in the mood for that sort of companionship.

When he got back to the apartment Frau Goetz was waiting for him.

'Are you alone?' she whispered hoarsely, trying to peer through the half-opened door into his room.

He threw open the door dramatically. 'Look under the bed, if you like.'

'Don't make fun of me,' she pouted. 'There was a telephone call for you. A girl.'

'Did she leave a message?'

'No.'

'Not even her name?'

'Nothing.'

'For heaven's sake!' he protested peevishly. 'She must have said something!'

'It's no good getting cross with me. I told her you weren't in and she hung up.'

It could have been no one but Karin. A damned shame she had telephoned when he was out, he thought, biting his lips in vexation.

Frau Goetz looked at him with greedy sympathy. 'Never mind,' she consoled him, 'the girl will call again. They always do.'

'Thank you. It's not important anyway.'

Martin closed the door on her and undressed slowly. *This is crazy*, he decided. *I just have to see her again. I can't wait until Monday.* He would go to East Berlin tomorrow and call at her home.

All night long Karin was in his dreams, punishing him for the arrogance of his rejection.

At Wittenbergplatz he got on to an East Sector train. With their shapeless bundles and air of weary resignation, the passengers looked like refugees whose lives were one long, meaningless journey between one point of departure and another. A middle-aged woman sat opposite him, her knees splayed, gazing ahead like a somnambulist with a profound, immovable melancholy. The cardboard box on her lap had begun to disintegrate, and as the train jolted over a junction in the line it slipped. A plastic doll fell on the floor. A momentary look of fright passed over the woman's face. She picked up the doll stealthily, rubbed its vacuous face with her sleeve, then cradled it protectively under her coat as if it were a living child. Martin looked away to spare her embarrassment. She was probably breaking some insane law by bringing it across the Sector boundary.

He alighted at Frankfurter Allee, not certain whether it was the right station. Yes, there were the heaps of rubble, the debris of rusted metal, and the excavated building lots with the outline of new tenements sketched in scaffolding along the skyline. The rain fell relentlessly on the sparsely populated streets. There was scarcely any traffic about – an occasional bus with a few passengers staring through the windows, a cyclist with rain dripping from the hem of his oilskin cape, a solitary car racing its own reflection along the glistening, empty road. Loudspeakers were relaying a brisk military march to the few pedestrians trudging by with the collars of their coats turned up against the weather.

Martin began to pick his way through the puddles that had formed in the broken pavements. At first the route seemed unfamiliar, but soon he began to recognise a landmark here and there until he found himself in the square, even meaner in daylight than he remembered it, with its deserted public benches and its patch of sparse grass churned into muck by the steady, monotonous downpour. His heart began to beat faster as he walked down a side street and turned into the tenement where Karin lived.

The interior was almost as dark by day as by night. A radio was playing loudly above the voices of quarrelling children. Someone was coughing, a harsh, dry, spasmodic sound like the bark of a dog. He ascended the stairs quickly, the breath tight in his chest. She lived on the fourth or fifth floor; arbitrarily, he chose the fifth.

A man opened the door in a sleeveless vest that showed the bony ridges of his ribs. 'Fräulein Paulus?' he said. 'One moment, I'll ask my wife.' She came and stood behind him, a big woman whose arms were covered with flour. Two children clutched at her skirts, staring at the stranger with large, fascinated eyes. 'There's nobody of that name here,' the woman declared firmly.

He had no more success on the floor below, nor on the sixth and the seventh. 'Karin,' he said desperately, 'a dark girl, seamstress, lives with her married brother?' But no one knew her. Like an anxious salesman turned away from too many doors, he returned despondently to the street and began to retrace his steps. There was another tenement near-by but it was clearly the wrong place – the passage was too wide, the stairs faced a different direction, and his strained senses detected a totally different atmosphere. He tried the next street. A small boy in knickerbockers stood in the doorway of a building bouncing a rubber ball against the brick portico to a play rhyme.

> 'Flieg, mein Ball, nur hin und her,
> Ei, das freut mich gar so sehr,
> Eins und zwei und drei und vier,
> Ball, komm wieder her zu mir.'

The words penetrated deeply into the layers of memory. It was perhaps the first rhyme he'd learned, and invoked with a brief, incredible violence the flavour of his fragmentary childhood. Strange that one's earliest memories always hurt the most, that the first years remain imperishable, as if the child is the last thing to die in a man. And with the abrupt re-emergence of that lost world, Martin made a moving discovery. Karin was linked with it. It was no accident that she had attracted him so strongly at their first meeting. Those dispassionate but gentle dark eyes, the sensual unhappy mouth which shaped itself in speech as though words were strawberry-soft on the tongue, the slight roughness of the black hair as it brushed against his cheek – they reminded him of the Silesian girl who had nursed him until he was four and whom he had loved with such intense possessiveness that he'd cried for weeks after she left to get married. Her name, he suddenly recalled, was Erika. Erika, Karin, he thought, inexplicably moved to sadness.

Aware of the presence of a stranger, the small boy bounced the ball silently and with less assurance and it rolled away from him. Martin retrieved it and handed it back. They exchanged polite greetings rather solemnly.

'Do you live here?' Martin asked.

'Yes,' the boy said. 'My name's Fritzi. I'm six.'

'Does Fräulein Karin Paulus live in this house?'

'Is she a little girl?'

'No, she not a little girl,' Martin said. 'She's grown up.'

The boy began to play with his ball again. 'I only know the little girls,' he said, 'and some of the grown-ups. My mother's friend is named Karin, I think.' He pointed down the street. 'She lives over there.'

'Can you show me her house?'

The child nodded and, with an appealing friendliness, took Martin's hand and led him to a near-by block of apartments. They went up several flights of stairs. On one of the landings three youths were sitting on a window-sill playing cards and ostentatiously puffing cigarettes.

'Hello, Fritzi!' they called amiably.

The small boy stopped and pointed to one of the youths, a lad of about sixteen. 'It's his mummy,' he said. 'The man wants your mummy.'

For some reason the other youths sniggered. The first youth coloured with embarrassment. He looked up at the stranger with hurt, mistrustful eyes.

'There's some mistake,' Martin explained. Still holding the boy's hand, he left the building and stood indecisively on the pavement staring helplessly at his surroundings. The damp seemed to penetrate into his bones, emphasising the improbability of his quest. 'Fritzi, here's a groschen for being a good boy,' he said, handing the child a coin and walking away.

'*Flieg, mein Ball, nur hin und her*,' Fritzi was singing as he turned the corner. The words stayed with him a long time. *Komm wieder her zu mir* ...

At precisely five o'clock the factory machinery stopped with a slow expiring sigh. A few men came out brushing fluff and cotton threads from their clothing, followed by a crowd of women who spoke little and blinked their eyes in the daylight, looking as if they were still dazed by the noise of the machines. Karin was among them. She wore an old green coat and clumsy flat shoes and carried a scuffed fibre case of the kind working-men use to carry sandwiches. She moved awkwardly, like an adolescent who has difficulty in adjusting to an unfamiliar womanliness, and even in the midst of her companions she seemed solitary and preoccupied.

The sight of her affected Martin powerfully, like fear. 'You didn't expect me?' he asked, trying to smile.

Karin turned, startled. She was pale and strained and dark circles ringed her eyes. It was the face of a fugitive, haunted and unhappy, and, for a moment, the face of a stranger. It seemed impossible that he'd once held her close, her breath in his mouth, that he'd tasted her strangeness and remembered it.

'You're angry with me,' he said.

'No, no!' She bit her lip in vexation and stared miserably at her clothes. 'I'm so *shabby*. If I'd known——'

'You look fine. *Wunderbar!*' he lied.

Carefully averting her eyes she asked: 'Why didn't you come on Friday?' Her voice trembled and he realised how much she'd been hurt. But it wasn't a question that could be answered as simply as that. He could say he intended to meet her, right up to the last minute; he could lie – an accident, a telephone call, an unexpected or comic complication. Most difficult of all, a straightforward apology. *I'm sorry.* The words lay on his chest like a stone.

A man came out of the factory pushing a bicycle, and locked the door. 'Good night, Fräulein,' he said, glancing at them curiously.

'Good night,' Karin replied without lifting her eyes from the ground. In the same lonely voice with which she had spoken before she said: 'You haven't answered me. Does it embarrass you?'

Martin felt a spurt of irritation at her persistence. With an unreasoning resentment he blamed her for the long, bitter week-end, for not having been there when he'd looked for her, for the fact that he was now humbly grateful to be with her again.

'Do you want me to go down on my knees, right here on the pavement?' he demanded, with more pain than mockery.

She began to cry, but the muscles of her face remained rigid. 'Don't humiliate me any more,' she whispered in a shaky voice, beginning to walk away. After a few yards she broke into an awkward run.

'What have I let myself in for?' Martin thought, dismayed at the depth of her misery. A paralysis of indecision overcame him. He would never see her again and a certain mutilation would remain, so that at moments this vague panic would return and he would remember this street, the smell of petrol, wet asphalt, and garlic sausages from a nearby grocer's, the cold touch of misery prickling his skin, and Karin diminishing, a random and indistinguishable figure submerged in the crowd. Suddenly he began to run, re-enacting a persistent nightmare.

When he caught up with her she was walking very slowly, crossing the Ludwigsplatz towards a small park in the centre of the square.

'Please go away,' she said.

'Karin, believe me, I didn't mean to humiliate you.'

'I'd rather not talk about it.'

'I want to explain. If I didn't come, it wasn't because I didn't respect you.'

'You don't mean that.' She looked at him mistrustfully and glanced quickly away.

'Of course I mean it.'

'How can I possibly know? I feel so ashamed.' Her voice trembled, and it seemed as if she might cry again. Instead, the tears came into his own eyes. 'You must believe me,' he insisted vehemently.

They stood beside a fountain in the park, moved by an inarticulate shyness. The wind blew a fine spray of water against their faces but they were reluctant to move, afraid that if they did so the fragile, precarious moment would be destroyed and they would be separate again. Suddenly there seemed more air to breathe. The harshness of the city was neutralised by the un-historical smell of grass and flowers and the shrill chirping of birds. The sky was rinsed with a watery sunset, children scampered under the trees, women were knitting with coloured wools, and old men sat on the benches in a stupor of contemplation like old men anywhere in the world. They smiled with unexpected relief, as if all the tensions in their blood had been washed away by a surge of spring-time.

'I'm hungry, are you?' Martin said. 'Wait here, I'll get some food.'

There was a small street market near-by and he wandered among the fruit stands, frankfurter kiosks, and bakery stalls, intoxicated by the sweet smell of new bread, the scent of apples and oranges and over-ripe melons, and the savory garlic smell of steaming sausages. Just then happiness seemed childishly accessible, a matter of amiable raillery with street traders, an armful of food in paper bags, and a girl waiting under the lime trees in the park.

When he returned Karin had taken off her shabby winter coat and looked gay and relaxed in a red jumper that revealed her smooth honey-coloured arms and the warm curve of her throat. She shook out her hair so that it fell over her shoulders.

'You're not hungry, you're greedy,' she smiled, glancing at the quantity of food he laid out on the bench.

He grinned back. 'You stimulate my appetite,' and soon they were laughing for no reason at all. Karin giggled at the noise he made in eating an orange. 'Like a fat man drinking soup.' He agreed cheerfully. 'But you! Now, you're an elegant eater. You eat with style,' and he mimicked her with the mannerisms of a feeding monkey until, choking with laughter, she had to plead with him to be more serious.

Later they went to a movie and sat close together in the darkness. She stirred uneasily as his hand moved to encircle her waist and then gently pressed her breast. Her breath came more quickly. She sought his mouth and kissed him with desperate passion. Almost giddy with desire, he said haltingly: 'Let's go to my place.'

It was different this time. As soon as they entered the room they embraced and with trembling hands he helped her to undress. When she was naked he switched on the light. Startled and shy, she offered her big shapely body to his conquering gaze, her hands limp by her sides. With lustful incoherence Martin thought that this was how he must have always imagined a German girl would look – the full, melon-firm breasts, the soft ripe belly, wide hips and big, round Amazonian thighs, and yet a submissiveness that invited all the cruelty, the passion, the tenderness of the male embrace. It was a strange body; an alien and forbidden body, tender, corrupt, and beautiful, formed in enmity, instinct with a complex guilt, dizzily perilous. He had never desired a woman with such intensity, and he took her with a storm of passion that swept aside her momentary terror when she lay beneath him in the dark, her teeth clenched and her eyes enormous with fear. And then the rage of it was transmitted to her, too, and she wrestled with his body, biting his flesh in a paroxysm of tenderness.

'I love you!' she moaned, and the confession was tortured and frightening. 'I love you! I love you! Oh!' she shuddered, 'I love you!'

He awoke sometime later. Karin was lying on her side looking at him with brooding concentration. In the thin milky light of the moon that shone through the uncurtained window her face seemed hollow and touched with a peaceful melancholy.

'Are you sorry?' he asked.

She smiled faintly, but her expression remained serious. 'Of course not,' she replied.

'There's something I must ask you,' Martin said.

Karin touched his cheek lightly. 'Yes?'

'Why did you come to me the first time?'

'It doesn't matter now, does it?'

'It matters to me. Why? You were so afraid.'

'I'm not afraid any more. I'll never be afraid of you.'

'Was it pity?' he said in a low voice.

'For a woman, there's always pity. One can't always explain in words.' She spoke gently, as if pacifying a child.

'Please try and tell me,' he insisted. 'You let me love you as if – you know what you told me about the soldiers. Afterwards I felt ashamed. That's why I didn't come to meet you on Friday.'

His words distressed her. She turned her head away and spoke into the darkness. 'You mustn't remember it like that,' she pleaded vehemently. 'How can I explain it? I had to come to you. I felt that I wanted to be able to love you. And then it was so ugly and sterile, as if I wasn't a woman but a creature without sex.'

Karin's voice faltered. The bars of the window threw shadows on the wall, imprisoning them in a world of threatening silence. Martin fumbled for his cigarettes and lit one, briefly exposing the ugly, reassuring furniture of the room. Now he was afraid of the confessional dark and the grotesque phantoms that had emerged from it at his insistence. Staring at the point of fire made by the burning cigarette, he said: 'I'm sorry, Karin. It's all over now. Let's forget it.'

'But that's not all,' she said. 'I must tell you.'

'No, don't. I shouldn't have asked you. It wasn't necessary.'

She stopped his protest with a kiss. 'Don't you understand, Martin? It's a story with a happy ending,' she said fondly. 'I want to tell you. Something wonderful happened afterwards. I was sitting at my machine in the workshop, absent-mindedly listening to the radio and the girls chattering over their work. Suddenly I thought of your name. I said it over and over to myself as though for the first time it really meant something to me. "Martin," I said. "Martin." It brought your face to me so vividly that I felt I could almost touch you. And then I knew I wanted you. My body had suddenly come alive. It was such an overwhelming feeling that I left the machine to try and calm myself. Then I thought that I'd be seeing you again that evening and you would know how differently I felt. The day seemed to go on for ever, I was so impatient. But you weren't there. I waited an hour, thinking you might have mistaken the time. It was the longest day and the longest night of my life. On Saturday evening I couldn't stand it any longer, so I telephoned – I was ready to beg you to see me. You weren't in. Yes,' she went on in a low voice, 'that was a bad moment. I thought you must be out somewhere looking for a girl who would enjoy making love. I could have killed myself with jealousy then.'

He stubbed out his cigarette blindly. All the tenderness he had been restraining surged through him. Now he was ready to make his own surrender.

'I love you,' he said quietly. Her mouth was against his mouth. Her breasts, her warm belly, her heavy languorous thighs set him on fire. 'I love you,' he repeated, this time urgently, with a demanding passion.

7

Goldberg stopped outside Krantz's and inspected the window with critical disdain. Ladies' clothes and jewellery, he thought disparagingly. What a way for an intelligent man to make a living! A small ticket attached to an emerald trinket caught his eye. He twisted his neck and peered near-sightedly at the price. Enough to support a family for a whole month, he reflected with judicial severity, shaking his head from side to side in public token of disapproval. Krantz was not a man of principle. Maybe he made big profits, but what sort of person could he be to do business with such people? With the blood on their hands, all they could think of was buying themselves luxuries and beautifying their women.

Entering the shop, his moral indignation was extended to the soft carpet, the subtle perfumed air, and the elegant perspectives reflected by many mirrors. Two rich and handsome women were discussing a purchase with an attentive assistant. Goldberg glanced away from their slender, nylon-sheathed legs with guilty despair, his mind scalded with erotic images. Even the wire dummies in the window tormented him with their suggestion of femininity, reminding him how long and irksome had been his celibacy. Since the concentration camps and the death of his wife and children he had almost forgotten what it was like to lie with a woman. He was not a man to go off with someone in the street. But what was one to do? One was still a human being.

Approaching the manageress, he asked quite humbly if it was possible to see Herr Krantz. A cool, assertive person accustomed to fending off importunate travelling salesmen, she automatically looked for the big case of samples or the brief-case stuffed with advertising leaflets. Their absence only increased her suspicion of a man who seemed to have no credentials but poverty, and looking from Goldberg's worn but well-polished shoes to his glistening earnest face, she asked with icy scepticism: 'You have an appointment, of course?'

'Not exactly,' Goldberg began. He was about to explain that he had come on a matter of the highest importance, it was imperative that he see her employer, but suddenly decided that there was no reason why he should explain himself to this woman, this mere employee of his acquaintance, Herr Krantz. She thought she could treat him like dirt. Who paid her wages, after all, that she should behave like the mistress of a Nazi general? 'My name is Goldberg. Please announce me!' he ordered angrily.

'Certainly,' she said, calm and unruffled. 'Can I state what your business is?'

'Private, if you don't mind,' Goldberg barked, and turned his back on her.

She returned some moments later and led him through an office at the back of the shop to the elevator. As he ascended to the top of the building, he felt an agreeable glow of triumph. That was the way to treat such people. No nonsense. Unfortunately, no one understood the Germans the way he understood them.

He was fighting against the world, and the thought gave him a melancholy satisfaction.

In his penthouse office, Hugo awaited his visitor with little enthusiasm. On several occasions he'd been useful to Goldberg, mainly in the provision of small loans, and the man didn't trouble him often. But a visit from Goldberg was inevitably a depressing experience. One recognised one's own sickness in him, like a voluntary patient in a mental hospital whose room is entered by an incurable lunatic. 'Come in,' he said testily as the buzzer rang.

Goldberg hurried into the room like a man with pressing business. 'I've got some news that will shock you, Herr Krantz,' he said in a solemn voice. He sat down and glanced round the apartment with ill-disguised contempt. 'I see you've had the place decorated since I was here last. With you it's always the latest style.'

Hugo shrugged deprecatingly. 'What else should I do with my profits?' He watched Goldberg with wry, paternal pity. 'What have you discovered that's so shocking?' he asked mockingly, convinced that it must be some trivial matter, an ex-Nazi working in the post office or an anti-Semitic conversation overheard in a café. He was, in fact, taken aback when Goldberg began to rant about the scandalous behaviour of Martin Stone. Goldberg had seen a woman come out of his room early one morning. A whore, he was sure of it. Now she was sleeping there every night. The place might just as well be a brothel, what with that actor bringing in his fancy boys and Stone, a Jewish man, keeping a street-walker in his room.

'That's enough, Goldberg!' Hugo commanded sharply. 'In the first place, what Martin Stone does is not your business. In the second place, you have no right to call the girl a whore. In the third place, if you don't like it you can go and live somewhere else.'

'All right, maybe she's not a whore,' Goldberg argued, 'but she's a German.' He implied that the distinction was too fine to quarrel over. 'It's disgusting!' he insisted, spraying Hugo across the desk with tiny gobbets of spittle. 'After all, Herr Krantz, we're only a few Jews in Berlin. We have a standard to keep up.' He stretched his hand stealthily towards the cigar-box, as if not responsible for the movement of his arm.

'Have a cigar,' Hugo invited maliciously, wiping the spittle off his face with a snow-white handkerchief.

'Well, if you insist.' Goldberg showed a row of ill-fitting dentures in a humourless parody of a smile. 'You understand, Herr Krantz, I'm not a scandalmonger,' he said, leaning back in his chair and puffing reflectively. 'What somebody does is, as you say, not really my business. But, after all, you recommended your friend to the house and it's not nice for you. It reflects on your own reputation.'

'My reputation will survive,' Hugo said dryly.

'But, of course! Everybody knows you're not the man to go with loose women.' The faint innuendo did not go undetected.

'Goldberg, we're all flesh and blood. Don't you ever have a little temptation? Say, when a nice curvaceous little blonde smiles at you?'

'With a German woman? Faugh! I would rather go to a doctor and have an operation.' He levelled his forefinger at Hugo's face and declared sternly: 'Don't forget, Herr Krantz, these people are murderers. You can't trust even the best of them.'

'*Ach! Schweig!*' Hugo snapped. Why on earth did he tolerate Goldberg? Hadn't he done enough for him, helping him to get a pension, lending him money, even putting up with his querulous interference? Goldberg was, for him, a deformed symbol of all the ghettos of the world; of the sour-smelling, rubbish-littered streets; of the big-breasted mamas with chicken feathers and dried blood on their aprons, their bellies big with babies and their great spongy hearts dripping mother love; of the smell of garlic and pickled cucumber and slightly rotting meat and black bread; of kosher signs on shop windows and small back-street synagogues reeking of bad drains and perspiration and crowded with bearded men whose eagled profiles spoke of pride and intolerance.

Goldberg was the thin sour fruit of the ghetto. It wasn't just the concentration camp that had made him. For years his soul had rotted in the sunless streets of some Polish ghetto, staring at the thin, hard-muscled peasants and arrogant gentry, hunger raging in his guts, his shambling flesh falling away from his big, ugly, suffering Jewish bones. Without that conditioning, without the years of existing on rotten potatoes and cruelty, he could never have survived the camps. But because of that survival they shared something, they belonged together. He loathed Goldberg. Goldberg brought out the anti-Semite in him. But he knew that Goldberg deserved his survival. He had accepted his ordeals and endured them with a queer perverse pride that contained some human dignity.

'Listen,' Hugo lectured him wearily, 'you're not being paid to improve the moral climate in Berlin. People will go on being wicked if they feel like it, whatever you do. Why don't you go back to Israel? You've got your pension now, there's no reason why you should stay here.'

There was, of course. Something to keep Goldberg alive, a passion that united him with people. Hate. Between him and the Germans there would always be this obsessive intimacy.

'I'll go,' Goldberg assured him. 'As soon as I can make arrangements I'll go. I've got to find enough money for the fare. And in Israel, because of the immigration, living is not cheap.' He sensed his advantage. A Jew had heart, even a man like Krantz. You could make him feel ashamed. 'Perhaps you can lend me a few marks?' he suggested, complaining that the Germans were bloodsuckers. They took away from you everything you ever had; they destroyed your health and strength; then they gave you a pension you could hardly keep your soul in your body with.

'Yes, yes,' Hugo interrupted testily. He handed over some money with the feeling that he was buying some peace for his conscience, bribing Goldberg not to reproach him with his presence. And Goldberg was grateful; it was very kind of Herr Krantz. But a man of principle is not deflected from his moral duty by material benefactions. 'Please, don't forget to have a little talk with your friend Herr Stone,' he insisted. 'We can't have a Jewish young man making a big scandal.'

The tone was authoritative, rabbinical. It was a Jewish tradition that a sage took precedence over a man who was merely rich, even a Rothschild.

The moment he went, Hugo poured himself a drink, but Goldberg's gossip had left a bad taste that lingered even after the second and third brandies. Martin's philanderings had nothing to do with him. He was behaving pretty normally, by all accounts.

He felt vaguely disgusted, as if he'd found a layer of dandruff on the shoulders of his coat. It was none of his business whom the fellow slept with. Goldberg was a busy member of the Jews' trade union, but he, Hugo, was one of the disaffiliated, long ago convicted of non-union practices. And yet he was unable to suppress an irrational uneasiness, thinking of old Silberstein and the grief he would feel if his son became involved with a German girl. In a sense, it was his duty to act as a father surrogate, or at least as an uncle. If the affair were merely a casual one it wouldn't matter that much, but it was inconsistent with the little he knew of Martin that the latter should be unserious about love. The intensity, the lack of humour, and, most dangerous of all, the abnormal feelings about Germany. Coming to Berlin exposed one's nerves. One was sensitive to all stimuli, to the extremes of love, hate, guilt, and remorse. It was a condition in which one's whole existence could be imperilled by a single impulsive act. Like marriage, he reflected ironically – the short honeymoon and the long repentance. It was a man's duty to save a friend from that idiotic folly.

An idea occurred to him. He would invite Martin over for dinner and a quiet chat. A discreet reconnaissance. Heinz Dieter could take a note around right away.

'Heinzi!' he bellowed in the direction of the kitchen. His voice was absorbed in the cushioned silence and he called again impatiently. The kitchen was empty, so was Heinz Dieter's room, so was the apartment upstairs. He buzzed the manageress downstairs in the shop and said sharply:

'Have you seen my secretary?'

'I saw him go off in the car, Herr Krantz,' she said smoothly. 'About half an hour ago. He must have gone to the post office because he collected some letters here.'

He thanked her curtly. She was covering up, of course. The solidarity of the employed against the employer: and the silly bitch had a soft spot for the boy, like so many other sentimental women.

Heinz Dieter had probably slipped off for a rendezvous with his latest girl friend, and the manageress was aiding and abetting him under the illusion that she was assisting in a great romance.

Obeying a sudden impulse, he went back to the young German's room. A book lay open on the divan, its lurid cover showing a half-naked girl menaced by a giant beetle, and in the background the red planet Mars swinging in blue-black space. The boy was reading something for a change, he noted ironically.

His irritation evaporated, replaced by the quick, facile pity he always felt for Heinz Dieter's naïvetés. He picked up the book to replace it on the bookshelf and looked around for something to mark the page. There was a twist of paper in the waste-paper-basket, and as he smoothed it out a scrawl of writing attracted his attention. It was a carelessly torn fragment of a note. '…Usual place tonight 22.00. I will expect you,' it read. The signature, if it had existed, was missing.

Carefully inserting the paper between the pages, Hugo put the book on the shelf with only a flicker of curiosity. The love life of Heinz Dieter, he reflected with a bored yawn, reminded him that he was supposed to be preoccupied with somebody else's love life at that moment. Returning to his desk, he dialled Frau Goetz's number.

'Hello, darling,' he said lightly, leading the conversation through the routine pleasantries until it seemed a discreet moment to invite her gossip. But Frau Goetz was only too eager to talk, and squeaked her story with kittenish relish. 'It's not an affair,' she shrilled, 'it's a grand passion. Believe me, I have a nose for these things.'

'You're a disgraceful bitch,' he growled. 'You spend too much time squinting through keyholes. What's the girl like?'

Frau Goetz giggled unbecomingly. 'You know the type, Hugo. Behaves as if she's spent the night on her knees in church. Comes out in the morning all solemn and purified.'

'You're the most cynical woman I know,' Hugo said sourly. 'You'd better go back to your kitchen and read the Bible.'

He replaced the receiver and shrugged at the empty room. I've got troubles of my own, he thought. Damn Goldberg!

He had no relish for the task. If he stood for anything at all, it was for more fun and games, and to hell with puritanism. Sweet copulation was the last human freedom, the precise antithesis of the little eggs of death that lay in subterranean iron nests ready for hatching. And here he was, at eight o'clock of an evening made for drinking and pleasure, on his way to warn a young man that he'd be better advised to sleep with strumpets than to fall in love with a good German woman and risk planting his seed in her German womb. It was his way of discharging an old debt, one loan the one-time banker, Silberstein, had made that at this late hour was producing interest. But was it bad or good, this advice he was so reluctantly prepared to offer? How could one know? Perhaps Germany needed another Jewish blood transfusion; perhaps the only way to resolve the bitterness was to mingle the blood of the murderer and his victim. The uselessness of these speculations wearied him. What it really came down to was that he had to go to Martin like a sentimental uncle and say: 'Whatever you do, don't break your old father's heart.' And the rôle was totally out of character.

He rang the bell of the apartment three times before Frau Goetz admitted him, shrieking with dismay because she'd just got out of the bath and her hair was still in curlers.

'Hugo, you bad boy, why didn't you phone first?' she reproached him.

Without the disguise of cosmetics she looked a hundred years old. It occurred to him then that she was his oldest friend, perhaps the only one, and that the affection she felt for him was something he valued. It must mean a great deal to her that he was one of the few people who could remember when she was young and pretty.

He stooped and kissed her cheek. 'Run along, little mouse,' he said, as if addressing a child. 'I haven't come to visit you tonight.'

'You never do,' she replied grumpily to hide her pleasure. 'But you're wasting your time if you want Herr Martin. He's not in.'

'It doesn't matter. I'll wait in his room.'

Frau Goetz trotted in behind him, a devoted Pekingese. 'If you're waiting, come into the sitting-room and talk to me. I hardly know a thing about you these days.'

'Of course not,' he said dryly. 'If I want to advertise I'll take space in the newspapers.'

'You dreadful man!' she exploded. 'I won't ever say another word to you,' and, with mock indignation, drew her kimono more tightly around her skinny body and flounced away.

As soon as she left, Hugo prowled about the room, shamelessly prying into cupboards and drawers. It was a faintly depressing experience, reminding him of the time he'd spent in this apartment when he'd first returned to Berlin. His return had seemed then a doomed gesture, an act of desperation. Now the feeling revived, and with it the memory of those last few lacerating weeks in England when he knew that the strain of living like a middle-class English intellectual, the ordeal of pretending to be

Marion's ever-loving husband, had brought him to the verge of complete breakdown. The mask of urbanity with which he had confronted society had begun to disintegrate until the dreadful night he realised that he couldn't carry on; unless he broke away he would fall into a rage of self-destruction.

It had been one of those dinner-parties for which he and Marion were famous. The guests were, as usual, talented – a careful blend of the biggest and smartest reputations. If a novelist scored a *succès d'estime*; if a painter provoked controversy with a new exhibition, or a young politician with a brilliant speech in a House foreign affairs debate; if everyone was talking about a new young actress or playwright or poet, he or she would appear at the table of the next Hugo Krantz dinner-party, cleverly offset by people of more established position, eminent critics, publishers, impresarios, and cultured financiers who rescue such occasions from pleasant frivolity by the aura of power and influence they generate.

On that particular evening one of the guests was a young Caribbean poet. Hugo had been drinking steadily all day, and as the wine and the conversation circulated more and more headily around the table his wit and iconoclasm waxed until even Marion looked pleased at the impression he was creating. And then, for some crazy reason, it entered his head that the Caribbean poet was queer. But he was still muddled on that point. Perhaps he hadn't thought anything of the sort, but was obscurely driven to an act of self-exposure in revolt against the hypocrisy that compelled him to conceal his true nature when everybody present knew of his homosexuality and made sly jokes about it behind his back. Whatever the motives, he made crude advances to the young Negro. Even drunkenness was no excuse for creating such hideous social embarrassment. Marion stared at him, her face the colour of dirty tallow. The poet moved away, distressed, and left after mumbling polite excuses. People went on talking in strained voices. He himself was more shocked and ashamed than anybody, not so much at what he had done, but because he had chosen to do it to a young Negro. It seemed to him then peculiarly significant that he had selected as victim someone whose race was more despised than his own, whose persecution at the hands of white civilisation was even more clearly a perverted form of sexual aggression than the Nazi brutality towards conquered peoples. I'm no better than Putzi, he told himself with revulsion, and walked out of the house, leaving Marion and his guests to extricate themselves as best they could from the mess he'd left behind.

Some hours later he returned sober but numb, as if his blood had congealed in his veins. His clothes were wet and muddy, although he hadn't been conscious of rain and was only vaguely aware that he'd spent the time walking about the streets. Marion was waiting up. She was still dressed for a social occasion, and her enamelled elegance and careful composure seemed unspeakably macabre.

'I can't stand it any longer,' he told her. 'I must go away.'

She looked at him with cold yet impersonal dislike. 'Don't be silly,' she said crisply. 'You behaved disgustingly, but everyone could see you were drunk. I've been thinking it over while you've been gone. We'll take a trip to Majorca for a few weeks. When we get back the whole thing will be forgotten.'

'It doesn't matter. I can't go on like this.'

'If I can stand it, so can you. The only thing I insist on is that you mustn't disgrace me in public. Never again.' How passionately she cared about respectability, he thought at the time, ready to sacrifice herself entirely on its behalf.

She said: 'Now get yourself cleaned up and go to bed.'

In the bathroom he was punished by all the mirrors. For some time he stared at his own ugliness with a feeling that went far beyond self-hatred. He judged and condemned himself.

'Hugo! What are you doing?' Marion screamed.

Blood was spurting from his left wrist. She took the razor from his hand and threw it into the bath. 'My God! All I need is for people to say my husband killed himself. You're so damned selfish!' she said venomously.

The next day he left for Berlin.

Martin came in loaded with packages and looked at him with dismayed astonishment. 'What on earth——' he began.

Hugo smiled with gentle mockery and held up a warning hand. 'Don't say it!' he urged. 'It's bad enough that you've been neglecting me.'

'Sorry, it was such a surprise.' Martin put the packages on the table rather self-consciously and a savoury smell of smoked sausages and cheese filled the room. 'Saving money,' he mumbled apologetically. 'It's much cheaper to eat this way. Anyhow, it's nice to see you.'

He wasn't very good at pretending, Hugo noted. The visit was obviously damned inconvenient, an interruption of a quiet little meal between two lovers. They were, after all, in the middle of a honeymoon of sorts. He examined Martin narrowly, as if he were seeing him for the first time. He, Hugo, stood between the generations of father and son and had never felt really close to either of them despite a long history of friendship with the family.

Old Silberstein was a man who had inherited wealth and been mellowed by it, so that even in bereavement and exile he retained a certain kindliness and charm. Martin had inherited bitterness, poverty, and rootlessness. He had the aggressiveness, the neurotic tension of someone who had always felt himself alien, first in the country of his birth and then in his place of refuge. He was more truly involved in the classic Jewish dilemma than his father could possibly be, because the Nazis didn't stop old Silberstein from being a German, they destroyed the Germany to which he belonged.

'You've changed since you arrived in Berlin,' Hugo said. 'The process generally takes longer.'

Martin pretended to be casual. He took out a packet of cigarettes and pressed one politely on Hugo. Exhaling reflectively, he said: 'How do you mean, changed? Do I look older, fatter, less harassed? I've only been here about two weeks, so it can't be anything drastic.'

'No, not drastic. It's routine, really. You're in what I call the second stage. We know the first – everybody looks like a Nazi, no one can say anything without its being examined for some sinister double meaning, you hate the air around you and the people who breathe it. Something like first-degree schizophrenia. In the second stage you're more relaxed. People have shrunk to normal size and you're prepared to believe that fundamentally the Germans are no different from anyone else. In fact, you wonder if the British or the French would have behaved very differently if Hitler had been a Welshman or a Gaulois. You haven't even, as far as you know, actually met a Nazi and are inclined to believe they were almost all packed off to jail or the gallows at the Nürnberg Trials.'

Martin smiled indulgently. 'This is quite a lecture,' he commented. 'Is there a third stage?'

'Yes, there's a third stage,' Hugo said gravely. 'It goes on for a long time. I'm still in it.' He noticed that his companion was listening with concentrated attention, lying on the divan with his face turned to the wall in the receptive position of a child captivated by a grim fairy-story but anxious to conceal his fear. 'The third stage is, in a sense, the worst. You don't know which side you're on. You're neither neutral nor committed. You've learned that everyone was compromised a little. It's no longer a question of who are the guilty and who the innocent. All are guilty in some degree and none are entirely without innocence. So where are you? Madder than ever, but in a condition of moral paralysis. You begin to hate the dead more than their murderers, because their death imposes on you a problem you can neither solve nor dismiss: it hangs around your neck for the rest of your life.'

Hugo suddenly stopped talking, depressed by his analysis. Sometimes it seemed that for twenty years he had thought and talked of nothing else, so that this painful dialogue in a shabby Berlin pension had the quality of a recurring nightmare in which every word and gesture, every sound, no matter how remote, was utterly predictable. And all the time, behind everything he said, was the thought of Putzi, somewhere in East Berlin, and of Heinz Dieter, who might also betray him because love incurred betrayal. And he, Martin, was thinking of his German girl.

'It would be a bloody good thing if we could all forget about it,' he said wearily. 'Someone ought to invent a drug that would give the world a collective amnesia.' And then it would begin again. Every creature had its prey, and the prey of man was man.

Martin went to a cupboard and produced a bottle and two glasses. 'It's time for some alcoholic amnesia,' he joked feebly, pouring the drinks with an unsteady hand. He walked to the window, lit a cigarette, and stared down at the street below with an intense preoccupation. A car drew up outside the neon-lit doorway of the *Spiel-Casino* and two men went in, the light glistening on their bald heads. A man and woman were talking under a street lamp. There was the tip-tapping of high heels hurrying along the pavement, the feeble wailing of a restless infant somewhere in the warren of apartments below, the inevitable grinding of mechanical music from a tireless radio.

'It's unreasonable,' he muttered helplessly, searching for reassurance in the commonplace street. 'What you're saying is that no one can be acquitted. Eighty million Germans and their unborn children are guilty by association. If someone commits a murder, is the entire neighbourhood responsible?'

Hugo swallowed the cognac in one gulp and poured himself another immediately. 'Of course it's unreasonable.' He rubbed his eyes as if he hadn't slept for a long time. 'We're all lousy with guilt, anyway. But what happened here in Germany has no relation to simple murder. The nearest analogy would be with an epidemic. It was a fever that raged among a whole generation. Perhaps the tragedy of Germany is that it provided an ideal breeding-ground for the disease. This is the epicentre of the epidemic. Cruelty germinates here more virulently than anywhere else in Europe. The Nazis couldn't have happened without the Germans.'

'We'd be happier if we could bring ourselves to bury the past.'

Hugo grimaced impatiently. One thought of the past as a collection of dusty photos in the attic of the mind, a bundle of old letters, a grief that the years had dulled. But the past was never over. It was here in the room with them. It was the enemy on the other side of the city.

He stood up and approached Martin almost menacingly, standing face to face with him and staring into his eyes. 'Don't think you can pull out,' he said softly. 'Whatever you do, be aware of the consequences.'

Martin pushed his hands into his pockets to hide their trembling and stared back at Hugo with dislike of his heavy, sardonic face and the angry sincerity of his bloodshot eyes behind the thick lenses of the horn-rimmed glasses. It didn't help that it was a German face. 'You're being oracular. It doesn't suit you,' he said coldly.

'In plain language, you've got yourself a girl. You're in love. And you have to tell yourself that she, at least, was not compromised. You want to acquit her of being German so that when you sleep together your conscience will lie easy.'

'God! you know how to twist the knife,' Martin said. He looked wretched and ill, defencelessly young. It moved Hugo to a peril-ous tenderness, a hair's breadth from desire. With difficulty he restrained himself from putting his arm around the younger man's shoulders. Instead he poured another drink and squinted through the amber at the light.

'What do you know about this girl, anyway – bedroom confes-sions apart?' he asked brutally.

'There isn't any point in prolonging this conversation.' Martin moved back to the window and gazed with concentration at the sky above the roof-tops. 'You've done your duty.'

'I've shocked you. Coming from someone like me, it's hard to take. But there's a point to that question that has nothing to do with

sex – normal or abnormal. This is a nation that set up vast factories
to gas and burn millions of people. It stocked its war plants with
armies of hungry, maltreated slaves. Cattle-trucks crammed with
frightened men, women, and children passed through its towns
and villages. They collected the gold from the teeth of the dead,
the hair from their heads, and the shoes of murdered children
to put on the feet of their own. They sold cakes of soap marked
"Pure Jewish Fat". It's an old story and even in primitive Indian
villages it's known by heart. But here, where it all began, there are
still many people who refuse to believe it, who saw no sign of it.
You can search from one end of the country to the other before
you find a man who admits to being a concentration camp guard,
or even someone who remembers serving a concentration camp
guard with a cup of coffee in a canteen. When they tell you about
themselves certain things are omitted. Often they are no longer
aware that they are omitting them. It isn't only that they want to
mislead you; they want to mislead themselves, because how else
can they live with themselves? Self-induced amnesia, in fact. The
trouble is that while they have forgotten, we can't forget. Ours is
a different, incompatible insanity.'

So, he had said it; and it left him empty, emotionally eviscerated.
He stood in the centre of the room, hands hanging limply by his
side, the very flesh sagging on his bones with weariness and defeat.
Like everything about him, his behaviour had been too melodramatic. The big guns of argument had been brought up to batter
a young man's poor love, and now the cause seemed contemptible,
an arbitrary act of cruelty whatever the professed motives.

'Well, the lecture's over,' he said brusquely. 'You can kick me
out now.'

'Feeling like that, how can you possibly go on living here?' Martin asked bitterly. 'That seems to me the worst kind of dishonesty.'

'It's the story of my life, I suppose. I always thought of myself as a German, but Germany had no place for me except in its crematoria.' Again he thought of Putzi. He would have expected no more than a gesture of friendship. Somehow it would have made the subsequent years more tolerable. 'Perhaps just being here is an act of revenge; it doesn't make any other kind of sense.'

Standing irresolutely in the doorway, he said: 'Have you noticed one thing, Martin? We've spoken hardly anything but German. It's my language, but does it have to be yours?'

Downstairs, as he walked out of the elevator, he collided slightly with a big, dark girl carrying some flowers. Their glances momentarily interlocked and she murmured a polite apology. 'I'm sorry,' Hugo said. 'I'm sorry.'

There were the stubs of cigars in the ash-tray, the two glasses and the cognac, stale traces of tobacco smoke in the air, a premonition. The room bore the invisible impress of conflict, the way death lingers on in a place after a funeral.

Karin hesitated in the doorway, waiting for him to kiss her. But he just said hello with a preoccupied, weary smile and she was still insufficiently sure of herself to court a rebuff. Instead she unwrapped the food and laid it on cardboard plates, then crossed the room, brushing by his knees, and arranged the flowers in a tumbler.

'I wrote a poem today,' she said. 'You didn't know I wrote poems.'

No, he didn't know she wrote poems. He knew her intimately and painfully, the feel of her body, the huskiness of her voice in the night, details of her private suffering. He knew things about her no one else could know. And yet what of the stranger in the skin of the woman he loved? One couldn't begin to count the number of things he did not know. When you thought people were revealing themselves they were in reality erecting a careful disguise.

'No, I didn't know you wrote poetry,' Martin said. They sat side by side like people casually sharing a table in a restaurant. 'What do you know about me?' he countered abruptly.

She shrank from the hostility in his voice. 'Why do you ask?'

'It's natural, isn't it? We sleep together. We make love. You must want to know everything about me.'

Karin stared at her plate. 'The important thing a woman wants to know about a man is that he loves her.'

'Is that all? It's the sort of thing they say in women's magazines, but is it true? Doesn't she want to know about his past, his friends, if he likes children, or hates Negroes, or believes in God?'

'Yes, she wants to know those also. But they're less important to her.'

'You know how I feel about Germany.'

'Yes.'

'Does it matter to you?'

'I don't blame you for the way you feel,' she replied in a subdued voice. 'I don't think it should make any difference to us.'

Yes, there were women like that. They had strictly personal loyalties, discounting everything but love, forgiving everything but the withholding of love. A man to them was a world entire, and they could live in him as a nun could live in Christ.

She touched his hand. 'Don't be so depressed, Martin. Have some Liebfraumilch, it's very good,' proffering the wine as she would give a child her breast or a man her body. It would be pleasant to surrender to it, taking the peace she offered along with the wine, had Hugo not planted a painful doubt in his mind. The temptation of Samson, he thought ironically, the Borgia's poisoned cup. Whichever way one looked at it, it had been turned into an absurd melodrama because of the millionfold dead Hugo had chosen to flourish in his face. As if anything mattered to the dead – to his mother, or Lise, or the cousins, or Uncle Franz, or Uncle Heinrich, with his Iron Cross on his dead chest to show he was a son of the Fatherland to the end. The dead belonged only with the dead.

'Show me your poem,' he said, moved by a complex impulse of curiosity, contrition, and mockery.

'You really want to see it?' she asked eagerly.

'Of course.' He watched her with an intense physical pleasure as she crossed the room to fetch her handbag, imagining their mutual surrender to sex and thinking of her body with an unfamiliar profanity. Their relationship had awakened in him an erotic violence that had lain dormant and unsuspected throughout all his brief and casual intimacies. He had never thought of himself as an aggressive lover; one of the reasons none of his occasional infatuations had turned into marriage was that he'd conducted the skirmishes too irresolutely, as if he'd needed tension as an aphrodisiac. She was a forbidden strangeness, and the enmity of race enhanced the antagonism of sex. The thought of it was sufficient to make him want to take her then and there and repeat his conquest.

Karin brought the poem over and stood with her hands behind her back like a child before its teacher. She seemed overcome by shyness. As he unfolded the sheet of paper, she suddenly left the room. He heard the bathroom door close behind her. The poem was headed, in a neat, sloping hand:

'The Desert
For M.S.'

It was embarrassing, a love poem, but its awkward sincerity disarmed him. She was the desert, and he was the sun and rain. He fertilised her and made her green, he made her womb stir, he restored her to life. It was sentimental, erotic, and adolescent, but it made him want to take her gently in his arms and ask her forgiveness.

An argument had broken out in the corridor. At first he was too absorbed in Karin's poem to pay attention to it. Then Goldberg's voice penetrated through the plaster wall, rumbling abuse. 'Disgusting!' he was shouting. 'Like a brothel!' And Frau Goetz screeching with outrage: 'Don't you dare call my house a brothel! You don't own the bathroom!'

Martin got up from the chair quickly and went to the door. He felt a strange, light-headed anger, followed by a quick gust of fury that set him trembling violently. All this ugliness was being directed at Karin. It was she who had unwittingly aroused the sick ravings of Goldberg, but it was Hugo who was ultimately responsible. Hugo did not have the excuse of insanity. He'd committed an act of aggression, coldly and malevolently. Everything he'd said was merely an excuse to justify his interference in a relationship whose normality he loathed and envied.

'What's the trouble?' he demanded ominously.

Goldberg was standing by the bathroom in his suspenders, his mad eyes protruding and the congested veins in his neck knotted like ropes. Frau Goetz was clawing the air with one hand while the other held grimly to the bathroom door-knob.

'You're to blame!' Goldberg screamed. 'You bring these women into the house!'

'Nobody brings women into the house!' Frau Goetz shouted, stamping her tiny foot and showering them both with her fiery spittle.

Martin pushed them aside and wrenched open the bathroom door. Karin had retreated to the wash-basin, looking ill and frightened. 'Get into the room,' he ordered quietly. 'It's all right.' She hurried past him with an anxious glance at Frau Goetz.

'Yes, go and fornicate!' Goldberg hissed after her.

Martin struck him hard in the mouth, dislodging his upper dentures, which fell to the floor. Goldberg stared at him with clownish dismay. His lips swelled under the impact of the blow and blood trickled down his chin. Dazed with shock, he bent down and fumbled on the ground for his teeth; then, with a curious gasp, toppled over and lay face downward, breathing heavily and irregularly.

'He can go!' Frau Goetz was saying. 'He can pay me what he owes and go!'

But Goldberg continued to lie in an unnatural posture, his breath rasping in his chest. With an appalled fascination, Martin said: 'My God, he's ill! Please get a doctor.'

He lifted the sick man up by the armpits and dragged him with lolling head down the corridor to his room. Frau Goetz was frantically telephoning for emergency medical aid.

She came in when he'd laid Goldberg on the bed and glanced at the unconscious form with shrewd compassion.

'A stroke, poor man!' she said, deftly wiping the blood from his chin with a wet handkerchief. 'May God have mercy on his soul, it was his own fault.'

'He's not going to die?' Martin asked, deeply shocked.

'Who knows? Sometimes they live. You mustn't blame yourself,' she added anxiously. 'It could happen at any time. We won't say anything about the quarrel. There's nobody but us in the apartment.' She pressed his arm in a gesture of complicity. 'I'll go and tidy myself before the doctor comes. You'd better wait here.'

The sound of Goldberg's tortured breathing filled the room. Sometimes he muttered a few words in a croaked delirious voice. Martin loosened his collar and leaned over, watching desperately for signs of returning consciousness. The leaden face seemed already that of a corpse, but for the muscular spasms and the mad words bubbling from the lips. He was speaking a mixture of Polish and Yiddish, pausing to suck air hoarsely into his lungs, then beginning to mutter again.

Martin's breath also came painfully, as though he were trying to breathe for two. He was overcome by a stupid feeling that he had no right to be in this strange room. It was even shabbier than his own, the rugs more threadbare, the furniture uglier, the proportions more meagre. A narrow, waist-high window looked out at a blank brick wall, and below was a basement yard cluttered with coalscuttles, refuse-bins, and scraps of broken timber.

Goldberg's tidiness, like his own, bordered on the obsessive and, in a curious way, threw into contrast its author's poverty and self-assertion. A neat pile of Hebrew newspapers was stacked on a shelf in the company of a handful of books, ponderous manuals of law contrasting with thin, garish paper-backs. An array of writing implements was lined precisely along the top of a small table which evidently served as a desk. A shirt, some underwear, and socks hung on an improvised line that terminated at one end by the side of an imposing diploma. There was only one photograph, a family group consisting of Goldberg himself, some twenty years younger, a woman dressed in black satin with narrow-set eyes and a thin, worried mouth, and two children, one a rather handsome boy of about twelve, the other a small, solemn girl with ringlets. The photograph stood on the bedside table along with a Jewish seven-branched candelabrum and a Hebrew prayer book.

That memorial gesture brought home to Martin the full real-isation of Goldberg's loneliness. It was a symbol superimposed upon the shabbiness and bitterness of the man's life, making at once a personal and universal statement. From now on he would always be atoning for Goldberg. Putting pennies into blind men's cups with the same hand that struck the unlucky blow; inviting the wrath. The Lord giveth and the Lord taketh away.

The sick man stirred and began to groan: 'Help me!' he gasped. 'Help me!' His hand groped and seized Martin's fingers in a con-vulsive grip. 'I should go to Israel,' he panted. 'The climate here – it's bad for me.'

'Yes, you'll go. Don't worry.' He watched Goldberg relax into a kind of peace, noticing for the first time that the man had a childlike face, trusting and naïve and foolish. All the madness lay shut away behind the closed eyelids, leaving the personality healed but diminished. In a strange way Martin trembled on the edge of revelation. It was on the point of articulation, like a forgotten word on the tip of the tongue, then it vanished. Instead he thought of the capricious irony that had allowed Goldberg to survive the trampling, jack-booted years only to make him fall at the hand of a fellow Jew in a Berlin pension.

The door-bell rang. There were whispered voices in the corridor and Frau Goetz came in with the doctor, a young man with the pompous but uncertain manner of the newly qualified practitioner. 'A heart attack,' he said, after a brief examination, and prepared an injection. The needle slid into Goldberg's arm and in a while colour returned to the leaden face. 'I'll call an ambulance,' the doctor said, packing his instruments away. 'Any relatives?'

'No, he was alone,' Frau Goetz replied. She began to snuffle with easy tears.

Martin said: 'I don't think I'm needed any more.' Soon the German orderlies would come to carry the casualty away, the dead Goldbergs would stare out of the photograph, through the seven-branched candelabrum, at the empty room. *Yisgaddal v'yiskaddash sh'mah rabbo…* It was no desertion to leave the dead. One had to turn back towards life.

Slowly he went along the corridor to Karin.

8

After Hugo left the building, he sat for some time in the darkness of the car biting on an unlit cigar. It had been raining earlier, and he stared through the diamond-studded windscreen at the gleaming surface of the road with a flaccid inertia that signalled the onset of familiar symptoms. Soon he would be groping for the only medicine that could dull the pain of being Hugo Krantz, that could make him forget what a louse he'd been to Martin. Then the spurious elation, sitting at the wheel of the car and aiming it at the city, at pleasure, at shrewd boys with cold flirtatious eyes; and waking in the sub-normal temperature of some strange room with the despair alone intact.

Not that again, he told himself. He would go back to the apartment, call a few people, have a quiet little party. Anything. The engine jerked into a neurotic palsy and he drove towards the distant glare of the Kurfürstendamm. The blue Studebaker, parked some distance behind, moved off at the same time. When he turned left at the Hohenzollerndamm it swung after him, and, with a persistence that discounted coincidence, followed him down a series of small side streets. He jammed his foot on the brake and stopped sharply as the driver of the Studebaker, caught unprepared, swerved just in time to escape a collision and disappeared round a corner, but when he came to the Bundesallee it was behind him again.

Well, there were only two ways to stop being chased. You could either give your pursuer the slip, or you could allow yourself to be caught. Impulsively choosing the second alternative, Hugo pulled up outside a store where several people were window-shopping. The Studebaker stopped about a hundred yards behind. He got out of the car, deliberately lit his cigar, and strolled back along the pavement.

'Enjoying the ride?' he asked caustically.

Kane was listening to an orchestra concert on the radio. 'Oh, it's you,' he said in feigned surprise, switching off the music.

'I suppose you mistook me for Ulbricht or Grotewohl or Adenauer.'

'Not at all,' Kane said pleasantly. His eyes glinted with amusement in the dim green light of the dashboard. 'Fact is, I'm kidding. I knew it was you.'

Hugo said: 'You're wasting your time and you're getting on my nerves. There isn't a story in it.'

'Oh, the story!' Kane shrugged his shoulders disparagingly. 'I've had that figured for some time.'

'I'd like to hear about it.'

'I thought you would. Fact is, I've been looking forward to having a talk.'

Hugo smiled in a faintly ironic way, 'I get it,' he said. 'You want to talk with someone, so you follow him around for a couple of weeks waiting for the right opportunity.'

'I didn't have anything better to do,' Kane countered coolly. 'Let's go up to my place and have a drink,' he offered, understanding his man well enough to know that curiosity would make the invitation irresistible.

He lived on the eighth floor of an apartment house in Nollendorfplatz, in one large room with egress to a rusty fire-escape. The room was austere, on principle apparently, because it had something of the appearance of a gymnasium with its spare, functional furnishings, rope matting, and some Indian clubs, a coiled metal chest expander and sprung-steel hand-grips hanging prominently on one wall.

It made Hugo feel soft and unclean, uncomfortably aware of his unhealthy corpulence. 'You like to keep fit,' he commented with a sour mockery not untinged with envy, despite his temperamental addiction to luxury.

'Sure, it's one of my fixed principles,' Kane replied seriously. 'Every morning at seven I get on the fire-escape and work out for twenty minutes before breakfast.'

'Bread and water, I suppose.'

Kane gave him a one-sided grin and threw open the french windows. 'We're a long way from the ground. Have a look at the view,' he said. The roof-tops of Charlottenburg stood out like cold mountain peaks above the glow of the city and stretched away eastward until they merged into the blue-black of the sky beyond Communist Berlin. 'You can look homeward from here,' Hugo suggested dryly. 'You kidding?' Kane grinned. Across the tidy, bomb-ruined hinterland were the lighted apartments of a housing block in Motzstrasse. He pointed towards one window. A girl could be seen sitting on a divan in a kimono, shaving her legs.

'The things people do when they're alone!' he said with a grimace of displeasure, leading the way back into the room and closing the windows. 'It reminds me of when I was a kid in downtown New York. We lived in one of those districts that always stank of vegetable garbage. Folks sat around on the sidewalks in hot weather half naked, fanning the stale air with newspapers. You looked out of the window at night into other people's windows, watching them scratch their sweating bodies, old ladies shuffling around in thin nightgowns bawling out their husbands, kids crawling on dirty floors, even folks doing it in bed.'

Hugo shifted impatiently on a chair seemingly designed to inflict discomfort on the spine. 'I expect it's the same in Moscow,' he suggested maliciously.

'You still got that crazy notion,' Kane said. 'What'll you drink, Russian vodka?'

'Do you have a neutralist cognac?'

Kane laughed politely and brought a bottle of Bisquit and two glasses from a cupboard. For a while he sipped his drink and watched Hugo obliquely, his flat, puffy face with its sly, rubber-lidded eyes giving away nothing.

'You puzzle me,' he admitted eventually, offering his cigarette-case and smiling with the practised skill of an experienced interrogator. 'Why all this preoccupation with Sommer?'

Hugo accepted a cigarette and examined it. Inevitably, it was a Camel. The props were always correctly chosen. 'I thought you had the story figured. I've come to listen, not to answer questions.'

Kane drummed his fingers thoughtfully on the table and when he spoke did so with visible hesitation. 'Let me tell you a few things I've picked up about you,' he said. 'Age: forty-seven, forty-eight. Case history: Born in Berlin, Jew, lower-middle class, talented. You went into the theatre, turned to revue writing, became a success. For a time you were the boy wonder of Berlin. Smart reputation, lots of money, millions of friends. Then the Nazis came. You were arrested, released, went to Vienna. Got out just before the *Anschluss*, went to Prague. In 1938 went to London, had a thin time for a while, then married money. Right so far?'

'Brilliant,' Hugo murmured warily. 'Where's it leading to?'

'We'll soon come to that.' Kane began pacing with measured tread up and down the floor with the shrewd, preoccupied expression of a hard-fisted peasant calculating the value of live-stock. 'Now,' he continued, reckoning up the facts on the fingers of his upturned hand. 'Money made more money and you became rich, millions of friends again, including government big shots. You were right on top of the heap. Then you do something damned funny.' He shot a cunning, sidelong glance at Hugo. 'On 14 October 1952, you suddenly hop out of that cosy little nest, without a word to anyone, and wing it back to Berlin. How do you explain that, Herr Krantz?'

Hugo shrugged and looked into his glass. 'Why should I try?' he countered, 'It's not a newspaper story.'

Kane picked up a chair, moved it close, sat down, and, staring straight into his companion's eyes, said in a soft, significant voice: 'I'm in the newspaper business the same way you're in the dress business.'

A paroxysm of uncontrollable laughter seized Hugo until he gasped for breath. 'Have you been wasting your time!' he roared, his eyes watering. 'I've never heard anything so marvellously ridiculous outside Baron Münchhausen.'

Kane continued to observe him closely, quite undisconcerted, his powerful shoulders hunched forward and his eyes narrow and cold. He looked the sort of man who wrestled with mental problems physically, like some horny-handed labourer who bunches his muscles and perspires freely in the effort of writing out his own name.

'It figures all the way,' he persisted. 'What incentive did you have to come back? The Germans kicked you in the balls, and you're not the type to answer that with loving kindness. You had it soft, so you didn't need to scavenge around in Berlin for a living.'

'Perhaps I was homesick.'

'I thought of that, but if you're homesick for nearly twenty years you learn to live with it.'

Hugo conceded the point with an amiable grin, fascinated by the man's ingenious yet stupid deductions. 'I'll have another drink if you can spare it,' he said.

'Help yourself.' His host gestured towards the bottle. Lighting a fresh cigarette from the stub of the old one, he tilted his chair back and addressed the naked electric bulb that hung from the ceiling. 'I put it to you this way. Supposing I was a German Jew, living off the fat in London, getting richer every day – there's only one thing that could persuade me to come back to Germany: revenge, a chance to hit back at some of the bastards who'd given it to me and my people. And supposing a gentleman in London came along with a proposition and laid it on the line?'

'Where is this leading us?' Hugo asked with mild amusement. The chair straightened with a jerk and he found himself staring down Kane's index finger levelled between his eyes like the barrel of a gun. 'The fact that we're in the same business is only incidental,' the man said sharply, his harsh metropolitan New

York accent grating unpleasantly. 'What interests me is that I suspect we're working on the same assignment.'

In the use of the word 'assignment' Hugo thought he detected a clumsy attempt at flattery. It was at the same time perfunctory and melodramatic, indicating that Kane regarded his profession in a romantic light, as if he were performing a rôle in a Hollywood movie and were indulgently prepared to include him, Hugo, in the scenario. The idea immediately rendered the whole episode ridiculous and allayed his underlying anxiety. With a feeling of aiding in a juvenile charade, he removed his horn-rimmed spectacles, polished them thoughtfully, and, staring at his companion with near-sighted concentration, murmured: 'What is this assignment? I'm not quite clear.'

'I thought we understood each other,' Kane said. 'I'm offering you a straight deal. You tell me and I'll tell you.'

'What do you expect me to tell?'

'Why you're after Sommer.'

'Who is Sommer?' Hugo asked with quickening excitement. It would be an odd irony if he found his way to Putzi through an agent of a Communist *Apparat*.

'You don't know,' Kane said sarcastically. 'You've just been chasing around after him to give yourself some exercise. You can take one thing for granted, Krantz: I've followed you enough to figure out who you're after. All I want to know is, why?'

'Sommer's not an uncommon name. Are you *certain* you know whom I'm after?'

'Absolutely. Sommer, Wolfgang. Ex-Wehrmacht corporal captured at Budapest, re-educated by the Reds, repatriated June, 1949. If you give me what I want, I'll tell you more.'

Hugo added a final polish to his lenses and held them up to the light. 'Why are *you* interested in him?' he asked, trying to sound casual. As Hugo replaced the glasses on his nose, Kane's face came into focus. It was entirely without expression, like a face constructed not of bone, blood, and living tissue but of some inert synthetic. The eyes were terrifyingly impersonal, moving like steel ball bearings. It was the quintessential official filing-cabinet face worn by men in frontier posts, thumbing through dossiers in small, bare government offices, sitting on judgement benches.

Kane turned away and crushed his cigarette into an ashtray. When he looked up again, the mask had gone and he was smiling.

'We're playing games,' he said regretfully. 'I take it you're not ready to co-operate?'

'I've nothing to co-operate with,' Hugo said. 'You've got the wrong notion of me altogether.' His voice shook slightly as he realised he was alone, eight floors above street level, with a powerful, and probably ruthless, man. The rumours of Communist terror flashed through his mind, setting up a strong vibration of fear. In Berlin melodrama was commonplace. One only had to recall the case of Otto John, chief of Adenauer's intelligence service, smuggled or kidnapped into Eastern Germany. Or Helmut Kaufmann, editor of a well-known Social Democratic newspaper, who confessed at a dinner party that he could never leave his house unarmed because three attempts had already been made to kidnap him. In retrospect, he even mistrusted Kane's gesture in showing him the view from the fire escape. 'We're a long way from the ground,' the man had said. The search for Putzi was becoming excessively perilous, or else one's sanity was more rotted by drink and fear than one had suspected. 'We're not on the same assignment at all,' he went on huskily. 'Matter of fact, I've given up mine.' It was the wrong Sommer.

Kane stood up abruptly and pushed his chair away. 'I'll think that one over,' he said. 'Would you like another drink before I throw you out?' He spoke with a certain sadistic relish, pushing a fist into the palm of the other hand so that the knuckles cracked audibly. Hugo cast an involuntary glance over his shoulder at the french windows and made a comic grimace. 'Let's not end the interview violently,' he said. 'It's been not altogether unpleasant.'

'As long as I haven't wasted your time,' Kane said, looking at his wrist-watch. 'I'm expecting someone at twenty-two hundred sharp. Will you find your own way down all right?' He stood in the middle of the large, bare room, with his heavy, anonymous face and his unspent violence projecting an image of menace until the door closed between them.

Back in his own empty apartment, Hugo sat down amid the convalescent comfort and picked up a book lying discarded on the couch. It was Heinz Dieter's science-fiction romance opened at a chapter headed: 'The Insect Invaders.' A piece of paper fluttered out as he tossed the book aside. It was the torn note he'd read that afternoon. '…Usual place tonight 22.00. I will expect you.' Reading it now, a voice in his head seemed to be speaking the message: *twenty-two hundred sharp*.

The pain was already beginning. He went to the bar, poured himself a drink, and settled down to wait.

The click of the lock as the door was quietly opened woke him. The radio was playing and he lay awkwardly crumpled on the couch, staring at the white ceiling, a small hammer beating in his right temple. Slowly, he remembered.

'Heinzi!' he called. 'Is that you?'

Heinz Dieter paused at the door. 'It's me, Hugo,' he said.

'Come in here for a minute.'

The young German entered reluctantly, smiling with pale determination. He was wearing a padded overcoat that gave him the massive shoulders of a weight-lifter.

'*Heil*, Herr Superman,' Hugo grunted. He sat up and wearily ran his fingers through his thin hair. 'Had an interesting evening?'

'Not bad,' was the unenthusiastic reply.

'Don't tell me you actually found a girl who could say no?' The ridicule was reflex, a matter of habit. Over the years they had developed a certain formula to ease the awkwardness of their relationship. Instead of tenderness they used the bantering toughness that expresses affection in any exclusively male society, and Hugo exercised his dominance in the manner of a slightly brutal, worldly elder brother towards a younger. The middle-aged queer, he'd often thought, was forced to behave like an athletic coach. One got used to the ignominy. But it enhanced one's nostalgia for the old, youthful pleasures, when there had been an aura of Putzi in the quicksilver streets, the harebrained parties, the malice of cabaret humour, when he would lend his cynical intelligence to your conversation, twisting his lithe, graceful body into acrobatic postures of listening, catching an idea neatly, turning it inside out and tossing it back into your lap in an exhilarating game that made life effervesce like the bubbles in a glass of poisoned champagne.

Heinz Dieter had perched himself on the edge of a chair, still wearing his outrageous overcoat. He held a cigarette between his fingers but seemed to have forgotten it, and the smoke rose in a wavering column into the air. His hand was trembling and, observing him closely, Hugo noticed other signs of distress – a tenseness about the mouth, the eyes hurt and evasive, and an air of subdued desperation expressed in restless movements as uncontrolled as a nervous tic.

'You're worried about something,' he said. 'You have been for some time now.'

'I'm just a bit depressed. I must have caught it from you,' the youth replied sullenly.

'That's fine. Nothing like being miserable in the right company.' Hugo came and stood over him. 'Why don't you take off your overcoat?' he suggested mildly. 'You live here, remember.'

Something in his voice seemed to irritate Heinz Dieter. 'Stop fussing over me,' he blustered. 'Anybody would think you were my father.' With head bent, he slouched away and slammed the door of his bedroom.

Hugo automatically poured himself a fresh drink, went to the desk, and searched in one of the drawers for a small bottle of migraine tablets. He swallowed two and sat for a while waiting for the hammering in his head to diminish. In an odd way he felt calm and detached, as if he had surrendered all interest in his own affairs. Another odd thing was both the clarity and the vagueness of his consciousness. For example, he noted with a sensation of surprise that it was not yet midnight. The grain of the desk, the soft feel of the carpet beneath his feet, the rounded hollows of the figurine on the black terrazzo fireplace, vividly impinged on his senses. He was indescribably moved by a Modigliani nude he'd recently acquired, the only direct representation of a naked woman in the place and the one picture that pleased Heinz Dieter, because it alone had meaning for him. Yet he found himself standing by the window looking down at the gleaming shops of the Kurfürstendamm, its fast river of traffic and its midget people, with no recollection of leaving the desk. The cigar smouldering in his hand seemed to have materialised already lit out of thin air, and with an amazing absence of locomotion he now stood inside Heinz Dieter's room while the young German piled his belongings into a suitcase.

'I'm chucking it, Hugo,' he was saying. 'You'll have to find a new friend.'

'Any reason?' Hugo asked calmly.

'This and that.' Heinz Dieter banged the case about petulantly. 'We haven't been very good pals lately anyway.'

'I've always liked having you around, Heinzi. But you've been getting too damned independent. What are you thinking of doing?'

'I don't know. Maybe I'll go to Hamburg and get a job there.'

The mention of Hamburg released a flood of sadness. 'Remember the trip we made there three years ago? I took you down to the docks to look at the ships, and *voilà!* you were going to be a sailor for the rest of your life. You had to go straight off and buy a seaman's sweater. Afterwards you were sick on oysters. I never saw a boy swallow so many in one sitting.'

'You deliberately made me sick,' Heinz Dieter said resentfully, 'telling me that stuff about oysters pepping up the sex.' For the first time that evening he smiled. 'But I got my own back when I took you into that brothel. There was a skinny little thing who took a fancy to you – she thought you were my uncle. It was your turn to be sick.'

'It was fairly nauseating,' Hugo agreed meditatively. 'You might have picked a whore-house where the girls had decent shapes.' For a long time he'd remembered the episode as coldly disgusting. One of the women had touched him with playful obscenity and insisted that he accompany her to her cubicle. Afraid of a scene, he'd followed and sat by her side on the bed, fending her off with glib, desperate conversation. Even now he could recall with audible precision the curious, husky quality of her voice that made everything she said sound like a lewd confidence. Her sex seemed to reside in her throat. After a while she'd treated him with indulgent contempt and demanded fifty marks as the price of releasing him. 'What a man!' she told the other women as they came out of the cubicle, rolling her eyes and puffing her cheeks in mock tribute to his virility while he pretended the joke was agreeable. It was neither the worst nor the least of his humiliations, and gradually it had merged with other experiences of women that filled him with shuddering aversion. But now, he realised, he would even think of that with nostalgia.

'You don't have to leave tonight,' he said. 'You might as well stay until morning. No good leaving the room empty.' The thought of it, of being alone in the apartment tomorrow and tomorrow and tomorrow, filled him with a chill foreboding.

'The sooner the better,' Heinz Dieter insisted obstinately.

Hugo sat down on the bed, his head swollen and light as a balloon. There was a total unreality about what was happening. Somewhere along the line he'd lost the thread and now the experiences of the day were disconnected. He could no longer recall the conversation in Martin's room, or even the motives that had impelled him to go there. And yet it all seemed to have something to do with the fact that Heinz Dieter was leaving him, like a dream episode in which, unaccountably, the faces change and the situation alters but the underlying significance remains. A bad dream. Somewhere it contained the key that could render the totally unimportant tragedy of being Hugo Krantz comprehensible. But just now he wasn't asking for that, or for honesty; only that the illusion should not be entirely taken away and he be left nakedly alone.

'Has Kane ordered you to leave?' he asked in a quite, matter-of-fact voice that bore no traces of resentment.

Heinz Dieter stood motionless, holding a folded shirt in his hands, while his face tried out a few suitable expressions – bewilderment, injury, anger. Then he seemed to give up. 'So you know about that,' he said, carefully placing the shirt in the suitcase.

'Yes. Why did you do it? For money?'

'What kind of a bastard do you think I am?' Heinz Dieter burst out, this time with genuine anger. 'In any case,' he added cautiously, 'what do you think I've done?'

'I don't know. Showed him my correspondence. Told him my movements.'

'That's crazy. I've only met him a couple of times, four or five at the most. Anyway, why should he want to know what you're up to?'

'Apparently I'm big news in San Francisco,' Hugo said. 'How did you meet Kane in the first place?'

Heinz Dieter snapped the locks of the suitcase and threw himself into a chair. He smoked gloomily for a while, staring slowly round the comfortable room with obvious regret.

'It's been nice here,' he said. 'I've got used to it. He was in the Don Juan, on the corner of Wielandstrasse. There were a couple of girls. You know how they go for foreigners. We went up to his place and had a party.' He studied his polished toe-cap from several angles, as if to suggest that the conversation bored him.

'I suppose he told you I was working for the Communists and he'd pay you well if you gave him reports about me?'

Heinz Dieter laughed, a shade too boisterously. 'You've got a persecution mania,' he protested.

Even to a Berlin guttersnipe the cliché came glibly. All the time they thought of you as a sick Jew, an incurable psychopath whom it was politic to humour, entirely unaware that it was a case of the mad consorting with the mad.

'All right, Heinzi,' Hugo said tensely. 'Let's get in the car. We're going somewhere.' He stood up and kicked the suitcase out of the way.

'I'm not going anywhere with you,' the young German replied, staring at him apprehensively.

'You are! We're going to see Kane.'

'I'm not going there, Hugo.'

It was like confronting a recalcitrant child, but it was clear that the obstinacy was grounded in fear and Hugo felt the inevitable stab of compassion and the warm gush of love like blood pumping out of the heart. 'You'd better tell me what it's about, Heinzi,' he said quietly. 'It's the best way.'

'I suppose so,' Heinz Dieter said, capitulating suddenly, as if it were a relief to do so. He lit another cigarette and drew on it with quick, nervous puffs. 'Kane did ask me a lot of questions about you, but I didn't tell him much he didn't know already.'

'What, for instance?'

'About who your friends were, and about the shop – if it was a front or really made money. He asked me if I knew this old pal you were trying to find.'

'If you weren't taking money from him, why didn't you tell him to go to hell?'

Heinz Dieter stared at the floor. 'He knows something about me,' he mumbled. 'Why I left East Germany.'

Hugo felt a morbid excitement. The scene came back to him. The station at Charlottenburg. The boy cringing under the blows of an American soldier. Later, in the restaurant, the story of the one-legged father living off his son's immoral earnings and flogging him with Prussian severity at home. Dry-mouthed, he asked: 'Is it something to do with the stabbing of your father?'

'Yes,' Heinz Dieter said. He crumpled his cigarette between his fingers and watched the grains of tobacco fall to the floor. 'Kane said the old man died. I didn't believe him, but he showed me a clipping from a newspaper.'

'Why didn't you tell me? I would have looked after you, Heinzi. We could have gone to Switzerland for a few months.'

'Kane said the police can have you picked up anywhere. You can't escape.'

Outside, a thin blue mist was coating the glass of the window like the breath of an invisible intruder. A few stars glimmered through broken clouds and the faint throb of the city vibrated against their ear-drums. The drowsy bee-drone of a plane passed diagonally across the sky towards Tempelhof, and for an instant Hugo imagined Berlin from the pilot's cockpit, the cold, nocturnal splendour thrown like a glittering net over the darkness. The image emphasised their insignificance. One sometimes forgot that even this was melodramatic. It was no longer possible to escape. The times made an ordinary history inconceivable; one survived the melodramas of the day by an arbitrary act of mercy only.

'You don't have to go now, Heinzi,' he said. 'We'll sort this thing out somehow.'

Heinz Dieter shook his head. 'That's not why I'm leaving.'

'What is it then?'

'Kane wants your diary. If I don't give it to him by tomorrow evening he'll send the police around. You'd have known I pinched it, so I'd have had to clear out anyway.'

Hugo said: 'It's not like you to be so self-sacrificial. I don't understand it.'

'No, neither do I,' Heinz Dieter admitted with a grimace. 'But I don't trust him. Once he got what he wanted, he'd probably double-cross me in any case.' Cynicism having been re-established, they both laughed.

'Let's go inside and have a drink,' Hugo suggested cheerfully. The brandy went to his head almost as soon as it was swallowed. He went to the desk and unlocked the private drawer. 'Tell Kane he can decode that, with my compliments,' he said, presenting the diary to Heinz Dieter with a flourish. 'It's full of useful scatological formulæ.'

He was happier than he'd been for a long time. Heinzi needed him; he hadn't betrayed him for profit. And he wasn't going away after all.

'Pals again?' he grinned.

'Pals again,' Heinz Dieter agreed a little uncertainly, holding the thick leather-bound diary gingerly, like a bomb.

Hugo walked into Resi's about midnight the following day, pausing by the door to scrutinise the crowd jostling on the dance floor under the revolving sherbet-coloured lights. A girl in low-cut evening dress detached herself from a group at the bar and paraded dutifully before him as was her custom with unaccompanied gentlemen.

'*Guten Abend, Fräulein,*' he murmured, sketching a smile to soften the inevitable rebuff.

The orchestra played a sugar-coated melody, with cloying violins to match the coloured gloom, and the massed audience responded eagerly to the sentimental dishonesty, nuzzling together as they danced or staring through rosy light into one another's eyes. The table telephones were ringing with flirtatious invitations, and canisters bearing love messages travelled by the pneumatic messenger linking each table with the central exchange.

He lit a cigar nervously before continuing his search. People in the mass bored and frightened him a little: they were trivial and menacing at the same time. Why had Boris insisted on this, of all places, for a meeting? For obvious reasons it hadn't been wise to meet in the apartment, but he'd expected Boris to propose a rendezvous more in character with his method of livelihood, a back-street bar or a dingy gambling club where business was executed with little more than a wink or an unobtrusive gesture.

'It pays to be seen in respectable places,' Boris maintained, and, true to his principles, he was sitting at a conspicuous table on the very edge of the dance floor, a small, swarthy man tapping his fingers in time to the music and gazing with a vivacious smile at the dancers. He seemed entirely gay and at ease; one would never have guessed that this was another case history of the concentration camp survivor.

'Thank God, my health is not so bad,' Boris grinned, waving Hugo to a seat at the table. Then he asked mournfully: 'Did you hear about Goldberg?'

'No,' Hugo said.

'He's dead. A stroke, or a heart attack.'

It was possible that he'd heard imperfectly. The band... the deafening saxophones... people conversing in loud voices... It was only yesterday, surely, that Goldberg had been sitting on the opposite side of the desk with his sour misery, talking about the wickedness of others.

'Poor Goldberg!' Boris said. 'It was his fate to die on German soil. I knew him in Auschwitz. You could only hear one thing from him: *Eretz*. He used to pray every every day that God should spare him to see The Land. But once he was there, the sun was too hot, you couldn't make a living, people didn't treat you with proper respect. So he came to get his restitution, and as soon as he was back in Berlin he began to pray again that God should spare him to die in *Eretz*.'

'Not everybody is grateful to his deliverer,' Hugo said. Goldberg had lived on the milk and money of hope and the strong meat of hate, but he needed the meat most. So now he was dead.

'*Ach!* He was a cripple like the rest of us. He began to die in Auschwitz, but he took a bit longer over it than most. The funeral is tomorrow. You'd better come. It's hard to get ten Jews, a *minyan*, together in Berlin.'

'I'll come if I can,' Hugo said, 'but it's too much like attending one's own funeral.'

Boris shrugged expressively. With mercurial swiftness his mood altered and his black eyes twinkled. 'Now let's get down to *tachlith*,' he said briskly. Although he spoke German, Russian, Polish, and English with varying degrees of fluency, he always adulterated these languages with occasional words in Yiddish. Like many Jews of his kind, people from the small Jewish towns of Eastern Europe who made garments or sold merchandise in all the world's capitals, Yiddish was for him a substitute motherland, a linguistic ghetto he never wished to leave entirely behind. 'Do you want to buy, or do you want to sell?' he asked. 'I can get anything you like in twenty-four hours. Selling takes longer.'

'I'm a respectable business-man,' Hugo remonstrated placidly.

'That's a matter of opinion. Krupps are also respectable now. The only difference between you and me is I don't mind admitting that I'm a bit of a *ganiv*, a thief. Neither of us works our fingers to the bone.'

'You talk like a socialist millionaire.'

Boris's wide, humorous mouth twisted into a wry smile. 'Long live the half-brotherhood of man,' he said. 'It's like the hippopotamus. Nobody but a gentleman hippopotamus would roll in the mud with a lady hippopotamus. That's how I feel about the human race.'

'Yes,' Hugo said, 'but the question remains——' he glanced at the sentimental revellers on the dance floor, thinking of Goldberg and Auschwitz – 'the question remains, how about the Nazi hippopotamus?'

'Do you expect me to have an answer for everything?' Boris retorted easily, rubbing a hand over the dark stubble on his chin. There was a soft thud as a canister landed in the pneumatic messenger at their side. 'Love always finds me,' he said, unscrewing the lid and glancing at the envelope. 'Not my night. It's for you.'

Hugo smoothed out a crumpled piece of paper. The message was written in English. It read: '*Keep your feet on the ground.*' It was unsigned. 'Some joker's having fun,' he said, searching among the pleasure-flushed crowds for one detested face. Lighting a cigar, he abruptly asked his companion: 'Can you get me some forged papers?'

'What's the matter? You in trouble?'

'Not for me, for a friend.'

Boris waved the cigar smoke away from his face and gazed at him with sad, reflective intensity. 'I'm not keen on getting mixed up with anything political.' He turned away and inclined his ear to the music as if there was nothing more to say.

A girl with swinging hips stood at the microphone snapping her fingers and singing in the American idiom. She wriggled suggestively and a group of stout men sitting with their homely wives began to applaud, pretending to be more drunk than they were.

Yes, everything nowadays is political, Hugo thought. The idea was, in an ironic sense, amusing. 'I suppose it's criminal,' he said. 'A youngster in trouble. Hurt someone in a fight.'

'You mean killed someone,' Boris corrected him.

Hugo hesitated briefly, then decided that frankness was necessary. He told him the story of Heinz Dieter and his father, omitting names and other vital details.

'Let's have a drink,' Boris said pleasantly. He called a tired-looking waitress over and took her hand playfully. '*Liebchen*, you're too beautiful to waste your time here,' he jested.

'I'll tell my husband,' the girl said. 'What would you like?'

Boris shrugged theatrically. 'If I was rich I wouldn't let a masterpiece like you slip through my fingers. Two cognacs, beautiful.' As she went to execute the order, he said: 'I know someone who'll do it. It's expensive, a thousand marks. He'll need some photographs and personal details – age, height, colouring, place of birth, that sort of thing.'

'There's something else,' Hugo said tentatively. 'A man named Sommer, Wolfgang Sommer. He works for the East German Government. Do you think you might help me find him through your contacts in East Berlin?'

'This is definitely political.'

'Not political. It's someone I used to know and I'd like to meet him again.'

'Why don't you just go along and ask for him? It's not a crime.'

'No, but I have reasons.' Hugo could almost see Boris's shrewd, quick intelligence at work, the sudden flicker of satisfaction in the black, lively eyes as his brain came up with the right answer.

'You're *meshugeh*,' the little man said, waving his hand in a gesture of disparagement. 'It doesn't pay, that sort of thing.' He leaned forward and spoke in an impassioned voice. 'Do you think I haven't thought of it? Sometimes I lie awake in the night thinking of Eichmann, the genius of the gas chambers. He's alive today somewhere and I kill him a hundred ways before I can get to sleep. But if he walked in here right now and sat down at this table and said: "Good evening, I'm Adolf Eichmann," – if that happened, do you know what I would do? I'd just walk away and cry. Because it's no damn use at all. No use!' The waitress came with the drinks. He took some coins from his pocket and threw them on the table. 'You know what?' he said to her. 'You're not even a little bit beautiful. Go and tell that to your husband. Tell him the Schwartze Boris said so.'

'He's drunk,' Hugo said anxiously. 'Take no notice.'

Boris looked hopelessly at the startled girl. 'Not drunk, just *verrükt*, like the rest of us. Why do you think we stay in this madhouse?' The coy violins were still making a pretty decoration interwoven with the rhythmic throbbing of drums, and dancers whirled among the revolving beams of coloured light. Boris said: 'Even the cognac's lousy tonight. Wait for me, I'll make a phone call.'

He stood up, a short, cocky little man in a sharp suit, and pushed his way through the crowd. The pneumatic messenger whirred like a cuckoo clock about to strike as another canister dropped. '*Co-operation could save us both a lot of trouble,*' the message read. '*What are you discussing with Boris?*'

Boris had a satisfied smile when he returned. 'I've fixed it up about your friend's papers,' he said. 'Let me have the details and the photographs tomorrow and they'll be ready in two or three days.'

'Can you help me with the other matter?'

'I'm against it. But I'll do what I can. It can't be difficult.'

'Thank you, Boris,' Hugo said. 'I hope you don't mind if we leave here separately.'

People were drifting on to the floor as the band struck up a catchy Latin-American rumba. 'You'd better go now,' Boris advised him. He indicated the direction with a nod of his head. 'There's a back entrance over there. I've used it before. I hope you have *mazil*.'

There was not, after all, any need for Boris's assistance with the 'other matter'. Hugo came back from Goldberg's funeral late the next morning and the telephone was ringing. It was Gustav Ulrich. They chatted casually for a minute or two, then Ulrich said: 'By the way, Hugo, a client of mine would like to meet you. A certain Herr Sommer.'

He was thinking of Goldberg lying with the other exiles in the Jewish cemetery. A crop of new marble tombstones had been planted there since the end of the war, carved with Hebrew characters. The solemn words of the ancient burial service had sounded thin and alien in the chill east wind sweeping across from the plains of Prussia, an immemorial, futile gesture. It seemed a waste of pain just then that Jews should still be buried in German soil and he shuddered at the thought that it would probably happen to him, too; although he could think of no place where his body would not lie strangely except, perhaps, the sea. Martin had been there, but his feelings were probably similar and they said little to each other.

'I'm sorry, Gustav,' Hugo said, puckering his forehead in the effort of concentration. 'What were you saying?'

'Herr Sommer,' Ulrich repeated distinctly. 'He thought you'd be interested in talking to him.' Hugo had difficulty with his breathing: 'Hello! Hello!' the lawyer said sharply. 'Are you there?'

'Yes… please go on.'

'He's here in Berlin for a few days,' the smooth, professional voice resumed. 'You'll find him at the Hotel Marienbad, room 109.'

'Good-bye,' Hugo said. The telephone clicked against his ear but it was some moments before he remembered to replace it on the cradle.

For the first time he was really frightened.

9

Handfuls of dirt had been thrown on the coffin and the rabbi was already walking away down the narrow path between the graves, his black robe flapping hard against his legs in the wind. A dozen middle-aged or elderly men followed, huddling into their overcoat collars and staring mournfully at the ground. Even Hugo seemed less coarsely alive in the black mourning clothes and respectable black Homburg that gave him the appearance of a synagogue elder.

'I hardly expected to see you here,' he remarked when they left the cemetery, turning briefly to shake the hand of a small man with a wispy blond beard flecked with grey, and eyes distorted by thick pebbled glass. 'Long life, Herr Bindermann,' he said dispiritedly. Herr Bindermann gave them both a melancholy smile and trudged away, one shoulder held higher than the other. Some of the other men were congregated on the pavement shaking one another's hands as if they were saying good-bye for ever. 'I never come to funerals,' Hugo grumbled in a low key. 'But Goldberg…' He shrugged massively. 'The proper way to celebrate this sort of thing is to get drunk and sing bawdy songs like the Irish. Or plant trees like the Israelis.'

Martin said: 'Did you have any idea that he'd die so suddenly?'

Hugo took off his hat and contemplated the crown. 'When you

get to a certain age you always hear about sudden death. People are around, and then they vanish.'

'Yes, but Goldberg…' Martin persisted with an uncomfortable urgency. 'A survivor of the concentration camp. He must have been dying for years.'

'I suppose so, but there was something terribly alive in Goldberg. He was a candle burning for the dead. He wouldn't let you forget. He came here, a bitter, flaming ghost, to haunt the Germans. He walked the streets accusing everybody with his two mad, hating eyes. That's all he lived for, but what a raging life it was, with the grief of all the Goldbergs in the world burning in it.' He released a weary sigh from the depths of his body. 'That's quite a funeral oration,' he said wryly. 'Can I give you a lift into town?'

Martin gazed away, down the avenue of trees that lined the street, his remorse unassuaged. 'No, thank you,' he said.

'Long life,' Hugo said as he got into the car and drove off.

When Martin reached the streetcar stop, Herr Bindermann was there peering with his near-sighted eyes at the timetable. He bobbed his head politely and smiled with the meek effacement of a man long accustomed to being a nobody, but when they sat out of politeness side by side on the car he directed several curious sidelong glances at Martin. Eventually, timid and ingratiating, he said: 'Excuse me, I did not catch your name.'

'Martin Stone,' Martin said.

'You are originally from Berlin?'

'Yes, I was born here.'

Herr Bindermann nodded gratefully. 'Ach, so,' he murmured. 'Ach, so.' The eyes blinked thoughtfully behind the thick lenses before he essayed a further impertinence. 'In which part?'

'The Grunewald, near Königsallee.'

The little man showed signs of suppressed excitement. 'You must forgive me,' he said, agitated and eager. 'It is not right that I should question you so much, but are you related to Herr Silberstein, the banker?'

'The banker' was an incongruous title when applied to the tired old man living frugally in Swiss Cottage on an income a banker might spend on cigars alone. It evoked a sharp but fleeting nostalgia for the prosperous world of childhood that had seemed so deceptively durable, when his father had been an urbane symbol of authority surrounded by soft-spoken, deferential men, and the harshness, the cruelty already abroad in Germany was kept waiting outside the door like a brutal policeman who yet knew his proper station in life.

'If you mean Otto Silberstein,' he said curiously, 'I'm his son.'

'Of course! I knew it immediately. Such a strong family resemblance! Your father's chin and the same broad, calm forehead. Such a kind man, Otto Silberstein, but how he could make us tremble with just a look!'

'Did you know my father then?'

The old man's eyes glistened with reminiscent tears. '*Aie, aie!* did I know your father! I worked for him for seventeen years. You tell him when you see him. Bindermann, from the Legal Department.' He put out a shaking, freckled hand and rested it on Martin's arm. 'I remember you, too, like yesterday, a small boy in knickerbockers. You would sometimes come to the office with your mother, such a beautiful, gracious lady.' The tears began to spill and Herr Bindermann blew his pointed red nose apologetically. 'I'm sorry,' he said. 'So few of us are left alive.

It's a great happiness for me to meet the son of my old employer.'

He went on to talk eagerly about the old days. Every year at Christmas there had been a banquet for the staff of the bank, and Herr Otto made a witty speech, and the directors danced with the wives of employees, and everybody got a little drunk, and the champagne corks you collected for luck! Then, in July, Herr Otto always hired a steamer for a trip down the Spree, with a band of musicians on board and plenty of sausages and beer, and everybody got a little drunk again, and they picked four-leafed clovers for luck! But there was no luck, after all. Young Herr Silberstein must forgive him once again if he could not control his tears. But it was a good omen to meet the heir of the Silbersteins in Berlin, and perhaps there would still be luck.

He spoke as if Martin could somehow reinstate the past: reopen the bank, put Bindermann back into the Legal Department, and continue the speeches his father had apparently been fond of making.

'Herr Bindermann, my father will be delighted to hear that I met you,' Martin said. 'Were you in a concentration camp?'

There was a nervous cough and the high shoulder rose apologetically. 'Would you believe it, my dear friend? I never left here at all. Not the whole time. It was foolish of me, but I thought things might get better. Then it was too late.' He went on to tell a remarkable story. His wife, he said with a hint of pride, was an Aryan. For more than four years she hid him in the house.

Again tears sprang to his weak eyes and he took off his thick bevelled glasses and wiped the lenses with a handkerchief: 'Every day she went out to work and locked the door. I would creep around like a mouse. She was the only human being I saw for four years, because I was afraid even to peep out of the window. We shared her rations, down to the last bread crumb. I owe my life to her, Herr Silberstein. I always think of that when I see the sunshine, and the trees, and the children playing in the streets.' He nodded his head several times and looked up with a shy, complacent smile. 'It's not so easy to hide yourself for four years without a soul knowing you exist. You have to think out every step you take, and ordinary things like going to the w.c. or having a bath can be quite a problem, really a difficult problem.'

Martin was deeply moved, not so much at the old man's ordeal as at the courage of his wife. Every good German justified Karin. *She* would have done it for me, he thought. And unexpectedly he remembered Erika, his Silesian nanny, and her big shadow in the warm glow of the nursery fire.

'Frau Bindermann must be a great woman,' he said fervently.

'*Jawohl*,' Herr Bindermann agreed. '*Ganz bestimmt.*' Suddenly the mild expression on his face slid away, replaced by something sly and loony. 'Mind you, Herr Silberstein, sitting in the cupboard all day long I used to ask myself: "Supposing somebody had a little white mouse in a cage and the landlady of the house said no mice allowed and if I catch one I'll feed it to my big savage cat, they'd also keep their little mouse hidden in a cupboard!" Don't you think so?'

'It wouldn't eat half your rations,' Martin objected tersely.

'That is correct, of course.' Nervously, Herr Bindermann rubbed the freckled skin on the back of his hand. 'It was wicked of me to think such thoughts. My wife, she was sensible and kind. She taught me to knit, and when we could get the wool I made socks and scarves and balaklavas. People used to buy them for the soldiers. It wasn't much, but it made me feel a bit more useful, you know.' He seemed oblivious to the irony. On the contrary, he smiled with satisfaction at the recollection of his labours and it was evident that he'd never allowed himself to connect the comforts he knitted 'for the soldiers' with their recipients, the Nazi troops who froze on the Eastern front. 'But it's all over now. Some people think it's wrong for Jews to stay here. Yet some of our people were here before the *Völkerwanderung* brought the Germanic tribes from Scandinavia and Denmark,' he went on in the pedantic accents of a professor instructing a backward student at a *Hochschule*. 'Now we have our synagogue, our small community, our Jewish schools. And so, in a strange way,' the old man continued with pathetic dignity, 'we have defeated Hitler, after all.'

The conviction these words were intended to convey was somewhat marred by the fact that they were spoken in a cautious undertone, with occasional uneasy glances at the other passengers on the car, as if Herr Bindermann nervously anticipated contradiction. Now his voice dropped so low that Martin had to incline his head until his ear was almost in contact with Herr Bindermann's wispy moustache. The near-sighted eyes darted frantically from side to side. 'Unfortunately, Herr Silberstein, there is still much anti-Semitism. You wouldn't believe it! Jewish cemeteries desecrated, people saying that not enough of us were gassed, big Nazis in the government! Every day it seems to get a little bit worse. We are having a meeting tomorrow to talk about it. Would you be so good as to come?'

Embarrassed and vaguely irritated, Martin declined. Herr Bindermann seemed much too anxious to involve him in an unwanted predicament. He felt like protesting vehemently that he was not the son of a German-Jewish banker any longer. He was Martin Stone, product of an English public school, an ex-private of a Welsh infantry regiment, at home drinking bitter ale in a London pub or reading the *Guardian* on the Stanmore line of the London Underground.

'Please,' Herr Bindermann said with gentle insistence. 'One of the great Berlin families, the Silbersteins. It would give us all encouragement if you could find the time. Just like having your father with us once more.' Again the reiteration of family honour, of inherited responsibility. 'In the old days there was no public dinner at which a Silberstein was not a principal speaker. They gave to every charity. They were princes in Berlin.'

Martin felt his resolve weakening. So the tradition of the House of Silberstein was not entirely extinguished. Two hundred years of history, which he'd thought reduced to a bundle of old documents, had left its traces in Germany. It reminded him of something he'd conveniently chosen to forget. There were Germans who shared his blood – third and fourth cousins, descendants of Silbersteins who had married Christians, who had shed the embarrassment of their origins and become provincial pastors, German aristocrats, *Bundestag* deputies, even followers of Hitler. Perhaps he did have an inherited responsibility.

Herr Bindermann scribbled an address on the back of a visiting card. 'We will expect you,' he said politely. With a profoundly respectful bob of the head he left the car and went slowly out of sight, watching his feet as though the habit of walking silently remained with him. And for the rest of the journey it was as though the Bindermann mouse nibbled at Martin's heart. He remembered;

perhaps, others, too, remembered. All at once it made Berlin seem a different place – a place one belonged to a little.

After all, was he so English? How would they be remembered in London, he and his kind? As temporary residents among the many thousands who occupied furnished rooms in the big, hospitable metropolis? As one species among a host of refugees from every land of intolerance, a class apart, with a voice, a manner, a shrillness that belonged nowhere in the strictly stratified society of England? As something of a burden on the conscience of liberal socialists; too-many-of-the-chosen-people-in-the-professions to the strident housewives of the Conservative Association; white Negroes to the League of Empire Loyalists? The kind and sentimental might think of Daniel Deronda. The others, the enemy, of Shylock, or Eliot's Jew squatting on the window-sill of the decayed civilisation he owns, or of Colleoni in *Brighton Rock* – the Tempter who looked like a man who owned the whole visible world, cash registers, police, prostitutes, parliament, and law, and whose face was the face of any middle-aged Jew, the mythological Wanderer trapped, as they saw it, in the web of his own evil. Judas.

That's how it was written into the civilisation of Europe. It was the classic Jewish dilemma. Once they offered you conversion, the forgiving embrace of an alien church; then the chimerical brotherhood of man. But all roads led to Auschwitz, to the Warsaw ghetto. Now there were only orange blossoms, kibbutzim and the Histadrut, and that might have been possible for him, too. But not after Karin; not – in a strange way – after Goldberg; not after the bitter, unforgettable taste of the city where you were born, which filled you with nostalgia for things you couldn't possibly remember.

The slight jolting rhythm of the streetcar, the blur of faces outside the window, the flow of traffic like a turbulent river, the sound of the dream-like symphonic city induced in him an unfamiliar depth of meditation. A clear bitter voice seemed to be speaking in his mind.

The truth, it said, is that you have been condemned to homelessness. Each generation passes on to the next its virus of insecurity. You learn the technique of survival, fearing ostentation as if it were a vice, censoring the act or gesture that may be pilloried as strangeness, observing yourself constantly through the eyes of an enemy. In a fortunate time a hundred years may pass and you will remain unmolested. You become incautious and show a coloured feather, a hand with six fingers, and another King arises to say: *Behold, the people of the children of Israel are more and mightier than we: Come, let us deal wisely with them; lest they multiply… and join also unto our enemies.* You who survive go out to the wilderness for forty years, the space of a generation, until a new, hard people advance upon another land of promise. The others, the Goldbergs, remain.

When the car stopped Martin alighted, stiff and cold as if he'd slept for hours in a position of cramped discomfort. And that's not the whole truth, he thought sombrely.

He was standing by the window, brooding over the events of the day, when there was a discreet knock at the door. It was Frau Goetz, with her little string shopping bag full of groceries. 'How did it go?' she asked anxiously. 'Poor Herr Goldberg, I've been praying for his soul.'

'You should have been praying for ours,' he said, remembering their complicity.

'I knew you'd take it like that.' Her face was creased with worry, and pink powder flaked from her skin like eczema. She looked ancient. 'Did you know he had a diseased heart? They told me at the hospital. They held an autopsy and the doctor said death could have come at any moment.'

'Nature was just hastened along,' he said.

She stared up at him, eyes gleaming fanatically. 'Nature has nothing to do with it. The Lord appoints the time.'

Martin felt an impulse to take hold of her and shake her violently. 'You were in Buchenwald. You saw them die in thousands. How can you possibly believe that?'

'I believe it. That is how it is.' Abruptly, she smiled with her usual bright good nature. 'Come and have some hot coffee,' she cajoled. 'I've bought a lovely cheesecake.'

'Not just now.' He was suddenly struck by the silence in the apartment. 'Isn't the Professor practising?'

Frau Goetz muted her husky, strident voice. 'Not today,' she said. 'It wouldn't be respectful.'

But soon there would be a new tenant in Goldberg's room, and tomorrow the perfectionist Japanese would be playing Mozart again, and the baritone voice of Richter would be declaiming new lines through the thin walls, and he would wake in the night to find Karin warm and womanly at his side. Even the feeling of remorse would have become weaker. God appointed things that way, too.

That night they dined at the Maison de France with Fred Adler and his little actress, Hedy. It was a kind of farewell celebration. Hedy was leaving for London to be auditioned for a part in a film and Fred was following her a few days later to fulfill a contract for a television play. They were buoyed up by Rhine champagne and Fred's contagious, slightly tipsy high spirits as he ushered his pretty partner on to the dance floor for yet another flamboyant fox-trot to the sedate music of the small band. Now they were making their way back to the table, laughing at some secret joke.

'What's funny?' Martin asked.

Fred's mobile face, adept at disguise, pretended bashfulness. 'You tell them, Hedy,' he urged.

'No,' she giggled. 'You tell them.'

Martin banged the table with the flat of his hand in exasperation. 'For heaven's sake, somebody tell us!'

They were all speaking English, and Karin, not understanding, looked at them with the puzzled, searching expression one sees on people who are deaf. She smiled anxiously from one to the other.

'Well, I will say it,' Hedy began, 'but you mustn't be cross with me. Promise?' She crossed her hands demurely in her lap, glanced at Martin from under her long lashes, and giggled again. 'You see, Freddie was watching you both when we were dancing, and I was watching, and – oh! I can't,' she spluttered. 'It's so silly.'

'Please speak German,' Karin pleaded. 'I would also like to laugh.'

But Fred was already rather bored. He thought for a moment and said: 'It won't be funny at all when we tell you. It was just the way you both looked. I said to Hedy: "You wouldn't think love agreed with them. They've only just got to know each other, but you'd think they'd been married twenty years!" 'Well', he ended lamely, 'that's all it was. It just touched our funny-bone, I suppose.'

'You should have it seen to,' Martin observed dryly. Karin's work-roughened palm touched him under the table and their fingers clung together in a brief gesture of affection. After a moment he gently pushed her away, but the movement dislodged a champagne glass, and as it splintered on the floor a few fragments were crushed under his foot. He was immediately reminded of the Jewish marriage custom, when the bridegroom seals the ceremony by stamping on a wine-glass; the significance was not overlooked by Fred, either.

'*Mazil tov*,' the latter murmured slyly. 'That always means good luck. Talking of marriage,' Fred went on in an elaborately off-hand manner, 'Hedy and I have an announcement to make, and this is as good an occasion as any.' He kissed the nape of the girl's neck and she shuddered deliciously. 'We're engaged. No ring, no fuss, no celebration. We're saving it for London. It should make a good paragraph in the evening papers. "Actor marries German sex-kitten."' He smiled nervously and tried vainly to catch Martin's eye. Karin gave the little actress a sisterly kiss and they called for a fresh bottle of champagne and drank a toast to the future bride.

Perhaps it would work for them, Martin thought enviously. Hedy would decorate London and be adored. But he couldn't imagine Karin wifely in Golders Green, jostling with Jewish matrons in the super-market, or sipping cocktails at parties with the young Jewish intelligentsia who were his friends. Even less could he visualise her coming back with him to the mouldering old house in Swiss Cottage, climbing the stairs to the second-floor flat, being introduced to old Mrs Klausner, Dr Ollendorf, and the other refugees. Some of them would, perhaps, nod politely and pass on, too mild and defeated to do more. But his father was different, as bereaved and bitter as Goldberg.

Pushing the thought aside, he asked Karin to dance, surrendering to the spell of her closeness. It was extraordinary the way her physical presence could console him, but the mood of departure seemed even to have invaded the music, so that it became the last waltz, the farewell embrace before the train and all its lights dwindle away into the dark.

She said: 'How much longer are you staying?'

'I'm not sure,' he replied evasively.

'I must know how long we've got. A month?'

'Less,' he said.

'A fortnight? A week?'

'Maybe a week,' he said. 'I have to think of my job. They only gave me a month's leave. And there's my father. He doesn't even know where I am. So far he thinks it's Switzerland. I asked somebody to mail him postcards from Zürich.' When he got back they would still be there on the mantelpiece in his father's room, tucked into the book-ends along with the views of foreign lakes and winter mountains and Cornish fishing villages, souvenirs of other, forgotten, travels. The dust would gather and in time this would be forgotten, too. He didn't believe it, but he had to go through the motions of belief. She would burn in his body like a fever, like a long delirium in the mind, and then, maybe, the slow convalescence would begin.

Karin said: 'If I came to England, do you think we could meet sometimes?'

'Perhaps I've got a wife,' he said. 'You never asked me.'

She turned her face away. 'I'm asking you now.'

'There's no wife,' he said. 'That's not the problem.'

'Is it impossible for you to forget that I'm German?' she demanded quietly.

'Let's try not to hurt each other,' he pleaded.

'It's too late to think about that, isn't it?' She said it without reproach and with a kind of resignation, wielding the scourge of meekness with skill, he thought with a grudging tenderness.

'Yes, it's too late,' he said.

Later, he was with Fred Adler in the men's room. The actor combed his sleek, brilliantined hair and stared meditatively into the mirror. 'I bet you were surprised about Hedy and me,' he said, elaborately casual. 'It shows you're never safe. I thought I was too fond of women to get married and wives are more expensive than mistresses.'

Martin said: 'Perhaps it's none of my business, but what will your family say?'

'Oh, I don't know,' Fred replied with an uneasy laugh. 'No one could object to Hedy. She comes from Württemberg, a simple, provincial girl. Her father's a cellist, non-political, a real nice chap. He's played in the Festival Hall half a dozen times.'

'How does he feel about it?'

'Oh, fine. He's quite pleased. But then, artists are a kind of inter-national.' Fred gave an unexpected grimace of resignation. 'You see, I'm trying to take everything into account. You wouldn't think marrying a girl was so complicated.'

When they left the Maison de France great clusters of people were coming out of the cinemas, moving uncertainly in different directions like ants drunk on aphis milk. They said good-bye rather awkwardly.

'We'll all meet again in London,' Fred said, sentimental with champagne. 'We'll have a reunion party in the Ivy, or in the Fitzroy. Good old English beer.'

Martin said: 'I'll give you a ring when I get back.' Karin stood looking at him with dumb, reproachful misery. He shared the same pain, needed the same sympathy, but thought: What else can the union of our bodies produce but this sterility?

The meeting was in a private room over a restaurant. The smell of cooking came up from below and the window framed a view of engine-sheds and rusty metal rails curving into the *Bahnhof Zoo*. A score or so of elderly men, several of whom he recognised as having been among the mourners at Goldberg's funeral, sat on rows of hard chairs arranged in the centre of the room. There was only one woman, middle-aged and well dressed, who sat by the door at a small table taking the names of people as they arrived.

'It's unusual to see a young man here,' she said, gazing at him with a frankness that bordered on insolence. 'Can I have your name?' He gave it to her and she acknowledged the information with a nod of her sleekly coiffured, greying head.

Clearly she had once been beautiful, and Martin saw immediately the bitterness that had ruined her looks. She had a broad, calm forehead and luminously intelligent eyes of clear amber. The nostrils of her small nose were delicately flared, giving the impression of a proud and spirited character, her skin was still smooth and supple; but bitterness had eaten into her lips like acid. They were permanently pursed and withered in a way that lipstick could not disguise, and the effect was somehow appalling – a lovely image ruined by one small, hideous detail. It was the kind of face that could haunt one for a lifetime.

'Don't you get young people at these meetings?' he asked, trying hard not to avert his gaze.

'There are no young people,' she said with a bleak smile.

Herr Bindermann hurried over and fussily introduced him to several people. 'Herr Silberstein, the banker's son,' he said over and over while Martin shook hands with a succession of grey little men who smiled and nodded their heads with anxious friendliness.

Eventually the chairman called the meeting to order and, in somewhat perfunctory tones, as if repeating a familiar brief, spoke of the efforts of the community to establish normal relations with the German people, of the sympathy they received from the authorities, and the problem created by the continued existence of Nazi sentiments in certain unregenerate but – he was happy to say – as yet uninfluential sections of the population. Then began a rather lengthy recital of recent anti-Jewish incidents, of former Nazis reinstated in public positions, and of the delaying tactics employed in certain courts when Jewish claims for compensation were being considered.

This recital had a profoundly depressing effect upon Martin, as, indeed, upon the rest of the assembly. The old men exchanged vague glances of foreboding, and one of them rose unsteadily and began a rambling account of his experiences in various concentration camps until he reached a point of confusion from which he retreated by abruptly sitting down again. He was followed by a stout, flustered man who entered into an impassioned explanation of the reasons why he had returned to Germany from Israel. Others also spoke, often irrelevantly, but whatever was said evoked the same sad agreement from the elderly audience. It was apparent that the true function of the meeting was to bring these people together, to offer them a brief escape from the ordeal of their lonely, comfortless existence.

Suddenly Herr Bindermann put up a timid hand and caught the chairman's eye. 'I wonder if perhaps our guest, Herr Silberstein, would care to say something?' he suggested.

The chairman smiled approvingly and the old men turned eagerly in his direction, hoping for once that a voice would speak to them with vigour, confidence, and hope. But he knew he had nothing to offer them.

Unlike Goldberg, they seemed too apathetic even for hatred, existing only as a memorial to the dead, the living ghosts that reminded one how final was the dissolution of the German-Jewish civilisation of Lessing, Heine, Einstein, and Freud. He stood up and apologised for not having anything to say, watching them shrug away yet another disappointment, aware of the woman smiling at him with her bitter, withered mouth, and of the meek reproach of Herr Bindermann's lifted shoulder.

After the meeting had passed a formal resolution noting with concern the recrudescence of anti-Semitic incidents in Germany, coffee was served and the occasion became a social gathering. The woman crossed the room, walking erectly and with a certain arrogance past the groups of elderly Jews, as if she disdained them.

'Have you a cigarette?' she asked. 'I've used up all mine.' She spoke in English, with an imperceptible accent, and Martin had the impression that this, too, was a rejection of the company in which they found themselves.

'You've obviously lived in England,' he said, offering her his cigarette-case.

She produced an elegant gold lighter and shared the flame with him. 'Actually, no, but I spent the war years in America. My husband died there.' Her lovely amber eyes held his glance. 'He was a magistrate here in Berlin and much older than I. I married when I was eighteen. I'm not quite as much of a museum piece as the rest of them.' She interrupted his polite gesture of remonstrance. 'Oh, don't bother to say anything. I'm sure you wonder why I'm here at all. The truth is I have expensive tastes and my widow's pension isn't exactly munificent, so I supplement it with some secretarial work. It's not much fun for a woman.'

'Haven't you got many friends here?' he asked. Even without looking he knew, by the shape of the words she uttered, that her mouth had twisted up.

'What sort of friends can I have?' she countered, her voice hard and metallic. 'German men? The storm troopers of the bedroom?'

Where else in the world would you walk into a room, be engaged in conversation by a stranger, and witness so naked an exposure of a corrosive loneliness? 'You shouldn't stay in Germany,' was all he could say.

'Why are you here?' she asked quietly.

He began to explain, but she stared piercingly into his face so that her gaze seemed to transfix him with its remorseless insight. A faint mocking smile touched her embittered mouth.

'Yes,' she said. 'I've told myself the same thing. A temporary visit, a matter of expediency. But it isn't convincing, is it? We come here because we hope to begin again. We refuse to accept our rejection. But we find that Germany still causes us pain, and the temptation offered by suffering proves as compelling as the temptation of love. Perhaps it's the sort of thing a woman understands better than a man.'

'It must be,' he said harshly. 'I'll never really know because I'll be leaving in a few days.'

'You'll be back again,' she said. 'A pity you're not twenty years older. Hell might be a more congenial place if two people shared it.' With a courteous nod she left him, panic rising, watching Herr Bindermann advance stealthily across the room to remind him again of his unwanted, inescapable responsibility. And soon he would be with Karin again, the tender burden oppressing his heart, entrapped in her compulsive embrace like a fly in a silken web.

10

The telephone rang with a repetitive insistence that made Hugo's body shudder even before the sound penetrated his sub-conscious. He opened his smarting eyelids reluctantly and a chink of early morning brightness struck his eyeballs like a shower of sand. Immediately he remembered that this was the day when he would finally come face to face with Putzi von Schlesinger. His heart began its uneven knocking. It was pain to roll free of the rumpled blue sheets, to walk unsteadily to the window and drag the curtains together to shut out the light; pain to think that today, after twenty-five years, he would reach the end of an obsession that had persisted half his lifetime. Most of the night, watching cigar after cigar smouldering in the darkened bedroom, he'd rehearsed the meeting in different ways, exploring the half-obliterated contours of the past until many memories became scaldingly alive: fragments of conversation, the texture of voices, caresses, leather thongs biting into his flesh, and the experience of lying on a stone floor staring up at the Brownshirt who bestrode his body with polished jack-boots. Pig, filth, Jew, degenerate. Urine pouring on to his face from the obscenely erect penis. How much he had learned in that terrible moment about cruelty!

And he'd come back to the thought of Putzi, flailing him with anger and contempt, reminding him that the murder of a

Canadian prisoner of war had made him a war criminal, that his impersonation of a dead corporal would no longer protect him. Then, again, Hugo'd rehearsed another encounter in which he neither threatened nor accused but only asked: Why? That was what he needed more than anything, the nakedness of confession. Lying sleepless in the dark, hypnotised by the red glow of his smouldering cigar, he'd thought that only truth could compensate for the wasted years. There was no justice, no retribution, only the hope that by achieving understanding one could at last begin to recover. The long night had ticked away interminably, ending in an exhausting conflict with his imagination in which he'd sought to visualise Putzi corroded by the years, the Portland-blue eyes faded, the narcissistic features blurred and coarsened, the lean youthful body corpulent and middle-aged. But the image of his betrayer remained as incorruptible as a Greek marble, inflicting its mocking punishment even when sleep took his tired brain by surprise.

The telephone was still ringing, a high-pitched, neurotic signal of warning. Eek... eek... eek... eek... 'Yes, what is it?' he asked tersely.

The manageress's voice replied, rather flustered: 'I'm sorry to disturb you. There's a man to see you.'

'A man?' His heart troubled him again, hammering with fear. The meeting was at three in the afternoon, at the hotel. It would be characteristic of Putzi to devise an unexpected strategy, ambushing him while his mind was still clogged with sleep. 'Did he give his name?'

'Yes, Herr Krantz,' she said, cool but astonished. 'Boris. Shall I ask him to make an appointment?' Her manner implied that the man was clearly undesirable and that she would be happy to save her employer the trouble of getting rid of him.

'That's perfectly all right. I'll see him now,' he said with a feeling of reprieve, and immediately buzzed Heinz Dieter. 'Breakfast ready?' he asked almost gaily. 'I'll need two glasses. Your new identity is on its way up.'

Boris brought the cold brisk air of the street into the stuffy bedroom, his pouchy twinkling eyes taking in its luxury with evident amusement. He twitched the curtains apart the better to see the rich carpet, the tinted mirrors, and the enormous sybaritic bed, and smiled at the room with sardonic approval. 'Could I borrow it for a special date?' he asked. 'I might want to impress a baroness some time.'

His wiry, shoulder-shrugging Jewish wit was precisely the right antidote for the depressed mood of the morning. It made Hugo feel a whole lot better. 'A housemaid would be more impressed,' he said cheerfully, mocking his own vulgarity. Self-esteem was not one of his vanities; he was among the least admirable men he knew. 'You'll stay for breakfast, Boris?'

The little man shrugged. 'Why not?' He pulled an envelope from his pocket and laid it carefully on the bedside table, a gesture of salesmanship that emphasised the value of the goods. 'A lovely job,' he said respectfully. 'You won't have any trouble with this.'

The forged passport was made out in the name of Adolf Porsch, but it bore the smiling photograph of Heinz Dieter. Hugo had a strange feeling that it accomplished more than a nominal change of identity. The handsome young German smiling eagerly out of the photograph reminded him of other young Germans, goose-stepping in athletic formations round the *Sportspalast*. One could imagine the case history. Date of birth was given as October, 1936; place, Nürnberg. He was probably named after the Führer at a secular christening in a stuffy middle-class parlour crowded with provincial bourgeois in their Party uniforms, among his baptismal gifts a dagger decorated with a swastika. The end of the war would have interrupted a *Herrenvolk* education and he would have watched Hermann Göring descending from a prison van at the Nürnberg Court with awed astonishment, not understanding why the toy Brownshirt uniform and the swastika dagger must be hidden away, not understanding any of it at all, but modelling himself for a while on another hero, the G.I. spendthrift with chocolate and canned meats. It might be Heinz Dieter's destiny to continue the development of Adolf Porsch and abandon his own.

All over Germany people had been changing identities. New names and new histories appeared on their passports, and often it seemed that they had accomplished a miraculous trans-formation into affable citizen-democrats of the Federal Republic, their aggression peacefully channelled into work or business enterprise. It made one wonder if there was something in the ancient magic of names: a new name, a new persona. Perhaps even Putzi. He might turn his face to the light and look at you with the eyes of a dead S.S. corporal...

'Do you see anything wrong with it?' Boris asked, a trifle worried by Hugo's lengthy scrutiny of the document.

'No,' Hugo said. 'Your artist must have had plenty of practice.'

'Passports are one of the most thriving rackets in Europe. There are always refugees.'

'And secret agents,' Hugo added, thinking of Kane.

Boris smiled tolerantly at the other's naïveté. 'There's no room for private enterprise there. Every government has its little gang of forgers busily producing documents. Whatever else is wrong, the papers are always in order.'

Heinz Dieter came in with the breakfast-tray. 'Good morning, Herr Porsch,' Hugo greeted him. Heinzi grimaced. 'Is that the best name you could find?' He held the passport at arm's length, admiring his own picture. 'I don't look like a Porsch. With a name like that you need a pig's snout.'

'That can also be arranged,' Boris murmured dryly, perplexed and repelled by the relationship that was reputed to exist between the men, for one of whom, Hugo, he entertained a warm affection. He flattered himself that he was a student of human nature, but was puzzled that among the Jews who felt impelled to remain in Germany so many were sexually abnormal. The country seemed to exert a morbid fascination over them.

Hugo interpreted these reflections with fair accuracy, for Boris's shrewd black eyes were his most articulate feature. 'Have some coffee,' he suggested amiably. 'Or cognac. We have to live the way we are, Boris. With or without our pig snouts.'

The reply was an immense, expressive shrug, a whole philosophy of resignation in the face of an incomprehensible existence. 'As long as you've got your health and strength,' Boris said inevitably, accepting both the coffee and the cognac. 'Where's your friend going for his holiday?'

'How about Tangier?' Heinz Dieter suggested enthusiastically.

Boris vetoed it with a wave of his hand. 'You've been reading too many books. What would a respectable boy from Nürnberg be doing in Tangier? France is an idea, or England. A working vacation with some student organisation.'

'What a thoroughly Porsch-like idea!' Hugo commented with a dry laugh. 'I approve of that, don't you, Heinzi?'

'Anything you say,' Heinz Dieter agreed apathetically. 'I'm not afraid of work.' He trailed out of the room, crestfallen.

An awkward silence intervened, but this time Hugo did not seek to interpret it. He thought uneasily that not many hours were left. It was as though something in his life was coming to an end, and it seemed like a premonition of death.

'I'm meeting my friend Sommer today,' he said.

Boris looked at him sharply. 'You found him, then?'

'He found me.' He explained it all – the telephone call from Gustav Ulrich, the special delivery messenger bringing a type-written note, the appointment at three in the afternoon.

'You're not falling for that?' Boris exclaimed incredulously, spreading his palms in a wide-open gesture of appeal. 'What kind of a *shmock* are you?'

'I'm the kind of *shmock* you think I am. I'll be there.'

'This is the twentieth century,' Boris said sombrely. 'Don't drink anything you're offered. Don't turn your back. Keep your hand on the door-knob. Best of all, don't go.'

He dressed himself with special care, choosing the right suit, the right tie, discreetly expensive cuff-links. Hoping to look at least reminiscently like the young Hugo Krantz leaving his flat in the Tiergarten to attend a rehearsal of his latest revue, he succeeded only in impersonating a gross Teutonic business-man with a prosperous shop in the Kurfürstendamm. Then, at a quarter to three, he was walking in the cool spring sunshine among the crowds of window-shoppers, a light breeze ruffling his thin hair. It was Wednesday, an ordinary afternoon. In the window of Kranzler's the same plump women manipulated their pastry forks with devout absorption; vaguely familiar faces glanced at him from the glass-enclosed terrace at Kempinski's; a girl in a leather coat flourished the early edition of *Der Abend* before passers-by. A lump rose in his throat and he experienced a vague sense of loss. It had always meant home to him, his birthright, and he would never belong. Nothing would compensate for that rejection. Now it was as if he was preparing to bid it a final farewell, and he would have liked to do so sadly and leisurely, driving slowly through the Grünewald and stopping somewhere by the river, watching the boats on the lake, the water sparkling with sunshine, the lovers walking under the trees...

At two minutes to three he was crossing the empty foyer of the hotel, talking to the desk clerk through a muffled silence that made his voice sound penetrating and impersonal, the metallic voice that speaks out of small boxes, announcing the departure of trains, impending catastrophes. Every movement seemed inevitable, synchronised to the explosive zero. As the electric clock began to strike the hour a page-boy led him past the banked flowers in the florist's windows, the girl manicuring her nails at the desk of the theatre ticket agency, the white-coated barber seen through glass bending devotedly over the upturned face of his client like a surgeon conducting a grave and delicate operation. With a feeling of automatism he ascended to the first floor and trod docilely behind the diminutive, uniformed figure along the airless corridor. Room 109. A small gloved hand opened to receive his coin and the boy retreated, dwarf-like and symbolic, the glossy back of his head reflecting the dim white lights of the long ceiling. Hugo's finger hesitated on the bell. He stood motionless, in a state of blank reverie, and stared at the polished surface of the door. Farther along the corridor an elderly man emerged from another room, walking stiffly through the dream with a polite greeting and a casual glance from his bored, hooded eyes.

The hypnosis suddenly wore off, leaving things hard and clear but still incredible. He pressed the bell once, an interval of silence, twice. The silence now seemed one of somebody listening in a concealed place. Cautiously he tried the knob. The door opened.

At first the room seemed empty. Curtains were drawn, allowing only sufficient daylight through to block out the shapes of furniture and disclose the tidy, untenanted solitude of the place. But as he turned his head a shadowy figure was outlined in a doorway, standing with its back to the light. 'Putzi?' he said tentatively, taking a step forward. The figure stepped forward too. Then he realised that he'd addressed his own reflection in a full-length mirror attached to a wardrobe. There was the click of a door opening and a man in shirt-sleeves entered from an adjoining room, adjusting his tie, as if interrupted in the process of dressing.

'Good afternoon,' he said. 'I am Wolfgang Sommer.'

The shock of the stranger's unexpected appearance was immediately succeeded by a horrible dismay. It wasn't Putzi! The man was perhaps forty years old, middle-sized, with a barrel-chested military bearing. He looked authentically like an ex-corporal who had become soft on sedentary duties. His pallid complexion was disfigured by blotches, and spots of blood on the shaven areas of the face had been dabbed with a chalky powder. 'I know who you are, and you know who I am,' he said, observing Hugo guardedly. 'Perhaps you can explain why you've been so interested in me.' Extracting a cigarette from a packet which bore an East German brand name, he rolled it round his tongue to wet the tip before lighting it, then settled into an arm-chair and relaxed into a posture of receptive attention.

'Are you really Sommer?' Hugo asked in a tone of disbelief.

The man inhaled a mouthful of smoke and nodded silently.

'I have reason to doubt that,' Hugo said.

With an ironical smile, as if indulging the whim of an amiable lunatic, the stranger produced a wallet from his pocket and extracted from it an identity-card which he held up to view. It bore a recognisable likeness of himself and was made out in the name of Sommer, Wolfgang.

Hugo stared at it in bewilderment; it was like being in the midst of an hallucination that brought into question his whole existence. Twenty-five years. He repressed a hysterical impulse towards laughter, thinking that at some point the border-line had disappeared, he'd begun to believe in his own extravaganza. The long quest for Putzi had brought him face to face with his own reflection in the wardrobe mirror of a hotel room. At any moment the quiet, strong men in white would enter and take him back to his haunted loneliness.

'There must be some mistake,' he said, turning to go. 'I expected to find someone else.'

Sommer dropped his cigarette into an ash-tray and slowly got to his feet, barring the door. 'That's not good enough,' he said gruffly. 'You've been chasing me and I demand a full explanation.'

'You demand an explanation.' Hugo laughed shortly. 'I'm the one who should demand an explanation. You have no business being here at all. You were killed in Budapest in 1944 by a shell splinter. You're a dead man.' He felt giddy and light-headed. 'Maybe we're all dead,' he said, smiling. 'That's probably the answer.'

While he was talking the man watched him grimly, uncertain of how to interpret these curious remarks. 'Don't try and turn it into a joke,' he said. 'My name is Sommer. I'm alive and kicking.'

Hugo performed a stiff ironical bow. 'I congratulate you,' he said. He was about to push past when a sudden suspicion entered his head. If Putzi was, in fact, alive, he would be capable of inventing precisely this situation. He, Hugo, could only recognise Sommer from a fifteen-year-old snapshot of three men, one of whom was Putzi, another Gross, the man in East Berlin who had told him that Putzi had been taken prisoner. The third man was pointed out as Sommer. Hardly a satisfactory basis for identification, and Putzi would find it amusing to devise a trick of this sort. Almost any German of the right age could claim to be Sommer, and how could he disprove it?

Then he remembered Stuttgart. The cottage reeking of boiled linen and the old asthmatic woman wiping her eyes on the hem of her apron as she wept for her long-lost nephew. Frau Herta Sommer, he'd called her, but she corrected him. Not Herta. Herta was dead! She herself was the spinster sister, Rosa Kraft.

'What's your aunt's name?' he asked cunningly.

Sommer looked nonplussed. 'My aunt?' he said.

'Yes, the one in Stuttgart.'

'Why the devil should I tell you my aunt's name?' the man blustered. He stepped close and seized Hugo's lapels in both his hands. The blotches on his skin showed blood-red. 'Just remember one thing. I don't like you prying into my affairs. I want no more trouble from you.' Reluctantly he relinquished his grip and stepped aside, but as Hugo was about to leave, the man caught his arm and stared into his face with demonic hate. 'Why don't you get out of Germany?' he said. 'We don't want any of your kind.'

The sun was still shining in the Kurfürstendamm, striking a glitter from glass and chromium and glossy cars. But Hugo walked down the bright road as through a dark corridor, exiled from the life around him because he alone seemed to have no sense of direction, no destination. The search for Putzi had sustained him in a way he could not pretend to understand fully. It had become a substitute for religion, ambition, friendship – incomprehensible by any rational standards. And yet if he never confronted Putzi he would never be free of him. Only that meeting could cut away the diseased past. The day he looked Putzi in the face would be the day Putzi died, and he would at last be able to forget the ugly history of Germany, along with his hatred of the man who had betrayed him. Somehow or other, therefore, the search must continue. The place to begin was at the point where his inquiries appeared to have gone wrong. He must return to East Berlin and find Gross again, have another look at that snapshot, if necessary set off in an entirely new direction.

Having reached this conclusion, he was immediately impatient to lose no time. Life had resumed its irresistible momentum; he had recovered his sense of purpose. The car was parked outside the shop, and as he drove away the powerful engine communicated its vigour to his body, reminding him what it was like to be young and optimistic. With a careless disregard of traffic regulations, he drove recklessly through the city, pulling up with a long screech of brakes for the cursory police examination at the Brandenburg

Gate. The West Berlin policeman was in a surly mood and insisted on searching the luggage compartment.

'I'll have a body in it on the return journey,' Hugo told him maliciously.

'Cut out the funny stuff!' the man snapped, and waved him on.

He had no difficulty in finding the street where Gross lived. Some children were playing in the stone-flagged passage of the house and a grey, withered little man with a leather apron came down the stairs carrying a steaming jug of coffee. Gross, he remembered, lived on the second floor, but the piece of white cardboard on which his name and trade had been written was gone. For a long while no one answered his knock; the person who did so came from the other side of the narrow landing. She was a young woman, harassed-looking, whose fair hair was drawn into a severe bun at the back of her head.

'Herr Gross isn't in?' Hugo asked with a profound sense of discouragement at this new disappointment.

The woman said: 'He doesn't live here any more.'

'Do you know where he's gone?'

'People go. They don't always tell you where,' she replied with unexpected bitterness.

Hugo was conscious of the envious scrutiny that was directed at his prosperous clothes. She mistrusted him for not being poor, and he caught something of her misery, like an infection. 'I'd be most grateful if you could help me,' he said. 'How long is it since Herr Gross left?'

She shrugged, looking at him steadily; then, with a smile, leaned against the frame of the door, exaggerating the curve of her hip. 'I'd like to help you,' she said in a husky voice.

The gesture embarrassed him as feminine coquetry always could. If it was only money—— 'About Herr Gross,' he began again uneasily.

'Would you like to come in for a moment?' The woman still held his gaze hopefully, and smoothed her skirt with a slow, sensuous gesture like a caress.

'I haven't the time,' he said. 'I'm very anxious to find Herr Gross.'

Perhaps his instinctive revulsion had communicated itself to her, or she'd suddenly become afraid. 'You'd better ask the police,' she said angrily. 'I can't tell you anything.' The door slammed behind her and he was left alone on the dusty landing, oppressed by his own inadequacy. Downstairs he entered the leather shop in search of information. The withered little man whom he'd passed in the passage was sitting at a bench cutting out handbags.

'Gross, the carpenter?' he said, lifting his spectacles on to his forehead and scratching the bridge of his nose. 'He was arrested.'

Hugo had an uncomfortable presentiment. 'Do you know why?' he asked.

The little man obdurately shook his head. 'I know nothing about that,' he said. 'Nothing at all.'

He drove back to Berlin, the old depression settling like marsh gas on his mind. Body and spirit craved relief, the alcoholic euphoria that made everything seem trivial – pain, disappointment, futility. Dusk was rising like a cloud of blue smoke. He remembered the exhausting conflicts of the long sleepless night and decided to take a hot bath, a sedative, and go to bed. At the Brandenburg Gate the same policeman waved him to a stop and looked into the luggage compartment again.

'Looking for the body?' Hugo asked sourly.

The policeman moved round to the side of the car and peered through the glass. He wrote something in his notebook. 'You can't take chances', he said, stepping back into the road and signalling him on. 'And watch your driving, or there will be a body in the car.'

Too tired to argue, he moved on past the burned-out Reichstag, the Russian war memorial, the ruined acres of the Tiergarten. They projected an image of desolation which confirmed all that was most pessimistic in his mood, and he thought idly that it would be an apt irony if he aimed his car at the Column of Victory, accelerated, and smashed himself into that arrogant phallus of German chauvinism. It stood for everything that had finally destroyed the Germany he loved – the Germany of pickled pork and gargantuan drinkers; of Goethe and Schiller and Heine, and even more the Germany of Max Ernst, Reinhardt, Caligari, of rib-tickling, bottom-slapping obscenity, of the Black Forest, the Rhine wine harvesters, the gravely pompous Hanseatic masters and merchants; the Germany that had once been vulgar, robust, and intelligent and had sacrificed everything to its lust for cruelty...

When he reached home the apartment was deserted. There was no Heinz Dieter to run his bath, pour his drink, bore him with trivial gossip. The false passport was missing. Kane, he thought immediately.

He called down to the shop. The manageress was vague. She had seen his secretary leave with, she thought, another man. Or the man had met him outside the front door. About an hour earlier.

There was no sign of any packing having been done. Heinz Dieter's bedroom was neat, the wardrobe was still full of his clothes, and he'd left a wallet with money on the dressing-table.

But he didn't return that night. Nor did he show up sheepishly the next morning with a long detailed story of amorous adventure. Instead, at first it seemed by coincidence, the postman delivered a brown paper packet with the mail. It was the diary he'd allowed Heinz Dieter to give to Kane. Hugo noticed a strange thing when he examined it. Every single reference to Putzi, no matter how disguised, had been carefully snipped out. There was only one man capable of interpreting these references – Putzi von Schlesinger himself. And in the cryptogrammatic technique that this suggested, he read a message from Putzi, a challenge. Yes, Hugo Krantz, I am alive. And Heinz Dieter's disappearance was part of the cryptogram.

11

She said: 'You'll never forgive me for Goldberg. I can only say this now, in the dark, lying in your arms.'

She said: 'If we'd never met it wouldn't have happened. That's the answer to everything.'

And in the long shuddering moment, her breath coming fast, she said: 'Kill me! Kill me...'

He seemed to float for hours on the surface of sleep, enormously distended by darkness. Fantasies germinated, grew monstrously, and dispersed without trace. There was Goldberg walking with the million-footed dead, and the poor mad face was his own. His father passed through a narrow door and emerged naked, and that, too, was somehow terrible. In a stark white room, in a hospital bed, Karin said: 'Here is our child,' and the dead face of Lise, his sister, lay between her thighs. When even that had gone, when he recognised with an acute clarity that he was there by Karin's side and would never be able to reject her, that she would always be a burden of tenderness, he thought: 'It makes a whore of me. I'm selling myself for love.'

Then, abruptly, he was in the midst of a vivid dream, a child again. The flames of a winter fire made huge shadows on the nursery ceiling, and outside the window the deep winter snow also reflected the colour and shadow of flame. Erika, his Silesian nurse, came in with a strange man. '*I'm going to marry him,*' she said, seating herself and taking the man on her lap.

'*You're not going to marry him,*' he said, beginning to cry. '*When I grow up you're going to marry me.*'

Erika laughed. '*Your papa wouldn't like that. I'll be old, an old Christian woman.*'

'*You won't be old,*' he screamed. '*You'll never be old. I'll kill him and then you'll have to marry me.*'

The hammering on the door was an inevitable extension of this nightmare, so that he awoke, trembling, a prisoner of the past, imagining in one swift moment of terror the iron-visaged men, the journey through dark and silent streets, the cattle-truck to Auschwitz. By his side Karin's pale, startled face amidst her tumbled black hair was like a suppressed scream, and he realised instantly that her fear was grounded in a more contemporary predicament. But it was another aspect of the same history. Uniforms altered: the nocturnal rap on the door, the callous face under the peaked hat, the language of cruelty – these remained unchanged.

'Who can it be?' she asked, her voice small, infantile, shrinking into the room's darkness. And looking into her eyes, enlarged with fright, he knew how she was the day the soldiers came.

'It's nothing,' he said. 'I love you,' defending her against the pain of it. 'Put something on,' he added gently, watching as she pulled back the bedclothes obediently and stood naked on the threadbare rug.

'You're not wearing anything yourself,' she reminded him with a shivering laugh, as she got back into bed.

He hurried into his dressing-gown as the knocking was resumed. Frau Goetz could be heard in the corridor contending with a blurred male voice. Wide awake now, Martin was seized by a new misgiving. Perhaps his father had come from England to confront him. Or the police, something to do with Goldberg's death. He would almost welcome that; it might help to relieve the lingering unassuaged ache of guilt.

But when he opened the door it was to find Hugo on the threshold, his massive body incongruously leaning for support on the tiny frame of Frau Goetz. He was very drunk, but she looked more inebriate than he did, her dyed yellow hair straggling from under a disarranged hair-net, her kimono gaping open to reveal the stringy sinews of her neck, one hand inadequately clutching Hugo's big belly in an effort to prop him up.

'I couldn't stop him,' she gasped. 'He's in a shocking state!'

Hugo gave him a foolish, half-apologetic grin and sketched a gesture of greeting in the air. 'Trust I'm not disturbing you, old boy,' he said in carefully modulated English, and staggered a few steps into the room. Some dim war-time memory groped in his befuddled brain, a binge in Shepheard's in Cairo, blundering into the Adjutant's room. Rommel was near Alexandria at the time and he was celebrating the doom of a German victory. Doom, doom, doom! went the throbbing in his skull. 'The fact is,' he went on, collapsing into an easy chair, 'I'm feeling lonely. No one at home. No one at all…'

'Come on, *Liebchen*,' Frau Goetz said soothingly. 'It's the middle of the night. Let me make you some black coffee.' She was suddenly aware of Karin clutching a blanket to her bosom. 'Forgive the intrusion, Fräulein,' she murmured, a trifle stiffly but in formal tones as if anxious to regularise the abnormal situation. She would have found some formula to smooth out an earthquake or the intrusion of a company of apes.

'I've come to see my friends,' Hugo argued with drunken obstinacy. His expression remained fixed in a kind of unfocused amiability, and he, too, addressed Karin, explaining with a reserved, gentle courtesy that he'd had a little too much to drink. She mustn't be offended. He was extremely sorry to cause her embarrassment.

The light from the corridor fell across her face. It harrowed Martin with its look of submission. It was the face of the victim, indelibly meek, commanding compassion, and because of that he thought it the most beautiful face in Germany.

'It's all right,' she said. 'It's quite all right.' With resolute composure she got out of bed and walked across the room. 'Please make the coffee, Frau Goetz. I will see to him.' Deftly she began to unloosen the afflicted man's collar and tie. 'My brother also drinks,' she explained gravely. 'It's a stupid thing to do. Alcohol is a poison.'

Hugo's big bloated face looked up at her, smiling vaguely. 'I haven't taken a lethal dose,' he objected. A muscular spasm passed across his features, as though the faint irony caused him pain.

'You try hard enough,' Frau Goetz grumbled as she left the room. They heard her reassuring one of the tenants in the corridor that everything was in order. 'God watches over this house,' her trailing voice proclaimed. 'You can sleep in peace.'

In the room Karin had thrown back the curtains and opened the french windows, dislodging some rolled newspapers that plugged up the draughty gaps. Cold moonlight gleamed on the serried roofs outside and a gusty night wind scurried across the floor. She shivered slightly and went to put on a wrap. As she did so, Hugo clambered unsteadily to his feet and leaned against the window frame, drinking the air in through his open mouth. It took a moment or two before Martin reacted to the danger, fighting an aberrant desire to see the heavy body fall into the darkness, impelled by its instinctive desire for death.

'Hugo!' he said sharply, grasping the other's arm. 'Come away or you'll fall!'

'Does it matter?' Hugo said, turning back from the void beyond the stone veranda. His breath reeked of brandy, but there was no mistaking the desperate sobriety of his question. 'I'm not asking you, I'm asking myself. And the answer is no, it doesn't.' Karin's anxious face peered at him over Martin's shoulder and he addressed his remarks to her perplexity, perhaps to the mother in her. 'I've lived fifty years and that's probably the only important question I can answer. I say to myself——' he closed his eyes and grinned, the darkness revolving beneath the shut eyelids – 'here am I, Hugo Krantz, end product of a civilisation, if you'll forgive the eloquence. Its arts amuse, its religion deceives, its morality lies; all these diseases are carried in my flesh. Drunk as I am, I know that I'm all its loneliness, the loneliness of all its multitudes. I'm fifty years of Europe, heir of a thousand million dead and crushed beneath the burden of that insignificance. That's why I'm here in Berlin, standing at the window of the suicide room in the apartment of my dear friend, Frau Goetz, soaked in poisoned alcohol but not quite ready to die.'

Karin turned to Martin in perplexity, but Martin was himself adrift in the older man's despair. He felt too fatigued to cope with the drunken deluge of pessimism. All he knew just then was that although the vocabulary was familiar it didn't make for a common language. There was love and an obstinate vitality that could be described as faith. The sodium lamps in the street below spilled out an anaemic radiance. It was three o'clock in the morning, the hour when life dwindled in the bodies of the aged and midwives drew the newborn from the womb. There was a meaning in that, too, he told himself wearily.

'You're a sick man, Hugo,' he said. 'You need a doctor.'

Hugo smiled with some of his old mockery. 'Sure I'm sick,' he agreed. 'We're all sick. Is there a God in the house?'

At that moment Frau Goetz came along the corridor with the coffee, hoarse with protest at the blasphemy, hurrying to secure the windows and shut out the wicked night.

She had found time to dab some powder on and was now ready to treat the affair as a social occasion. A single bulb shone dimly in a faded parchment shade as she switched on the light and seated herself near Hugo. 'We might as well be cosy,' she declared. 'Who'd like some nice cinnamon cake?' Hugo stared at her, bemused. He fumbled in his pocket and produced a cigar-case, but it was empty and this triviality seemed to defeat him. Martin handed him a cigarette instead, and he crumpled it clumsily in the act of putting it to his mouth.

'You're in trouble,' Frau Goetz said, eagerly solicitous. 'Tell us about it.'

The strong black coffee had begun to clear Hugo's head a little. 'How do you know I'm in trouble?' he said, swamped by a black wave of misery.

She made a sharp sound of impatience and rattled her cup in the saucer. 'Do you generally burst in here drunk in the middle of the night? Of course you're in trouble. It'll do you good to talk about it. We're your friends.'

'You're my oldest friend,' he agreed with a tired smile. Her bony, shrewish face and scrawny neck moved him as it always did. It was part of his unhappiness. They'd been young together, sung duets, shared ribald confidences. They were almost an extinct species. 'Maybe you can even remember Putzi von Schlesinger.'

'Putzi von Schlesinger?' She thought for a moment, then gave a husky laugh. 'Of course – such an amusing boy, and terribly handsome. I wonder what happened to him? He was too smart to become a Nazi.'

'Too smart,' Hugo agreed, smiling strangely, and as he talked of Putzi, and then of Heinz Dieter, the taste of bitterness on his tongue, it was as though she and he were alone in the room.

About an hour later Martin drove him home. During the journey he seemed to have fallen into a stupor, lying back against the leather upholstery, his eyes closed and his hands hanging limply between his thighs, but when they got up to the apartment he began to walk about with an imprisoned restlessness.

'Take a couple of aspirin and go to bed,' Martin advised him.

'Don't go yet,' Hugo begged. 'Let's have a nightcap.'

'Haven't you had enough to drink for the time being?' protested Martin, unable to conceal his exasperation.

Hugo's gaze took in the empty apartment, lingering on every object with grim distaste. 'I'm too bloody sober,' he growled. 'We compulsive drinkers burn alcohol as fast as we take it in.'

The room was lit only by the angular lamp over the desk, and he disappeared into the surrounding gloom to emerge again with two tumblers generously filled with cognac. The nocturnal sky filled the big curved window and turned it into a solid wall of silence. They seemed to be suspended high above the night-deserted city in an intense isolation, and this impression was enhanced by the prolonged reflection of the shadowy room in the glass of the window. Martin was seated facing it, and he saw Hugo's bulky figure as a reflection, too, an image sketched upon unreality, and it created a symbol of loneliness that all his drunken rhetoric had only imperfectly conveyed.

He grew tense, anticipating another difficult confession. Ever since his arrival in Berlin, when they had met or spoken on the telephone, he'd felt that Hugo was on the point of making some painful private disclosure. The bitterness had been apparent from that first evening: in the reckless drive from the airport, the yelling at pedestrians, the half-monologue spoken in this bleakly pretentious room. Now they were back to it again, it seemed as if the entire month had been compressed into one long, interminable night.

And Karin was waiting for him, their precious hours running out. There was so little time left, only another day or two, he realised with a flutter of panic, resenting the fact that Hugo detained him, resenting even more his own inability to break the spell of the other's personality and leave.

Hugo trimmed a cigar with infuriating deliberation, killing time. The trembling flame lit up his sad, pouchy, intelligent eyes. 'Do you ever see Marion?' he asked. The attentiveness with which he awaited a reply betrayed a certain anxiety. They'd been divorced years before and yet he still spoke her name with an unmistakable accent of fear.

'Hardly ever,' Martin said. 'I run across her occasionally at parties.'

'What does she say about me these days?'

'I don't know. We don't often talk to each other.' He remembered her as a well-groomed, middle-aged woman, a cigarette-holder poised like a weapon between clenched fingers. One heard her brisk, uneven voice discussing people, the latest book or play, her favourite charity committee, perhaps. She belonged to a world he had never inhabited except as a casual visitor. Nor had Hugo, for that matter. They were both rootless, but a great dividing line lay between their generations. That was where his own immunity lay. Hugo, his father, the other middle-aged refugees, all that generation chronicled by Koestler, had been torn up in their prime by the living roots. Unadaptable, they had no defence against the virus of despair. But his own generation was acquiring the stubborn technique of survival, hardier, less weakened by optimism, convinced that life was still worthwhile even if religion and philosophy were unable to explain why. They were like those people who return to their town after a devastation and begin picking over the debris, finding, here and there, a serviceable piece of timber, a piece of tarpaulin, a few bent nails, and so begin to re-make their homes.

Hugo's reflection, more emphatic than his physical presence, moved restlessly in the glass of the window. 'I hope you won't discuss me with Marion,' he was saying. 'Wouldn't like her to know...' His voice trailed away uselessly.

'Of course not,' Martin agreed politely. 'I won't say a word.' The assurance was scarcely necessary. He had the feeling that they were drifting irrevocably apart: his own life had broken free from Hugo and his fate – and somehow from his father, too. The thought constricted his heart painfully. There was no way of rescuing them; they were petrified, looking back over their shoulders like the woman who fled from Sodom.

'Marion's not a bad person, I suppose,' Hugo continued, swirling the brown liquid in his tumbler. 'I did a terrible thing when I married her. She expected an uxorious spouse and all she got was me.' He tilted his face to the ceiling and swallowed, making a slight grimace. 'It's silly, but I can't bear the thought of her laughing at me. Let's have another drink.'

It was dawn, a sky as grey and cool as a dove's feather. The city was waking up. Milk bottles clattered, there were the infrequent footsteps of early-morning workers, the first buses coughed and groaned, and chilled engines growled as cars went by with a sleek, cold glitter as if they'd just come off the production lines. The first newspaper vendors, their voices still husky with sleep, were already shouting the new day's alarms, and all along the Kurfürstendamm the garish neon lights dwindled as daylight filtered along the pavements. It was all somehow exhilarating. A wind cool as water blew against Martin's forehead as he hurried back to Karin with a lover's impatience. Sometimes when he was separated from her he could scarcely realise her existence, but now she had moved into his untenanted heart and he was more certain of her than of anything else.

When he arrived, coffee was steaming aromatically on the hotplate and she was dressed, sitting at the mirror outlining her lips with lipstick. 'How is Hugo?' she asked mildly. 'You were so long, I thought something might have happened.'

'We talked,' he said, disinclined to discuss it.

'I'm sorry for him. He's so terribly unhappy, it's frightening. Surely he ought to have someone to look after him?'

She didn't understand at all. She knew what had happened but couldn't understand that Germany still had the power to make them suffer, that for people like Goldberg and Hugo there was no healing. Her incomprehension was the one thing that alienated him. But one day she would have to know, and the knowledge would pierce her with knives. For she would realise that when they first lay together, her heart beating against his breast, she had still been a symbol of the German evil, and he'd taken her the way a man takes the daughter of his sworn enemy, as a sacrifice on the altar of his hatred.

'The coffee smells like the beginning of a wonderful day,' he said, kissing her contritely. 'Let's have our breakfast.'

'It may be a wonderful day for you, but I have to be in the factory by seven,' she reminded him.

'To hell with the factory. Take the day off. We'll go down to the Tegeler See and have lunch in one of those beer gardens on the river.'

Everything went right for them. The sun came out warmly for early spring, and there were crocuses in the fields and early daffodils. They drank beer on a veranda overlooking the moss-green water and watched intrepid children splashing in mid-river like playful beavers. Later, when the water began to turn black and the stain of darkness spread across the sky, they walked silently among the trees, arms linked, religious with peace. And suddenly stopped; looked at one another; embraced. Karin's eyes were moist and bright. She put her arms around his neck and whispered: 'I want to celebrate this day.'

Afterwards they lay side by side on the grass, staring up at the starry sky broken by the branches of their sheltering tree and listening to the chirruping birds.

'I feel tonight that you may have given me a child,' Karin said. She sighed deeply, touched by an involuntary sadness, as though her heart had already accepted a new and tender burden.

Martin was suddenly cold. He stood up stiffly and brushed some earth mould from his clothes.

'We'd better go,' he said.

'Yes,' she said forlornly, 'we'd better go,' walking by his side distantly, with a different silence.

12

'**Y**ou're not a relative?' the policeman asked.

'No,' Hugo said. 'The young man was my secretary-valet.'

The policeman sat square and upright on the chair, knees pressed together, at attention in the prescribed sitting position. He recorded the answer in his notebook.

'You are the person who sponsored his application for a West Berlin residential permit?'

'Yes.'

'The permit was issued to him in the name of Heinz Dieter Schulz. Did you know it was a false name?' the policeman continued sternly. He was an official of *Abteilung V*, police intelligence, and scrutinised Hugo sharply, as though he were already a proven malefactor.

'False?' Hugo echoed incredulously, dismayed to discover that Heinz Dieter had deceived him in this, too. The habit of changing identities was not uncommon in Germany, but beguiled by the polluted innocence of those candid blue eyes he'd suspected nothing, taking the boy on trust as an engaging rascal, a post-war casualty forced by circumstances into a cunning struggle for survival.

'Did you know he was a deserter from the *Volkspolizei*?'

So the whole biography was false, not merely the name. But that was Germany, too, the symptomatic evasion of guilt.

After all those years Heinzi hadn't been able to trust him, and now he saw that they'd never communicated. There had been a performance: the characters had spoken their lines and departed. Now the curtain was rung down on the empty stage. Permitting himself a ghostly irony, he said: 'But is deserting from the East German police an offence? I understood they were given a medal for enlisting in the free world.'

'We like them to declare themselves,' the official pointed out dryly. 'Will you please answer the question.'

'I didn't know he was a deserter from the *Volkspolizei*.'

'You seem to know very little about the man, yet you sponsored him and gave him employment for several years.' A faint, derisive smile flickered over the policeman's compressed lips, and he tapped his thumb-nail with the end of his pencil, blatantly registering scepticism.

Hugo stared meditatively at the blank white blotter on his desk, his mind blurred with lack of sleep and the stale fumes of alcohol. He'd taken enough sleeping tablets to annihilate consciousness altogether, but the only effect was to induce an enormous lethargy. A fly flew waveringly around his head and settled finally on the glass paperweight, its sucker darting from its bulbous head like a snake's tongue. Waving it away, he said: 'I believed what he told me.' The dull pain groped again. He'd never been free of it since Heinzi disappeared. He felt as though his blood had congealed into lead and was being forced through his arteries. An imponderable weight pressed on his mind, making it impossible to think coherently. He seemed to see Heinzi lying, as he often did, on the floor in an old sweat-shirt and faded jeans, smoking and boasting about girls, a blond young animal as mindless and instinctive as a young tiger. Did it matter what he'd done? Was there anything to forgive? Some people were as incapable of guilt as they were incapable of morality. Or were they? In all this mental confusion he only knew that Heinzi's absence was a synthesis of all the absences he'd ever experienced, the echo of a slammed door in an empty apartment, the desolate unanswered ring of a hundred telephones, other people's laughter on the far side of a wall.

He lifted his head reluctantly and stared across the desk into the hard blue eyes of the man opposite. 'What exactly are they charging him with?' he asked.

'There are several possibilities,' the policeman replied dryly, shifting slightly to ease the stiffness in his buttocks. 'They think he killed a man.'

Hugo automatically reached for a cigar while he absorbed the shock. Somehow, he'd never been able to believe it, even when Heinzi told him it was the source of Kane's blackmail. 'His father? I thought that was an adolescent fantasy.'

The policeman looked at him sharply. 'What's that about his father?' he rapped out. 'You seem to know more than you've told me so far.' He paused perceptibly, waiting for Hugo to elaborate his comment, and then continued: 'As I understand it, the victim was a Russian soldier. He was found knifed and robbed in a barn. Apparently he picked up your young friend after a drunken evening.'

'I don't understand,' Hugo said stupidly.

The man smiled again, derisively. 'I think you do.' He leaned forward, pencil poised over the notebook, and went on in a level unemotional tone: 'What precisely was your own relationship with Schulz? Did you have sexual relations with him?'

'I think you're going too far,' he protested, faint with appre-
hension. Pressing his hands against his aching forehead, he sat
with eyes closed, hopelessly, superstitiously, praying that the
whole thing should turn out to be a nightmare.

But the interrogator was solid and inflexible, wearing his
authority with an unrelenting grimness. 'The question is material,' he insisted.

'I refuse to answer,' was all Hugo could say.

'You are listed in the records for a homosexual offence.'

'I've no recollection of it.'

'It was in 1934.'

'In 1934,' Hugo said harshly, 'I was arrested by the Gestapo.
They tortured me for days. Then they released me.'

'For a homosexual offence,' the policeman repeated, unmoved.

He was sweating. A distant pounding of surf sounded in his
ears as the blood seemed to rush to his head with the force of an
exploding sea. Congested with rage, he hammered his bunched
fists on the desk and shouted incoherently: 'You don't want to –
you dare to tell me – the damned Gestapo——'

The official remained cold, serious, and impassive. With a
sense of futility, Hugo collapsed in the chair like an old man, legs
trembling with weakness.

'Is there anything else?' he asked shakily. 'I'm not prepared to
answer further questions without legal advice.'

'That will be all for the present, but I must advise you that
we may require your attendance at headquarters. May I have
your passport?'

He handed it over with an ominous conviction that by doing
so he was being entirely cut off from human society, a feeling that

persisted long after the policeman left. The surrender was powerfully symbolic. It identified him as the representative victim of the age, without rights, without status, without protection, without a recognised identity. He could be imprisoned, beaten, and outraged in a hundred ways but none would intercede for him. The Nazis had confiscated his passport, too, and from that moment the search for identity had begun. He'd asked himself: 'Who am I?' and now, in pain and despair, he asked himself again: 'Who am I?'

There was still no answer, unless the silence was itself the only possible reply.

A handful of subdued men and women were seated in the waiting-room glancing taciturnly at one another, or stolidly staring at the scuffed brown linoleum of the floor. A strong, sweetish smell of disinfectant and an atmosphere of imposed silence might have suggested a hospital of the more primitive kind, but the uniformed policeman lounging by the door and the usual portraits of Lenin and President Ulbricht testified that the building fulfilled a sterner function. An official entered the room on some fleeting errand and the people looked up quickly, smiling with the ghastly, ingratiating amiability that so often disguises fear. One by one they came forward, explained their business to the receptionist, and were either dismissed or directed to the appropriate department of the establishment.

Eventually it was Hugo's turn. He went to the window and blinked uncertainly in the light of a hard, naked electric bulb strategically placed to expose the features of visitors. Now he was there, he was momentarily at a loss to explain his purpose and gazed absently at the pink, fresh face of the boyish police reception clerk.

'Yes, what is it, Comrade?' the youngster demanded impatiently. His skinny neck protruded awkwardly from the ill-fitting collar of his greenish uniform, undermining his attempt to impersonate authority.

Hugo smiled faintly, touched, as always, by inexperience, but it required a deliberate effort to overcome the torpor that had settled so tenaciously on his mind. Unhappiness could affect him that way, more than a prolonged bout of debauchery, producing both extreme physical debility and an inability to focus on even the simplest actions. The infirmity affected him now in an odd way, making him feel that he must speak loudly and simply to the person he was addressing, as if the other were mentally retarded. He began to explain about the visit from the West Berlin police, who had informed him that a former employee of his was detained on a serious charge.

'Yes, what do you expect us to do?' the youth asked indifferently.

'I expect you to be civil about it!' Hugo shouted. His eyes watered with mortification. The people behind him exchanged glances, half hopefully, half in fear, at the unexpected act of rebellion. The lounging policeman by the door stiffened and stationed himself closer.

'Can I see someone in connection with the case?' Hugo went on more quietly. 'The accused has no relatives or friends. It's my responsibility to help him if I can.'

'You must see the West Berlin authorities about that.'

Interpreting the formal reply as a calculated impertinence, he fought down an impulse to seize the youth by his thin neck and forcibly shake respect into him. 'This isn't a political matter!' he protested, the undercurrent of hysteria rising dangerously again. 'Will you kindly pass the matter to someone in authority.' The policeman was now standing quite close, undisguisedly menacing. Hugo looked him up and down with some of his old arrogance. 'Your superiors will probably take a different view from your own,' he told the clerk contemptuously.

The receptionist, because he was a little intimidated, or deciding to humour a difficult customer, drew out a form and began to fill in the details in a careful hand. 'Wait here!' he said curtly – no Comrade now – and climbed down from the high stool to confer with a colleague who sat at a table making card-index entries, paying little attention to the altercation. After a short conversation, during which they both consulted a book of regulations, the young receptionist went into another office. He returned crestfallen and red with embarrassment. 'Take this man to Room 42,' he said, immediately turning his attention to the next person in the queue.

The policeman straightened his tunic and signalled Hugo to follow. Their footsteps echoed desolately as they walked through a warren of shabby corridors, passing a window *en route* that overlooked a cement-paved courtyard where several men were filing into a police van under the vigilant eyes of an armed escort. One of them might have been Heinz Dieter, the same age, the same colouring, the same desperate swagger. Hugo passed on, his heart knocking violently.

Room 42 was a suite rather than a mere office. The anteroom was occupied by a young policeman in a well-cut uniform who greeted him with affable courtesy. 'So you found us, Herr Krantz,' he said. 'We're rather tucked away here, I'm afraid.'

Only later did it occur to Hugo that it was a curious remark to make in the circumstances. 'It's very kind of you to see me,' he said.

'Not at all. Would you care for a cigarette? The Chief won't keep you long.'

Bemused by the cordiality of his reception, Hugo selected a cigarette from the thin metal case offered to him and fumbled for his own gold lighter.

'Allow me,' the young officer insisted, smiling with distinctly bourgeois charm. His hands were well kept, white and smooth as a girl's, and his spruce, well-mannered coolness went oddly with his rank and profession. The setting, too, was unexpected. Folk art from the People's Republics softened the austerity of the buff-coloured walls, and picture magazines were piled neatly by the side of an easy chair arranged to give its occupant the benefit of a glowing electric fire. The rug underfoot was from Bokhara.

'I'm sorry you had some difficulty with our receptionist,' his host – it was impossible to think of him otherwise – declared pleasantly. 'A young recruit. Inexperienced and inclined to be a little over-zealous.'

'Really, it was nothing,' Hugo said dazedly. He was thinking that the charm was excessive and wondered what motive lay behind it. Not, surely, a determination to show that a Communist regime was as capable of good manners as a bourgeois democracy. 'You know why I'm here?' he asked, convinced that somewhere, somehow, a misunderstanding must have arisen.

'Certainly, Herr Krantz. It's this unfortunate business of Schulz. The Chief is studying the dossier on the case now.' The buzzer on the desk sounded discreetly. 'Ah! He's ready for you now. Would you kindly go straight in.'

Hugo ground out his cigarette in an ash-tray of Bohemian glass, thinking briefly and hopefully that perhaps the West Berlin police had exaggerated and Heinz Dieter was being held on a charge of lesser gravity than homicide. Then, not thinking any more, he went through the door. There was a faint odour of crushed flowers in the room. A tall, slender civilian with greying fair hair stood by the window looking down into the courtyard below. He turned with a smile and walked across the room, limping slightly. It was Putzi.

Hugo stood absolutely still except for the violent trembling of his limbs. The shock pierced his brain, his heart, his intestines, and then flooded him with an unbearable sensation of pleasure, immediately followed by a wave of relief – a lifetime of tension abruptly released. The persistent cloudiness that had affected his mind cleared away. It was really Putzi, and suddenly he was not surprised.

Putzi just smiled.

Physically, he'd changed remarkably little. The years had tightened the smooth skin of his face so that the bones showed through more sharply; his mouth had tasted power and become subtly reshaped, no less pleasure-loving but hungrier, indefinably more avid, as if what was once appetite had become an insatiable addiction. But there was no sign of the old exuberance; his eyes no longer crinkled with bright malice and it was impossible to imagine this spare, controlled, keenly observant man exploding like the old Putzi with rebellious laughter and publicly mocking convention. Even the slight odour of perfume seemed incongruous.

His vivid awareness of this personality was Hugo's second major shock. He recorded it as instantly and minutely as a camera might if it could encompass an object in all its phases and, at the same time, explore its detail with photoelectric insight. He was sensitive to every nuance of Putzi. Love and hate had engraved their compelling images on his heart until each became inextricably involved with the other, creating a chiaroscuro of emotion in which each changing mood could find an echo. With the force of revelation, he realised that all his loves had only been cherished insofar as they confirmed the conflicting images of Putzi. They were fleeting reflections of the first, the doomed, the corrupt and only love. Even Heinzi. And so the loneliness was inevitable, all things withering in the soil of the first betrayal.

'I had no idea,' he said, voice husky with pain. But it was untrue. The shadow of this meeting had fallen upon his life in the cellar of the Brown House. Thereafter he knew that, at any time, when he turned a corner, or fumbled in the dark of a cinema for an empty seat, or opened a door into an unfamiliar room, Putzi would be there. If he'd never advertised in newspapers, never seen Gross in East Berlin, never been dogged by Kane or betrayed by Heinzi; if he'd done nothing but wait, they would have arrived at this moment as surely as two planets are drawn into collision by each other's gravitation.

Putzi continued to gaze steadily at him, smiling with the muscles of his mouth. A clock on the wall ticked out second after second and he did not move or speak. Then, cautiously, probing the defences of an adversary, he broke the silence at last. 'You've altered,' he remarked. 'If we had met in the street I doubt if I'd have recognised you.'

The voice was unfamiliar. It had been mannered, mocking, a trifle womanish; now the timbre was deeper and there was an unrecognisable brusqueness. Even more than the subtle physical differences, it indicated how much the character of the man had altered. It was the voice of a harsh personality, of someone who had forcibly subdued his own nature and, by so doing, deformed it. The old Putzi could have spoken with such a voice, but he would have assumed it to caricature the kind of person he despised. Probably that was how it started when he became Sommer, a prisoner of the Russians determined to deceive and exploit his captors. He may have used the voice in the lecture-room when repeating the lessons of dialectical materialism, confident that his mentors would not recognise its mockery. But now the man and the voice were one, and it suddenly occurred to Hugo that perhaps Putzi had never really despised toughness and brutality, and that his contempt had concealed the fascination these exerted over him. When he joined forces with the Nazis it may not have been out of cynicism at all, but because their special lust for cruelty titillated his own appetite.

'You've changed, too,' Hugo said slowly, 'but I would have recognised you anywhere.'

'That ought to worry me,' Putzi said, screening his dark blue eyes so that the smile which accompanied the words became ambiguous. 'Please make yourself comfortable,' he said, pointing to one of two armchairs some distance from the desk. With an unobtrusive movement he touched a switch and an electric heater came on, making a high whirring sound that effectively muffled the rest of the conversation. 'A cigar?' he offered, pushing a box across the table that separated them.

Hugo declined stiffly, maintaining an attitude of hostility that, astonishingly, he didn't feel.

'A drink, then? Is it still cognac?'

It was the opening strategy, a hint of their former intimacy in the hope that it would disarm suspicion a little, enabling him to discover if the old weaknesses, the points of vulnerability, were still there.

'My doctor doesn't allow me alcohol before dinner.'

'I'm sorry,' Putzi said with concern. 'I hope it isn't serious?'

Dryly he replied: 'It's nothing. A slimming course.'

Putzi relaxed in his chair and puffed thoughtfully at his cigar. 'You once wrote a song about a man who looked in the mirror and complained that the other fellow, the one in the glass, had changed. January, February, 1931, wasn't it? In that musical comedy, "A Halo for Johannes Schmidt". It was one of the wittiest things you did. He laughed reminiscently. 'I've thought of that inflation scene a thousand times. The little fat Schmidt coming home with his wages, supervising a queue of porters carrying enormous parcels of paper money that they piled in a heap in the middle of the stage. Schmidt took off his shoes and clothes to pay them, then he climbed on top of the heap in his underwear and started to eat bread and sausage, wiggling his toes through the holes in his socks. Do you remember?'

This deliberate evocation of the past showed he still retained his cool effrontery and was gambling that even if it forced the bitterness to the surface, nostalgia would dissolve it. Hugo did, in fact, irresistibly recall the white glitter of that fabulous winter of success. The parties in the Tiergarten, racing in the open sports car through crazy, delightful Berlin, the two of them young and exuberant with optimism, from Kempinski's to the Adlon, from the Adlon to the Bristol, from the Bristol to Eldorado, and everywhere friends eager to flatter and to sun themselves in Hugo's popularity.

'A Halo for Johannes Schmidt'! Schmidt had been played by a talented little comedian, Binum Kisch, as a typical Jewish *nudnik*, and smart Berliners had gone wild over him. But the usual fate sought him out, and he went unhaloed with the others to asphyxiation. With grim humour Hugo said: 'You treat me like Lazarus risen from the dead in an old raccoon coat.'

The strategy hadn't worked. Outside in the courtyard a drill sergeant gave staccato orders to a platoon of men whose iron-shod feet rhythmically trampled the awkward silence and recalled more recent memories. Putzi increased the volume of the heater until the whirring sounded like the distant drone of an aircraft. 'You've been hunting me, Hugo,' he said, no longer smiling. 'All those newspaper advertisements, all those meetings with men from my old regiment, the persistent inquiries, the visit to Stuttgart. You went to a lot of trouble.'

'Did you know about everything?' Hugo asked.

'It wasn't difficult. If you'll forgive me for pointing it out, you are inclined to be naïve sometimes.'

'And Gross? You knew about him, of course.'

'Naturally. Poor fellow, he's very sick. Advanced tuberculosis.'

'This man Kane, who calls himself an American, is he one of your people?'

Putzi ignored the question, tapping the ash from his cigar with a steady forefinger. 'So you've found me at last,' he said. 'And now what?'

Hugo looked at him sombrely. 'Why should we pretend? I didn't find you, you found me. Furthermore, you brought me here.'

'I merely anticipated you'd come.'

The hatred that had until now lain dormant rose in Hugo's gorge, sour and hot as vomit. 'You made sure of it by hurting someone who means very much to me.' His voice was full of loathing. The anger he could no longer feel on his own behalf boiled up at the thought of Heinz Dieter. Had he not had this obsession, nothing would have happened to the boy. He would have gone on living in West Berlin unmolested. 'Did you get your tame ape, Kane, to slug him and drag him over here?'

'You'll never learn,' Putzi retorted pityingly. 'You were always as sentimental as a woman. A young scamp like Schulz! Do you really think it's necessary to use violence when one has only to offer him a simple inducement and he comes running? He's sold you more than once for a girl and a pocketful of money.'

'You've charged him with killing a man. Is that what you call an inducement?'

Putzi lowered his eyes. A tight, inward smile came over his face. 'I'll discuss that with you later,' he said. 'At the moment there's something else to clear up. What exactly is it you've got against me?'

The question was so grossly impudent that at first it struck him speechless, filled him with disgust. And then, because it was so impudent and unexpected, it made him think. What exactly was the root of this hatred? The cellar and its orgiastic cruelty, yes. In a sense, because it was easier to blame one known person than a million who were anonymous, he'd held Putzi responsible for all that happened, imagined him the author of the concentration camps, the gas chambers, the experiments on the bodies of living women and children, and all the unspeakable variations of cruelty that had been so inventively performed. But in all this Putzi had merely been a suitable object upon which to focus his bitterness. He was already hated before most of it had happened. And now he saw where the root lay: it was in that feeling of outrage and misery that came when Putzi, whom he'd loved almost idolatrously, rejected him.

'You blame me for joining the Nazis,' Putzi said, drawing him on. 'But I only did what all the others were doing.'

Hugo still said nothing, sitting with bowed head and holding his hands clasped together on his knees in an attitude of bitter resignation.

'Today it doesn't seem very smart. But in 1933 it was rather different. Society was nasty enough, and the Nazis weren't all that bad at the beginning.' He looked across the table with a direct, challenging forcefulness. 'You and I were both the same sort of people, living in the same sort of world. Neither of us was an idealist. We were cynical, hedonistic, out for all the fun we could get. The difference was that you couldn't join the Nazis. But if you hadn't been a Jew, would you have chosen to chuck up everything and become a refugee, or would you have made the same accommodation as I did?'

'I don't know.' He was compelled to admit it. Could anyone know how he would react to a temptation that had never presented itself? But with all the force of inner conviction he believed that he could never have done what Putzi did. They were not the same sort of people at all. 'I can only say,' Hugo continued with difficulty, 'that if our situations had been reversed, I would have remembered that you were my friend and I would have continued to behave towards you as a friend.'

The other smiled with sour mockery. He leaned forward and violently stubbed out his cigar in the ash-tray. 'This is a time for frankness,' he said, 'not for sentimentality. We were never really friends. You were the great Hugo Krantz, clever, witty, ambitious, convinced you were a wonderful fellow. I was there to admire you and flatter your ego.'

'Is that how you remember it?' Hugo exclaimed incredulously. He couldn't believe their relationship could be so misrepresented.

'That's precisely how it was.' Putzi spoke with passion, an old neurosis suddenly revived. It seemed that he was no longer entirely in control of what he said. 'Did it ever occur to you in those days that your vanity and arrogance might sometimes hurt me, that perhaps I was a little jealous of your success? You were a nobody whose talent brought him fame. Perhaps it was foolish, but I regarded myself as no less intelligent, no less witty, no less ambitious. And yet with all my advantages of birth and influence I could do nothing that you did as easily as breathing.'

Savagely, Hugo said: 'So you ran to the Gestapo and told them that the Jewish nobody, Hugo Krantz, had seduced you. And the Gestapo obliged by beating the upstart until he screamed for mercy!'

Putzi got up and stood over him, pale and angry, the skin taut over his cheek-bones. He seemed unable to trust himself to speak. Abruptly, he walked across the room and stared out of the window at the courtyard below. For a while the silence was broken only by the staccato voice of the drill sergeant shouting '*Links, rechts, links, rechts,*' and the clicking of the electric heater as an obstruction became caught in the blades of its fan. Putzi said harshly: 'So that's what you've thought all these years? I'm not exactly flattered.' He continued to stare out of the window for a few moments, then suddenly turned, and, with a visible effort, switched on a resigned, reproachful smile. 'Will you believe me? I didn't know until it was too late. The truth is that my jealousy was trivial. I was young and rather rash, but I hope you'll believe that I never wished you any harm, then or now.'

Yes, Hugo thought, none of them knew. He was disappointed that Putzi should make the same tired excuses as any other middle-aged German.

It was no longer worth continuing the argument. He glanced at the taut but smiling face and quickly looked away again, unable to bear what he saw. A few minutes had accomplished the corrosion of a quarter of a century. The image of Putzi he'd retained intact through the years had faded away and there was only this man, greying, implausible, and corrupt, a stranger like any other. Putzi had become generically German, and as, by killing the Jews, the Germans had sought to destroy something they feared and hated in themselves, their moral inferiority, so it now seemed that Putzi also had sought to destroy his moral inferiority by doing away with the one person who reminded him most painfully of it.

He felt like saying: 'Wolfgang Sommer, what have I to do with you?' He had once loved someone and been betrayed, and the betrayal had caused him great suffering; but it was all over now, one of many loves, many betrayals, and the last fragile and compulsive link that held him to the past had snapped. Free at last, he would leave here and mingle with the crowds, walk past the Gedächtniskirche, past the kiosks with their fragrant smell of boiled sausages and mustard, along the Kurfürstendamm with its parade of broad-bottomed blondes and their comfortably fleshed

escorts, past the lively, coquettish boys and girls merchandising
sex on the corners near the Augsburgerstasse – and nothing
would be quite the same. Berlin would be just another city.

And he would go up to his empty apartment, lonelier than ever,
switch on all the lights, put a record on, look out of the window
at the gleaming shop windows below and the midget people,
and wonder what on earth he should do with himself to pass the
evening and the night and the day and all the other interminable
days of passportless freedom that lay ahead.

'You do accept what I say?' Putzi was demanding, politely but
with an anxious insistence.

Hugo merely nodded, unable to bring himself to utter the lie.

'Good! I'm very relieved,' Putzi said almost jovially, rubbing the
dry palms of his hands together. 'It means a lot to me to be able to
explain things to you face to face like this. Although I must admit,'
he added with a laugh, 'that you rather forced me into arranging
this meeting. But now it's taken place, I hope we'll both feel better.'

'What about Heinz Dieter?' Hugo asked. 'Now that his arrest
has served its purpose, don't you think he can be released?'

'Ah, yes, the case of Schulz.' Putzi limped to the desk and
picked up a blue folder, flicking over the pages one by one. 'I'm
afraid it isn't quite as simple as that.' His expression had become
severe and formal, reminding Hugo that he was, after all, in the
presence of a high police official. 'Your young friend has been
on our wanted list for some time. His record is very bad. I can
assure you that his arrest would have taken place whatever the
circumstances. The law is the law, after all.'

Hugo's heart sank at the smooth display of hypocrisy. The
law was always applied selectively. A boy grew up in a shattered

world where death was arbitrary, casual, and indiscriminate. He killed a man, in God knows what circumstances, and now, several years later, the law was ready to turn him into a sacrificial victim of society's guilt. But here in Germany there were men walking in freedom, sometimes occupying important offices, who were administrative mass-murderers even if no single spot of blood had stained their soft, well-kept hands. For men like these the world suspended its laws. It was not only a German characteristic. 'So you won't help him?' he demanded harshly.

'That's another question entirely. I do have some influence in certain cases.' Putzi suddenly dropped the official tone of voice and glanced airily at the ceiling, to indicate that what he was now saying was casually conversational. The fingers of his left hand drummed nervously on the blue cover of the dossier. 'I'm bothered by one little thing. As far as I know, you are the only person who knows my true identity. Actually——' he laughed with some embarrassment – 'when I say true identity, I don't want to give the impression that it's of any importance. I have no particular affection for the family title and I changed my name for a very good reason. I believe you know the circumstances.'

There was a malignant gleam in the bland stare of the watchful blue eyes. A sudden uneasy thought crossed Hugo's mind. He was *not* the only one who knew Putzi's true identity. There was Gross, Putzi's batman, who had been in Budapest when the change of identity was accomplished and who had recently disappeared – 'arrested', the old leather-worker had said. The implication was frightening, even though it had been clear for some time that the pursuit of Putzi had become dangerous.

'It could be awkward for me if the information were to be

passed on,' the voice continued mildly. 'I'm comfortable here. I have my position. As long as you keep silent I have nothing to worry about.'

'Is it important enough for you to kill me?' Hugo asked. He felt cold, as if the temperature of the room had dropped sharply.

Putzi laughed uproariously, but the glitter in his eyes became intensified, almost insane. 'Good old Hugo! As sardonic as ever,' he said. 'I won't say it isn't an idea, even though it's a preposterous one. But what,' he asked, lifting a smooth, quizzical eyebrow, 'would I do with your body? Ask my assistant to clear it away?' He laughed again. 'No, it's much simpler than that, I believe. You can't really have any interest in telling anyone my little secret. And I can be quite useful to young Schulz.'

'I'm relieved you see it that way,' Hugo commented. The perspiration was damp under his armpits and he breathed with difficulty, as often happened when he was frightened. 'I assure you that I won't talk about it. How do you think you can help Schulz?'

'Well, I think we can show that there were strong mitigating circumstances. He was only sixteen, after all. The soldier accosted him and persuaded him to go to this lonely barn. The boy probably didn't understand what was happening until the man began to assault him. Naturally, he was shocked. I wouldn't be surprised if he gets no more than a nominal sentence.' He smiled, as if to say: 'See how cleverly I've arranged everything?' and held out his hand for a farewell handshake, the fingers stiff and reluctant. Hugo shuddered at the physical contact.

'We may meet again,' Putzi said affably on parting. 'This is the winning side. If you were wise, you'd join us.' Half mocking, half in earnest, he lifted his fist in the Communist salute.

For some time after leaving the building Hugo kept glancing nervously over his shoulder to see if he was being followed. Then, forgetting about it, he walked off in solitary freedom with an empty, exhausted feeling of anticlimax.

Kane paid off the taxi driver and turned his collar up against the driving rain that glistened on his black leather coat and dripped steadily from the brim of his wide hat. The noise of a thumping, old-fashioned *Tanzlied*, played on drums and accordion, disturbed the silence of the deserted street. Before entering the bar he walked a few yards along the pavement and inspected the surroundings: derelict buildings, an evil-smelling urinal at the foot of a row of stone steps, the Stadtbahn overhead and the railway arch supported by rusty iron girders projecting from shadowy recesses. But, judging by the number of expensive cars parked in the neighbourhood, Lili's Bar was well patronised. It specialised in counterfeiting the Berlin of the 1920's, a profitable nostalgia, by the look of it.

He pushed through the door and stood for a moment, shaking the rain off his clothes with violent movements, like a dog emerging from a swim, and scanning the jostling crowd through eyelids narrowed in protection against the dense eddies of tobacco smoke. Fat, middle-aged queers, were dancing clumsily with shabbily dressed working-class youths, and the only woman present was an elderly Lesbian sitting alone at a table, dressed in a masculine jacket, collar, and tie. Her hair was cropped and she wore gold-rimmed spectacles on a small, tight, clerkly face.

'I'm Lili,' she said, beckoning him over. 'Your first time here, isn't it?'

'Yes,' he replied, continuing to scan the crowd over her head.

'That's right, I never forget anybody,' she remarked complacently, and signalled a waiter. 'Find our friend a table,' she ordered, and, to Kane, said: 'I hope you have a good time. I'll always remember you now.'

He gazed at her phlegmatically, not happy at the prospect.

'Don't worry,' she reassured him with a gold-toothed smile. 'We're all good pals here. No names ever mentioned.'

On the far side of the place, half-concealed by an accordionist, he recognised a familiar figure, gross, dejected, and already drunk. 'I'm not worried,' he said thoughtfully. 'I like it here. Can you give me a table where I can see what's going on? I'd hate to miss anything.'

The waiter found him a place in a corner by the bar. Near-by, on high stools, a group of middle-aged men dressed as women stared indifferently into their drinks, ignoring the jollities. The clientele came for the boys. These were tourist bait performing a decorative function, Kane decided shrewdly. The creatures were almost ironically grotesque – raddled, ugly, with powdered masculine jaws, wearing silly little feminine hats. One of them had a pince-nez on the bridge of a large nose. He suspected that they were normal men, possibly unemployed actors, picking up some extra cash in an unusual way. His gaze wandered stealthily past Lili and the flushed men perspiring with effort as they propelled hefty youths around the dance floor. Through the drifting smoke it found Hugo again and rested on him with clinical concentration.

There was the talkative Frenchman and the boy with one arm amputated at the elbow. Hugo ordered a fresh round of drinks and smiled vaguely when the Frenchman said: 'This is a marvellous place. I'm writing a book.'

'Can I have a fag, mister?' the boy pleaded, his white, eager face turning from one to the other.

He was the age Heinzi had been when they first met, not much more than sixteen. 'Bring a packet of cigarettes,' Hugo called to the retreating waiter. Pity was the crippled child's enemy. It got him the drinks, the cigarettes, the small change from well-lined pockets, and so he became addicted to such beggary. But one day he would be no longer young and would realise, too late, that for all its sentimental tears the world was a heartless place.

'Tell us how it happened,' the Frenchman urged, swallowing his saliva.

The boy told his story glibly, smiling a shy, poignant smile. He'd been playing with his younger brother in some ruins. He'd found a hand-grenade and brought it home. Cleaning the dirt off it in the bedroom, it exploded. 'I saw my fingers flying up to the ceiling,' he said brightly. The detail was always effective, and he watched their faces proudly to gauge the reactions.

'Dreadful, dreadful!' the Frenchman said, closing his eyes and shuddering.

Hugo took out his wallet and shoved some money into the cripple's jacket pocket. 'Shut up and go home!' he growled.

The boy examined the notes and saw that they amounted to quite a lot of money. 'There's more than a hundred marks here!' he exclaimed, stammering with excitement. 'Thank you, Uncle!' Impulsively, he bent over and kissed Hugo's cheek.

'Go away, you little bastard!' Hugo muttered. Tears stung his eyes and he averted his head, embarrassed by the futility of his own gesture and the boy's ardent response. Coming to Lili's was an act of desperation. He'd hoped that its warm vulgarity would help to thaw his loneliness, or that he'd find some amusement in its grotesqueries. Instead, in a strange way, it mirrored his despair. The men jerking amorously in the arms of bored youngsters parodied a lifetime's sterility; the phony Weimar atmosphere of the place and its music mocked the nostalgia that had clouded his judgment and immured him in the dead past. He was like those pathetic castrated relics huddled round the bar, débris of an empty, tragic, and ridiculous age.

The crippled boy left with his windfall and the Frenchman, mellowed by several more drinks, waxed philosophical. 'What a strange people you are!' he declared. 'So brilliant and inventive, so industrious, so easily moved to self-sacrifice! How could you have tolerated a comedian like Hitler?'

Of course, he takes me for one of them, Hugo thought. It was one of those bad jokes. He grinned drunkenly into the other's face, performing an old trick of impersonation. 'Ah, we Germans, how little you understand us!' he said gravely and pompously. 'You do not realise that for all our qualities, our brilliant qualities, we are over-burdened with a sense of inferiority.' The Frenchman was listening avidly, no doubt delighted at obtaining such useful material for his book. 'Yes,' Hugo continued, parodying someone whose name for the moment eluded him, 'we have always wanted to be proud of ourselves as Germans, but it hasn't been possible. Hitler gave us an *ersatz* national pride and the world thought it was real. They were intimidated by it. But any good comedian could have done it. If your Monsieur Poujade had been a German we would already have made him President of the Republic.' He suddenly realised whose voice and manner he was aping. It was dear old Gustav Ulrich, the lawyer with the characteristic liberal readiness to make atonement for his ten per cent commission for handling restitution claims, the 'good' German, obtuse as well as shrewd, dishonest as much as well-meaning. 'We are rather hysterical about national pride,' he lectured the Frenchman. 'If we can't find a suitable object of hero-worship we make do with a successful German boxer, a German football team which has won an international game, a German film star. When our little actress, Hildegarde Kneff, became a success in Hollywood, we sent the *Burgemeister* of Berlin and all our civic dignitaries to the Tempelhof to do honour to her on her return.'

'She would make a charming President,' the Frenchman said gallantly.

'Why not?' Hugo said, swallowing his cognac with a grimace.

The Frenchman caught the eye of a handsome boy and stood up to dance. 'I must sample everything,' he smiled.

Across the room, behind the stamping, demonic revellers and the cacophonous music, Kane was watching him, but he was too giddy with talk and smoke and alcohol to see the pale, rubbery face at such a distance. And when, eventually, he got up to leave he didn't notice that Kane put on his coat and hurried from the bar before him.

There was no one in the street as he walked unsteadily through the pouring rain to his car, thinking vaguely that he was far too drunk to drive: one day, if he wasn't careful, he'd kill somebody; thinking of Heinzi in a prison cell and caring desperately that Putzi should keep his promise and help the boy to freedom; thinking that perhaps there was nothing but that to live for now.

Someone seized his arm. Too bemused to feel fear, he said: 'Why – what is it?'

'Don't be alarmed,' a voice said out of the darkness. 'I just want to talk to you.'

It was a familiar voice, but he couldn't quite place it. It seemed disguised, the voice of someone playing a practical joke. 'Who are you?' he asked, trying to sound brisk and sharp and giggling slightly because it was impossible.

'You know me, I'm your friend,' came the soothing reply.

He was being forcibly propelled under the railway arch and into the shadow between two girders.

He began to protest that he had no friends when the small tongue of flame stabbed and a heavy blow smashed into his chest. In that instant he recognised Kane and realised why the voice had puzzled him.

It had spoken in faultless German.

The last moment of pain stretched all his senses on the wrack. He was lying on the cold stones of the cellar, the moisture trickling, salt and horrible, into his open mouth and the cruel footsteps retreating. A wind of darkness tore through his shuddering body and, finally, irrevocably, he forgot his name.

13

There was still more than an hour before the plane left, and now he was restless and impatient, wishing it were all over. The two suitcases stood on the floor in the middle of the threadbare carpet and the room was neat and tidy, already vacant, waiting for someone else. It hurt him to see it that way; he'd got used to its ugliness, filled it for a while with the violence of living. It had been his habitation. Leaving it was like beginning another exile.

Karin pulled out several drawers to see if they were empty, taking a long time over it because any kind of activity was better than trying not to say the wrong thing. 'You've forgotten a tie!' she said in that bright empty voice she'd been using all morning.

'Never mind, I'll put it in my pocket.' Their glances clung, exchanging a swift confession of misery.

She said wretchedly: 'It's got a grease stain. I'll get it cleaned for you and send it on,' crumpling it tightly into the pocket of her coat.

Martin fumbled for a cigarette. Once he was gone she would smooth it out and touch it, as if it were a part of him. 'It's my favourite tie,' he said. Karin took the matches from his hand and gave him a light. Their bodies seemed to strain towards each other, separated by an invisible wall of glass, but recoiled immediately with a baffling shyness.

In another room the Japanese was delicately picking out a theme by Mozart, and it sounded like the sad tinkling of a toy music-box.

It was almost a relief when Frau Goetz came in with a bottle of whisky on a tray and a plate full of small, sticky cakes. 'I thought you'd like one for the road,' she said, red-rimmed eyes blinking in her grey, suffering face. Since Hugo's death she couldn't stop crying, most of all in the hours she spent alone reading the Bible in the stuffy little parlour. God had not yet consoled her: she had loved her friend too much. There was still black crepe around the frame of the faded picture that showed them singing a duet, and she'd dug up another youthful picture of Hugo, looking serious and very thin, which now stood, also edged with black, in the centre of the sideboard along with the crucifix, the pagan wood carvings, and other vaguely pious objects. It was the only shrine he would ever have, but somehow her muddled piety would accommodate it and she would be its priestess even in defiance of Jehovah.

'Well, Herr Martin,' she said, achieving brightness by sheer gallantry, 'may you have a safe trip and a wonderful journey.'

'Thank you, Frau Goetz.'

'It's been lovely having you. You've been such a gentleman.'

'You're being much too kind.'

'Nonsense! We'll all miss you.'

The sun was shining dustily through the curtain, searching out the room's shabbiness, the cracked leather of an easy chair, the faded tapestry bed-cover, the grease-marks on the vast mahogany wardrobe.

'It's a pity you're going just when the weather's getting nice. But it's good for flying.'

'Yes,' Martin agreed, 'that's one good thing.'

'You must come again, soon. I'll hate you if you're ever in Berlin and you forget to drop in to see old Marlene Goetz.'

It was the first time he'd heard her Christian name, and it sounded so comically inappropriate that he wanted to laugh.

'I wouldn't dream of it,' he assured her. 'Of course, I'd come to see you.'

Their glasses clinked and they drank cheerlessly, staring at one another with that inarticulate, smiling embarrassment that troubles all leave-takings. Frau Goetz sipped her whisky sedately and nibbled at a pink cake. Silence always tormented her; she even read the Bible with the radio full on. She put down her glass and smoothed her throat as if in pain.

'Nothing will ever be the same without Hugo,' she began, making a curious snuffling noise that sounded hopeless and dumb, like a dog's grief. 'And now, with you going, everything seems to be coming to an end.'

It was just a week since the newspaper with its hideous black headlines had been pushed through the door. It was the morning when, unsuspecting, you wake up to disaster and nothing, nothing in the world is ever certain again. Each day, each hour, each separate moment becomes a hazard blindly negotiated.

The photographs had been especially frightful. The body, in close-up, features blotted out so that the corpse became anonymous. A damp railway arch with smears on the cobbles that may have been blood, the doorway of a shabby-looking bar, a view of a derelict street: images of desolation. There were innuendoes of exotic vice and jealousy, partly supported by an interview with a maimed boy who achieved brief notoriety with an account of drunken advances.

Then an evening newspaper produced a sensational development. 'Berlin's Oscar Wilde,' it clamoured in large capitals, and that started an avalanche of obituaries recalling Hugo's brilliant, short-lived theatrical career, his taste for eccentric parties, the irreverent wit that had made him a legend in pre-Hitler Germany. Everything was much exaggerated, imbued with an inevitable nostalgia for the day before yesterday. Now there was even talk of reviving one of Hugo's revues at the Schlossparktheatre in Steglitz.

The tragedy had revived in Martin the shocked antagonism he'd felt when he first arrived in Germany, the feeling that the past had left an invisible corruption that infected all it touched with malice and cruelty. Reluctantly, almost as a gesture of expiation, he undertook the task of settling Hugo's affairs. A cable to his divorced wife, Marion, elicited no reply. Possibly she shrank from becoming involved in yet another, even uglier, scandal. After some hesitation Martin also cabled his father; it seemed his duty to do so, regardless of the consequences. His father sent a message: 'Stricken by your news. A terrible judgement,' convinced, no doubt, that Hugo's fate was a punishment divinely imposed upon a Jew who consorted with the mass murderers. A few hours later came another cable: 'Cannot understand your presence in Berlin. Please explain.' That reckoning would have to come, but the inquest, the funeral (the Goldberg mourners and the Goldberg rabbi), and the protracted discussions with Ulrich, the lawyer, drove the foreboding from his mind. Hugo had been less affluent than people thought, having been spendthrift and careless of money, and there was no will. Ulrich regretted that his property would go by default to the German authorities. 'It seems a shame that his own people won't get it,' he said.

But the irony was appropriate. It seemed to touch the very core of Hugo's tragedy.

A taxi hooted persistently in the street below. Karin went to the window and peered out. In a dry whisper she said: 'It's come.' Martin swallowed the dregs of the whisky. A last look round the room, thinking: 'I've mislaid something here,' something nameless and precious; Frau Goetz, curlers slipping from her dishevelled hair, crying without embarrassment, an aged, broken-hearted child; and the travel-stained suitcases were back in his hands, already cutting familiar grooves into the palms.

Karin clutched his arm tightly, and just as they were leaving, Frau Goetz put up her drawn face for him to kiss. Even Professor Hokoyama left his music and came smiling into the corridor with Oriental reticence to speak a courteous farewell. And then the apartment door closed on the whole episode.

They were alone again, sitting side by side in the taxi with too much to say and no way of saying it, the last minutes withering in silence.

For Karin this was more than pain, Martin told himself. It was always worse to be left behind, like a bereavement. They had awakened different things in each other. In him, a sense of the future, so that he was moving on, warily and not without misgiving, yet ready to trust his nerves. In her it had been an awakening to love; but she still felt the threat of sterility. She was mortally afraid of absence, afraid that without the evidence of the senses, the tangible act of tenderness, her nightmare would return. He was going and she couldn't allow herself to believe that luck would bring them together again. And although he was certain that they would seek each other out, blindly, in any darkness, as shoots instinctively grope towards the warmth of the sun, it was impossible for him to say it.

Even now, on the point of departure, there were things he could never say to her in Berlin. The violence of their love sprang from the very tragedy that made their union seem an unnatural one. As long as they were in Germany the violence would be there and every passionate encounter would seem a parody of other lusts.

He looked out of the taxi window with a heavy heart, wondering if their history would ever permit them to find the ordinary peace they needed so much. Sunlight brought out the solidity of the physical streets, the steel and concrete buildings, the flesh and bone of people. It wasn't so different from any other city in appearance, but as long as the story of man was recorded it would symbolise something cruel and monstrous. He had come here raging because those who made it so seemed immune from punishment, because nothing could be done to cancel out the killing of even one human being. Now he knew that guilt and punishment were meaningless, life-suffocating, abstractions. They changed nothing, and if the Day of Judgment were to come God would be left with nothing at all to say except: Begin again from the beginning. Be the first Man and the first Woman, so united in love that the pain of one is the pain of the other.

Life went on despite man's self-destruction. Because the loins were stubborn and passionate, because the moist vagina drew the impetuous seed into the blind, instinctive womb. And in the waters of that darkness a gentler civilisation might yet germinate.

Karin said: 'You often promised to show me where you were born. Is there still time?'

He looked at her in surprise and said gently: 'You often asked me to show you where I was born. Why are you so curious?'

'There's so much I don't know about you. Perhaps it's silly' – her voice stumbled – 'but… for some reason it's desperately important to me. I think if I saw the place I could imagine you as a child, going to school, playing with your friends…' The notion seemed absurd and she became silent, biting her lower lip in vexation.

'There's time,' Martin said, glancing at his wrist-watch with a feeling that even that practical gesture was ungenerous.

He leaned forward and gave the address to the taxi-driver. 'The house doesn't even exist any more. They're building a block of flats there. Please hurry,' he urged the driver.

'Are you sure we can manage it?'

'Just about by the skin of our teeth. It isn't far.' His own curiosity had been aroused and he was suddenly as anxious as she was. It would be another thing shared, an end-of-honeymoon memory. That made it important, too. Soon they would only exist for each other as a series of memories: the breakfasts in the dawn-lit room, messages left on the table, hurried lunch-time meetings outside the factory fearful of wasting the little time they had together, walking back after the cinema to undress in the dark aching with desire, and waking after love to smoke a cigarette and laugh in quiet, contented voices for no reason at all but the sheer happiness of it. Now this last journey, this parting.

The taxi accelerated as it left the crowded centre of the city, jolting them against one another, injecting a sense of urgency and adventure. Soon it was Dahlem, avenues of green suburban streets and the old landmarks returning, one after the other.

'This is where I went to school,' he said. 'See those flats? There was once a little shop there where we bought pockets-full of candy.' And, again: 'My friend Willy Schneider took music lessons from a Russian princess in the Thielplatz, just round the corner. There was a little blonde girl named Frieda in my kindergarten. We were sweethearts. She lived over there in a yellow stone mansion and her father once galloped her to school on a roan hunter.'

The smell of the Grünewald vivid with spring brought a piercing nostalgia as sharp as if the umbilical cord that joined him to the past had been abruptly severed, and he knew he would never feel it in the same way again.

'We're here, darling,' he said, climbing reluctantly out of the taxi. The last fragments of rubble that marked the site of his house had gone.

Karin held his hand and looked at the street with a curious kind of reverence, an almost religious silence. She was turning it into a pilgrimage, and at first he didn't understand: it embarrassed him. Then he realised that she was humbling herself before his dead. It was indescribably moving. These small intuitive gestures of hers helped to remove the oppressive burden of hatred.

This street was, indeed, his family grave, even though all traces of their existence had been obliterated from it. For a moment he tried vainly to visualise Lise solemnly skipping on the grass of these alien gardens by the neat row of prefabricated garages, her long brown hair blowing round her flushed cheeks. Again, he sought to imagine his mother stepping out of the dark blue Mercedes, supple in furs, and handing a pile of shopping parcels to Manfred, the chauffeur. But they remained frozen in the stillness of death, offering no reconciliation, no reproach, only the absolute indifference of non-existence. Yet their absence laid its silent curse on those who occupied the spaces they had signed with their pain.

Instead of the big ornate country house built by a Prussian landowner in 1806, the year Napoleon occupied Berlin after his victory at Jena, there was a seven-storey block of luxury flats, faced with black glass, as slickly styled as a Knightsbridge espresso bar, its flat roof crowded with television aerials like twisted ribs of a broken umbrella. The windows were neat and uniform, framing indoor plants or Swedish pottery, and a spiral of yellow stairs seen through a transparent wall pierced the site of his parents' bedroom and climbed through the nursery ceiling to penetrate their old sky. For him it could only be a tomb of glass his ghosts refused to inhabit.

It reminded him of Vienna, which once blazed with Jewish creative vitality and was now the city without Jews, bankrupt of their prodigal talents and hiding its sterility behind the most beautiful façade in Europe. The street and its stylish apartment were a symbol of all the *Judenrein* towns and cities here in the heart of Europe; and in all these places the absence of the Jews, after two thousand years, was the soundless shape of a multitude of silent voices that the deafening roar of traffic and the million noises of the living could not shut out.

Martin turned away, knowing that he had explored himself down to the harsh roots, and that it was time to move on.

'We'd better go now,' he said. She looked at him, and what she saw in his face made her begin to cry.

Then they were in the Tempelhof, the sun glinting on the metal wings of the planes, and only the last cup of coffee in the wide cork-lined corridor before the shutters dropped and loneliness became real.

Karin held his face in her gaze, afraid it would be lost the moment she glanced away.

'You will write?' she said.

'As soon as I get to Hamburg.'

'And when you get to London?'

'I promise. Darling, as soon as I get off the train. I promise.'

And again there was nothing to say that could be said without hurting. A straggling line of Pan-American passengers from New York filed across the black-top into Arrivals, yawning tiredly after the long tedium of the lower stratosphere. Mechanics were climbing down from the big Lufthansa plane, whistling and wiping oily hands on their blue dungarees.

Martin smiled through a tight constriction of the heart. 'If it always hurts like this, who wants to fall in love?' he said.

She spoke with slow vehemence, treating his anxious attempt at humour seriously: 'When I'm hurt, I'm alive.' They were so close that each of the tiny gold flecks in her charcoal-coloured eyes was separately visible. 'Whatever happens, I'm not sorry,' she said.

Women almost always said that, but this time it sounded new. 'We'll meet in Paris,' he said huskily. 'Soon. That's what's going to happen.'

'I've never been out of Germany in all my twenty-five years. I can't believe in something I don't know. Does Paris exist?'

'It existed the last time I saw it, about six months ago,' he reassured her solemnly. 'But there've been changes recently. If it's vanished we'll camp out in the Bois de Boulogne. The weather will be warm.' And then he realised that she was a factory worker, not well paid, for whom foreign travel was a prohibitive luxury. He could imagine her putting aside a few marks every week, skimping on food and other necessities. 'I'll send you the fare,' he said awkwardly.

'Oh no!' she protested.

A crisp voice was announcing his flight. She clung to his coat, tears trickling through her shut eyelids, with a violence of grief that made him shudder.

'We'll find a way,' he promised desperately.

'Yes?' she asked, a tiny note of hope in her voice. 'Do you really believe it?'

And, without waiting for his reply, she kissed some of her tears on to his mouth, so that he tasted the salt on his lips all the way to the plane.

'We'll have to forgive each other every day of our lives,' he thought sombrely as the plane mounted into the air, Berlin growing smaller, diminishing fast, until it was only a smudge below. Then they slid into the grey sea of cloud and there was nothing.

About the author

EMANUEL LITVINOFF (1915–2011) was born in Whitechapel, then a largely Jewish slum, to Russian-Jewish parents. His childhood, spent skirting the borderline between poverty and destitution, was unforgettably described in his memoir *Journey Through A Small Planet*. *The Lost Europeans* was Litvinoff's first novel. He also wrote poetry, radio scripts, plays and book reviews.

More from Apollo

NOW IN NOVEMBER
Josephine Johnson

> *Now in November I can see our years as a whole. This autumn is like*
> *both an end and a beginning to our lives, and those days which seemed*
> *confused with the blur of all things too near and too familiar are clear*
> *and strange now.*

Forced out of the city by the Depression, Arnold Haldmarne moves
his wife and three daughters to the country and tries to scratch
a living from the land. After years of unrelenting hard work, the
hiring of a young man from a neighbouring farm upsets the fragile
balance of their lives. And in the summer, the rains fail to come.

BOSNIAN CHRONICLE
Ivo Andrić

> *For as long as anyone could remember, the little café known as 'Lutvo's'*
> *has stood at the far end of the Travnik bazaar, below the shady, clamorous*
> *source of the 'Rushing Brook'.*

This is a sweeping saga of life in Bosnia under Napoleonic rule.
Set in the remote town of Travnik, the newly appointed French
consul soon finds himself intriguing against his Austrian rival,
whilst dealing with a colourful cast of locals.

THE MAN WHO LOVED CHILDREN
Christina Stead

All the June Saturday afternoon Sam Pollit's children were on the lookout for him as they skated round the dirt sidewalks and seamed old asphalt of R Street and Reservoir Road that bounded the deep-grassed acres of Tohoga House, their home.

Sam and Henny Pollit have too many children, too little money and too much loathing for each other. As Sam uses the children's adoration to feed his own voracious ego, Henny becomes a geyser of rage against her improvident husband.

MY SON, MY SON
Howard Spring

What a place it was, that dark little house that was two rooms up and two down, with just the scullery thrown in! I don't remember to this day where we all slept, though there was a funeral now and then to thin us out.

This is the powerful story of two hard-driven men – one a celebrated English novelist, the other a successful Irish entrepreneur – and of their sons, in whom are invested their fathers' hopes and ambitions. Oliver Essex and Rory O'Riorden grow up as friends, but their fathers' lofty plans have unexpected consequences as the violence of the Irish Revolution sweeps them all into uncharted territory.

DELTA WEDDING
Eudora Welty

> *The nickname of the train was the Yellow Dog. Its real name was the Yazoo-Delta. It was a mixed train. The day was the 10th of September, 1923 – afternoon. Laura McRaven, who was nine years old, was on her first journey alone.*

Laura McRaven travels down the Delta to attend her cousin Dabney's wedding. At the Fairchild plantation her family envelop her in a tidal wave of warmth, teases and comfort. As the big day approaches, tensions inevitably rise to the surface.

THE DAY OF JUDGMENT
Salvatore Satta

> *At precisely nine o'clock, as he did every evening, Don Sebastiano Sanna Carboni pushed back his armchair, carefully folded the newspaper which he had read through to the very last line, tidied up the little things on his desk, and prepared to go down to the ground floor...*

Around the turn of the twentieth century, in the isolated Sardinian town of Nuoro, the aristocratic notary Don Sebastiano Sanna reflects on his life, his family's history and the fortunes of this provincial backwater where he has lived out his days. Written over the course of a lifetime and published posthumously, *The Day of Judgment* is a classic of Italian, and world, literature.

THE AUTHENTIC DEATH OF HENDRY JONES
Charles Neider

> *Nowadays, I understand, the tourists come for miles to see Hendry Jones'*
> *grave out on the Punta del Diablo and to debate whether his bones are*
> *there or not...*

A stark and violent depiction of one of America's most alluring folk heroes, the mythical, doomed gunslinger. Set on the majestic coast of southern California, Doc Baker narrates his tale of the Kid's capture, trial, escape and eventual murder. Written in spare and subtle prose, this is one of the great literary treatments of America's obsession with the rule of the gun.

About the cover and endpapers

Unknown artist, *Berlin-Kurfürstendamm*, c.1957. Photographic postcard.